BROOKLYN NOIR 2

THE CLASSICS

BROOKLYN NOIR 2

THE CLASSICS

EDITED BY TIM MCLOUGHLIN

AKASHIC BOOKS
BROOKLYN

Published by Akashic Books
©2005 Tim McLoughlin
Brooklyn map by Sohrab Habibion

ISBN-13: 978-1-888451-76-4
ISBN-10: 1-888451-76-9
Library of Congress Control Number: 2004115735
All rights reserved
First printing
Printed in Canada

AKASHIC BOOKS
PO Box 1456, New York, NY 10009
Akashic7@aol.com, www.akashicbooks.com

Grateful acknowledgment is made for permission to reprint the stories in this anthology. "The Best-Friend Murder" by Donald Westlake was originally published in *Alfred Hitchcock's Mystery Magazine* (December 1959), © 1959 by Donald Westlake; "The Only Good Judge" by Carolyn Wheat was originally published in *Women Before the Bench* by Carolyn Wheat (Berkley Publishing Group, March 2001), © 2001 by Carolyn Wheat, reprinted by permission of Curtis Brown, Ltd.; "The Day of the Bullet" by Stanley Ellin was originally published in *Ellery Queen's Mystery Magazine* #191 (October 1959), © 1959 by Stanley Ellin, reprinted by permission of Curtis Brown, Ltd.; "Only the Dead Know Brooklyn" by Thomas Wolfe was originally published in *From Death to Morning* by Thomas Wolfe (Charles Scribner's Sons, 1935) and in the *New Yorker* (June 15, 1935), © 1935 by Thomas Wolfe, reprinted by permission of Eugene H. Winick, Administrator C.T.A., Estate of Thomas Wolfe; "Luck Be a Lady" by Maggie Estep was originally published on Nerve.com (2004); "Tugboat Syndrome" by Jonathan Lethem was originally published in the *Paris Review* #151 (Summer 1999) and is an excerpt from *Motherless Brooklyn* by Jonathan Lethem, © 1999 by Jonathan Lethem, reprinted by permission of Doubleday, a division of Random House, Inc.; "The All-Night Bodega of Souls" by Colson Whitehead was originally published in *John Henry Days* by Colson Whitehead, © 2001 by Colson Whitehead, reprinted by permission of Doubleday, a division of Random House, Inc.; "By the Dawn's Early Light" by Lawrence Block was originally published in *Playboy Magazine* (August 1984); "The Horror at Red Hook" by H.P. Lovecraft was originally published in *Weird Tales* Volume #9 (January 1927), reprinted by permission of Arkham House Publishers, Inc. and Arkham House's agent, JABberwocky Literary Agency; "Tralala" by Hubert Selby, Jr. was originally published in *Last Exit to Brooklyn* by Hubert Selby, Jr. (Grove Press, 1957), © 1957 by Hubert Selby, Jr., reprinted by permission of SLL/Sterling Lord Literistic, Inc.; "The Boys of Bensonhurst" by Salvatore La Puma was originally published in *The Boys of Bensonhurst* by Salvatore La Puma (University of Georgia Press, 1987), © 1987 by Salvatore La Puma; "Borough of Cemeteries" by Irwin Shaw was originally published in the *New Yorker* (August 13, 1938), © 1938 by Irwin Shaw; "Steelwork" is an excerpt from *Steelwork* by Gilbert Sorrentino, orginally published in 1970 by Pantheon Books, © 1970 by Gilbert Sorrentino; "Men in Black Raincoats" by Pete Hamill was originally published in *Ellery Queen's Mystery Magazine* (December 1977), © 1977 by Pete Hamill, reprinted by permission of the author.

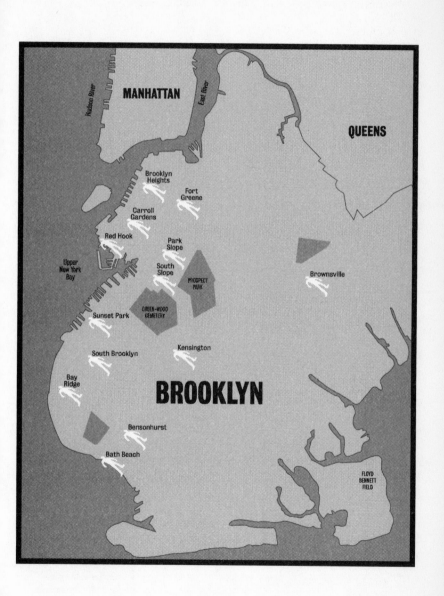

It is not upon you alone the dark patches fall,
The dark threw its patches down upon me also

—Walt Whitman, "Crossing Brooklyn Ferry"

TABLE OF CONTENTS

PART IV: WARTIME BROOKLYN

INTRODUCTION
SHAKEN, NOT STIRRED

When I first proposed what ultimately became the crime-fiction anthology *Brooklyn Noir* to my publisher, Johnny Temple, he seemed intrigued, and asked a series of questions for which I was not prepared. *How do you see it coming together? New stories or reprints? Strictly conventional crime? How would you pick the neighborhoods where the stories would be set?*

I'd presented the concept as it popped into my head, in a fairly offhanded manner, and frankly, I didn't have the answers. As I riffed and winged it, as he embraced some ideas and rejected others, the book began to take shape. We batted these and more questions around over the next few weeks, and compiled a dream list of contributors. After the first few writers agreed to craft original stories for the book, we decided that we would request new stories from all participants, written specifically for the volume. To me the book grew, almost organically, from there. A number of names from the list signed on, other writers heard about the anthology and submitted work, and I was able to include four stories from writers who had not been previously published. It became exactly the book I'd dreamed of when I pitched it, half-formed in my mind's eye.

But. There was a price to pay. By going with original pieces, I lost all the great stories that had given me the idea for such a book in the first place. I still wanted to collect tales that I felt had fallen between the cracks of time, or had never been grouped geographically, to paint the ominous portrait that I saw lurking behind every laundromat, nail salon, and Starbucks.

The success of *Brooklyn Noir*, launched in the summer of 2004, surpassed all expectations, I'm pleased to say. One story from the collection received an Edgar Award nomination, another is a Pushcart Prize finalist, and yet another won the Mystery Writers of America's Robert L. Fish Memorial Award. Two more have been selected for inclusion in *The Best American Mystery Stories 2005*. With my head properly swelled, I found myself once again on the phone with Johnny, riffing and winging it. So, here we are.

Working on this volume has been a different task than the first, in that there was little interaction, from an editorial point of view, with the writers, some of whom are deceased. This time I felt more like an archeologist, mining volumes old and new, looking for treasure. The rule for the first *Brooklyn Noir* had been that each story had to be previously unpublished. Here, just the opposite. *Brooklyn Noir 2* stories had to have been printed somewhere else before they hit the doorstep. That was about the only difference. I tried again to capture the special dread, tension, and solid writing that good dark fiction possesses. The scary feeling of watching the average Joe getting in over his head, or accidentally brushing up against something sinister on the way to work.

Figuring how to order the stories was an issue that resolved itself almost immediately. When I scanned the contents page in manuscript form, I was surprised to see that the first three categories from the original *Brooklyn Noir* applied, and the pieces were easy to assign accordingly. The fourth and final section in the first volume was "Backwater Brooklyn"—overlooked or forgotten neighborhoods. This time around, the stories in the last section all fall under the ominous shadow of World War II–era America. The image of a Brooklyn soldier—always a great dancer; often reading his love letters aloud to the rest of the company—was ubiquitous in classic war movies. My mother, a teenager during the war, told me that every block in her neighborhood, Sunset Park, had at least one "gold-star" family with a banner hanging in their window signifying a child lost in combat. It wasn't unusual to have three or more gold stars on a single street.

The argument can be made that it's odd to have a "New School" section in an anthology calling itself *The Classics*, but I think it works. Carolyn Wheat, Jonathan Lethem, Colson Whitehead, and Maggie Estep are in fact classic Brooklyn authors, but the territory they cover is very new school compared to the tone of the rest of the book. And you're not going to get much more old school than H.P. Lovecraft and Thomas Wolfe. I've always felt that, aside from the physical bulk of Wolfe's big guy with the map in "Only the Dead Know Brooklyn," he could have *been* Lovecraft, drowning in Brooklyn, as Lovecraft was in 1925, living in a rooming house on the edge of Red Hook, hating the city, becoming increasingly racist and withdrawn.

In the introduction to the first *Brooklyn Noir*, I said that what the writers captured brilliantly was the language of the borough, and that goes for this volume as well. Each story is a slice of neighborhood that rings true, whether the time machine has taken you back one year or eight decades. And, as in the first book, the tales cross all boundaries of past and present, well-known and unknown neighborhoods, literary and genre traditions. It all goes into that great cocktail shaker that is Brooklyn. As editor, I have the pleasure of picking the ingredients, mixing them, and serving them to you. And that makes me the luckiest bartender in the world. Enjoy.

Tim McLoughlin
Brooklyn, May 2005

PART I

OLD SCHOOL BROOKLYN

THE HORROR AT RED HOOK
BY H.P. LOVECRAFT
Red Hook
(Originally published in 1927)

> *There are sacraments of evil as well as of good about us,*
> *and we live and move to my belief in an unknown world,*
> *a place where there are caves and shadows and dwellers*
> *in twilight. It is possible that man may sometimes return*
> *on the track of evolution, and it is my belief that an awful*
> *lore is not yet dead.*
>
> —Arthur Machen

I

Not many weeks ago, on a street corner in the village of Pascoag, Rhode Island, a tall, heavily built, and wholesome-looking pedestrian furnished much speculation by a singular lapse of behaviour. He had, it appears, been descending the hill by the road from Chepachet; and encountering the compact section, had turned to his left into the main thoroughfare where several modest business blocks convey a touch of the urban. At this point, without visible provocation, he committed his astonishing lapse; staring queerly for a second at the tallest of the buildings before him, and then, with a series of terrified, hysterical shrieks, breaking into a frantic run which ended in a stumble and fall at the next crossing. Picked up and dusted off by ready hands, he was found to be conscious, organically unhurt, and evidently cured of his sudden nervous attack. He muttered some shamefaced explanations involving a strain he had undergone, and with downcast glance turned back up the Chepachet road, trudging out of sight without once looking behind him. It was a strange incident to befall so large, robust, normal-featured, and capable-looking a man, and the strangeness was not lessened by the remarks of a bystander who had recognised him as the boarder of a well-known dairyman on the outskirts of Chepachet.

He was, it developed, a New York police detective named Thomas F. Malone, now on a long leave of absence under medical treatment after some disproportionately arduous work on a gruesome local case which accident had made dramatic. There had been a collapse of several old brick buildings during a raid in which he had shared, and something about the wholesale loss of life, both of prisoners and of his companions, had peculiarly appalled him. As a result, he had acquired an acute and anomalous horror of any buildings even remotely suggesting the ones which had fallen in, so that in the end mental specialists forbade him the sight of such things for an indefinite period. A police surgeon with relatives in Chepachet had put forward that quaint hamlet of wooden Colonial houses as an ideal spot for the psychological convalescence; and thither the sufferer had gone, promising never to venture among the brick-lined streets of larger villages till duly advised by the Woonsocket specialist with whom he was put in touch. This walk to Pascoag for magazines had been a mistake, and the patient had paid in fright, bruises, and humiliation for his disobedience.

So much the gossips of Chepachet and Pascoag knew;

and so much also, the most learned specialists believed. But Malone had at first told the specialists much more, ceasing only when he saw that utter incredulity was his portion. Thereafter, he held his peace, protesting not at all when it was generally agreed that the collapse of certain squalid brick houses in the Red Hook section of Brooklyn, and the consequent death of many brave officers, had unseated his nervous equilibrium. He had worked too hard, all said, in trying to clean up those nests of disorder and violence; certain features were shocking enough, in all conscience, and the unexpected tragedy was the last straw. This was a simple explanation which everyone could understand, and because Malone was not a simple person, he perceived that he had better let if suffice. To hint to unimaginative people of a horror beyond all human conception—a horror of houses and blocks and cities leprous and cancerous with evil dragged from elder worlds—would be merely to invite a padded cell instead of a restful rustication, and Malone was a man of sense despite his mysticism. He had the Celt's far vision of weird and hidden things, but the logician's quick eye for the outwardly unconvincing; an amalgam which had led him far afield in the forty-two years of his life, and set him in strange places for a Dublin University man born in a Georgian villa near Phoenix Park.

And now, as he reviewed the things he had seen and felt and apprehended, Malone was content to keep unshared the secret of what could reduce a dauntless fighter to a quivering neurotic; what could make old brick slums and seas of dark, subtle faces a thing of nightmare and eldritch portent. It would not be the first time his sensations had been forced to hide uninterpreted—for was not his very act of plunging into the polyglot abyss of New York's underworld a freak beyond sensible explanation? What could he tell the prosaic of the antique witcheries and grotesque marvels discernible to sensitive eyes amidst the poison cauldron where all the varied dregs of unwholesome ages mix their venom and perpetuate their obscene terrors? He had seen the hellish green flame of secret wonder in this blatant, evasive welter of outward greed and inward blasphemy, and had smiled gently when all the New Yorkers he knew scoffed at his experiment in police work. They had been very witty and cynical, deriding his fantastic pursuit of unknowable mysteries and assuring him that in these days New York held nothing but cheapness and vulgarity. One of them had wagered him a heavy sum that he could not—despite many poignant things to his credit in the *Dublin Review*—even write a truly interesting story of New York low life; and now, looking back, he perceived that cosmic irony had justified the prophet's words while secretly confuting their flippant meaning. The horror, as glimpsed at last, could not make a story—for like the book cited by Poe's German authority, "*es lasst sich nicht lesen*—it does not permit itself to be read."

II

To Malone the sense of latent mystery in existence was always present. In youth he had felt the hidden beauty and ecstasy of things, and had been a poet; but poverty and sorrow and exile had turned his gaze in darker directions, and he had thrilled at the imputations of evil in the world around. Daily life had for him come to be a phantasmagoria of macabre shadow-studies; now glittering and leering with concealed rottenness as in Beardsley's best manner, now hinting terrors behind the commonest shapes and objects as in the subtler and less obvious work of Gustave Doré. He would often regard it as merciful that most persons of high intelligence jeer at the inmost mysteries; for, he argued, if superior minds were ever placed in fullest contact with the secrets preserved by ancient and lowly cults, the resultant abnormalities would soon not only wreck the world, but threaten the very integrity of the universe. All this reflection was no doubt morbid, but keen logic and a deep sense of humour ably offset it. Malone was satisfied to let his notions remain as half-spied and forbidden visions to be lightly played with; and hysteria came only when duty flung him into a hell of revelation too sudden and insidious to escape.

He had for some time been detailed to the Butler Street station in Brooklyn when the Red Hook matter came to his notice. Red Hook is a maze of hybrid squalor near the ancient waterfront opposite Governor's Island, with dirty highways climbing the hill from the wharves to that higher ground where the decayed lengths of Clinton and Court Streets lead off toward the Borough Hall. Its houses are mostly of brick, dating from the first quarter to the middle of the nineteenth century, and some of the obscurer alleys and byways have that alluring antique flavour which conventional reading leads us to call "Dickensian." The population is a hopeless tangle and enigma; Syrian, Spanish, Italian, and negro elements impinging upon one another, and fragments of Scandinavian and American belts lying not far distant. It is a babel of sound and filth, and sends out strange cries to answer the lapping of oily waves at its grimy piers and the monstrous organ litanies of the harbour whistles. Here long ago a brighter picture dwelt, with clear-eyed mariners on the lower streets and homes of taste and substance where the

larger houses line the hill. One can trace the relics of this former happiness in the trim shapes of the buildings, the occasional graceful churches, and the evidences of original art
and background in bits of detail here and there—a worn
flight of steps, a battered doorway, a wormy pair of decorative
columns of pilasters, or a fragment of once green space with
bent and rusted iron railing. The houses are generally in solid
blocks, and now and then a many-windowed cupola arises to
tell of days when the households of captains and ship-owners
watched the sea.

From this tangle of material and spiritual putrescence the
blasphemies of an hundred dialects assail the sky. Hordes of
prowlers reel shouting and singing along the lanes and thor-
oughfares, occasional furtive hands suddenly extinguish
lights and pull down curtains, and swarthy, sin-pitted faces
disappear from windows when visitors pick their way
through. Policemen despair of order or reform, and seek
rather to erect barriers protecting the outside world from the
contagion. The clang of the patrol is answered by a kind of
spectral silence, and such prisoners as are taken are never
communicative. Visible offences are as varied as the local
dialects, and run the gamut from the smuggling of rum and
prohibited aliens through diverse stages of lawlessness and
obscure vice to murder and mutilation in their most abhor-
rent guises. That these visible affairs are not more frequent is
not to the neighbourhood's credit, unless the power of concealment be an art demanding credit. More people enter Red
Hook than leave it—or at least, than leave it by the land-
wardside—and those who are not loquacious are the likeliest
to leave.

Malone found in this state of things a faint stench of
secrets more terrible than any of the sins denounced by citi-

zens and bemoaned by priests and philanthropists. He was conscious, as one who united imagination with scientific knowledge, that modern people under lawless conditions tend uncannily to repeat the darkest instinctive patterns of primitive half-ape savagery in their daily life and ritual observances; and he had often viewed with an anthropologist's shudder the chanting, cursing processions of blear-eyed and pockmarked young men which wound their way along in the dark small hours of morning. One saw groups of these youths incessantly; sometimes in leering vigils on street corners, sometimes in doorways playing eerily on cheap instruments of music, sometimes in stupefied dozes or indecent dialogues around cafeteria tables near Borough Hall, and sometimes in whispering converse around dingy taxicabs drawn up at the high stoops of crumbling and closely shuttered old houses. They chilled and fascinated him more than he dared confess to his associates on the force, for he seemed to see in them some monstrous thread of secret continuity; some fiendish, cryptical, and ancient pattern utterly beyond and below the sordid mass of facts and habits and haunts listed with such conscientious technical care by the police. They must be, he felt inwardly, the heirs of some shocking and primordial tradition; the sharers of debased and broken scraps from cults and ceremonies older than mankind. Their coherence and definiteness suggested it, and it showed in the singular suspicion of order which lurked beneath their squalid disorder. He had not read in vain such treatises as Miss Murray's *Witch Cult in Western Europe*; and knew that up to recent years there had certainly survived among peasants and furtive folk a frightful and clandestine system of assemblies and orgies descended from dark religions antedating the Aryan world, and appearing in popular legends as Black Masses and

Witches' Sabbaths. That these hellish vestiges of old Turanian–Asiatic magic and fertility-cults were even now wholly dead he could not for a moment suppose, and he frequently wondered how much older and how much blacker than the very worst of the muttered tales some of them might really be.

III

It was the case of Robert Suydam which took Malone to the heart of things in Red Hook. Suydam was a lettered recluse of ancient Dutch family, possessed originally of barely independent means, and inhabiting the spacious but ill-preserved mansion which his grandfather had built in Flatbush when that village was little more than a pleasant group of Colonial cottages surrounding the steepled and ivy-clad Reformed Church with its iron-railed yard of Netherlandish gravestones. In his lonely house, set back from Martense Street amidst a yard of venerable trees, Suydam had read and brooded for some six decades except for a period a generation before, when he had sailed for the old world and remained there out of sight for eight years. He could afford no servants, and would admit but few visitors to his absolute solitude; eschewing close friendships and receiving his rare acquaintances in one of the three ground-floor rooms which he kept in order—a vast, high-ceiled library, whose walls were solidly packed with tattered books of ponderous, archaic, and vaguely repellent aspect. The growth of the town and its final absorption in the Brooklyn district had meant nothing to Suydam, and he had come to mean less and less to the town. Elderly people still pointed him out on the streets, but to most of the recent population he was merely a queer, corpulent old fellow whose unkempt white hair, stubbly beard, shiny black clothes and gold headed cane earned him an amused glance and nothing more. Malone did not know him by sight till duty called him to the case, but had heard of him indirectly as a really profound authority on mediaeval superstition, and had once idly meant to look up an out-of-print pamphlet of his on the Kabbalah and the Faustus legend, which a friend had quoted from memory.

Suydam became a "case" when his distant and only relatives sought court pronouncements on his sanity. Their action seemed sudden to the outside world, but was really undertaken only after prolonged observation and sorrowful debate. It was based on certain odd changes in his speech and habits; wild references to impending wonders, and unaccountable hauntings of disreputable Brooklyn neighbourhoods. He had been growing shabbier and shabbier with the years, and now prowled about like a veritable mendicant; seen occasionally by humiliated friends in subway stations, or loitering on the benches around Borough Hall in conversation with groups of swarthy, evil-looking strangers. When he spoke it was to babble of unlimited powers almost within his grasp, and to repeat with knowing leers such mystical words or names as "Sephiroth," "Ashmodai," and "Samaël." The court action revealed that he was using up his income and wasting his principal in the purchase of curious tomes imported from London and Paris, and in the maintenance of a squalid basement flat in the Red Hook district where he spent nearly every night, receiving odd delegations of mixed rowdies and foreigners, and apparently conducting some kind of ceremonial service behind the green blinds of secretive windows. Detectives assigned to follow him reported strange cries and chants and prancing of feet filtering out from these nocturnal rites, and shuddered at their peculiar ecstasy and abandon despite the commonness of weird orgies in that sodden section. When, however, the matter came to a hearing, Suydam managed to preserve his liberty. Before the judge his manner grew urbane and reasonable, and he freely admitted the queerness of demeanour and extravagant cast of language into which he had fallen through excessive devotion to study and research. He was, he said, engaged in the investigation of certain details of European tradition which required the closest contact with foreign groups and their songs and folk dances. The notion that any low secret society was preying upon him, as hinted by his relatives, was obviously absurd; and showed how sadly limited was their understanding of him and his work. Triumphing with his calm explanations, he was suffered to depart unhindered; and the paid detectives of the Suydams, Corlears, and Van Brunts were withdrawn in resigned disgust.

It was here that an alliance of Federal inspectors and police, Malone with them, entered the case. The law had watched the Suydam action with interest, and had in many instances been called upon to aid the private detectives. In this work it developed that Suydam's new associates were among the blackest and most vicious criminals of Red Hook's devious lanes, and that at least a third of them were known and repeated offenders in the matter of thievery, disorder, and the importation of illegal immigrants. Indeed, it would not have been too much to say that the old scholar's particular circle coincided almost perfectly with the worst of the organised cliques which smuggled ashore certain nameless and unclassified Asian dregs wisely turned back by Ellis Island. In the teeming rookeries of Parker Place—since renamed—where Suydam had his basement flat, there had grown up a very unusual colony of unclassified slant-eyed folk who used the Arabic alphabet but were eloquently repudiated by the great mass of Syrians in and around Atlantic Avenue. They could all have been deported for lack of credentials, but legalism is slow-moving, and one does not disturb Red Hook unless publicity forces one to.

These creatures attended a tumble-down stone church, used Wednesdays as a dance-hall, which reared its Gothic buttresses near the vilest part of the waterfront. It was nominally Catholic; but priests throughout Brooklyn denied the place all standing and authenticity, and policemen agreed with them when they listened to the noises it emitted at night. Malone used to fancy he heard terrible cracked bass notes from a hidden organ far underground when the church stood empty and unlighted, whilst all observers dreaded the shrieking and drumming which accompanied the visible services. Suydam, when questioned, said he thought the ritual was some remnant of Nestorian Christianity tinctured with the Shamanism of Thibet. Most of the people, he conjectured, were of Mongoloid stock, originating somewhere in or near Kurdistan—and Malone could not help recalling that Kurdistan is the land of the Yezidis, last survivors of the Persian devil-worshippers. However this may have been, the stir of the Suydam investigation made it certain that these unauthorised newcomers were flooding Red Hook in increasing numbers; entering through some marine conspiracy unreached by revenue officers and harbor police, overrunning Parker Place and rapidly spreading up the hill, and welcomed with curious fraternalism by the other assorted denizens of the region. Their squat figures and characteristic squinting physiognomies, grotesquely combined with flashy

American clothing, appeared more and more numerously among the loafers and nomad gangsters of the Borough Hall section; till at length it was deemed necessary to compute their numbers, ascertain their sources and occupations, and find if possible a way to round them up and deliver them to the proper immigration authorities. To this task Malone was assigned by agreement of Federal and city forces, and as he commenced his canvass of Red Hook, he felt poised upon the brink of nameless terrors, with the shabby, unkempt figure of Robert Suydam as arch-fiend and adversary.

IV

Police methods are varied and ingenious. Malone, through unostentatious rambles, carefully casual conversations, well-timed offers of hip-pocket liquor, and judicious dialogues with frightened prisoners, learned many isolated facts about the movement whose aspect had become so menacing. The newcomers were indeed Kurds, but of a dialect obscure and puzzling to exact philology. Such of them as worked lived mostly as dockhands and unlicensed pedlars, though frequently serving in Greek restaurants and tending corner news stands. Most of them, however, had no visible means of support, and were obviously connected with underworld pursuits, of which smuggling and "bootlegging" were the least indescribable. They had come in steamships, apparently tramp freighters, and had been unloaded by stealth on moonless nights in rowboats which stole under a certain wharf and followed a hidden canal to a secret subterranean pool beneath a house. This wharf, canal, and house Malone could not locate, for the memories of his informants were exceedingly confused, while their speech was to a great extent beyond even the ablest interpreters; nor could he gain any real data on the reasons for their systematic importation. They were reticent about the exact spot from which they had come, and were never sufficiently off guard to reveal the agencies which had sought them out and directed their course. Indeed, they developed something like acute fright when asked the reasons for their presence. Gangsters of other breeds were equally taciturn, and the most that could be gathered was that some god or great priesthood had promised them unheard-of powers and supernatural glories and rulerships in a strange land.

The attendance of both newcomers and old gangsters at Suydam's closely guarded nocturnal meetings was very regular, and the police soon learned that the erstwhile recluse had leased additional flats to accommodate such guests as knew his password; at last occupying three entire houses and permanently harbouring many of his queer companions. He spent but little time now at his Flatbush home, apparently going and coming only to obtain and return books; and his face and manner had attained an appalling pitch of wildness. Malone twice interviewed him, but was each time brusquely repulsed. He knew nothing, he said, of any mysterious plots or movements; and had no idea how the Kurds could have entered or what they wanted. His business was to study undisturbed the folklore of all the immigrants of the district; a business with which policemen had no legitimate concern. Malone mentioned his admiration for Suydam's old brochure on the Kabbalah and other myths, but the old man's softening was only momentary. He sensed an intrusion, and rebuffed his visitor in no uncertain way; till Malone withdrew disgusted, and turned to other channels of information.

What Malone would have unearthed could he have worked continuously on the case, we shall never know. As it was, a stupid conflict between city and Federal authority suspended the investigations for several months, during which the detective was busy with other assignments. But at no time did he lose interest, or fail to stand amazed at what began to happen to Robert Suydam. Just at the time when a wave of kidnappings and disappearances spread its excitement over New York, the unkempt scholar embarked upon a metamorphosis as startling as it was absurd. One day he was seen near Borough Hall with clean-shaven face, well-trimmed hair, and tastefully immaculate attire, and on every day thereafter some obscure improvement was noticed in him. He maintained his new fastidiousness without interruption, added to it an unwonted sparkle of eye and crispness of speech, and began little by little to shed the corpulence which had so long deformed him. Now frequently taken for less than his age, he acquired an elasticity of step and buoyancy of demeanour to match the new tradition, and showed a curious darkening of the hair which somehow did not suggest dye. As the months passed, he commenced to dress less and less conservatively, and finally astonished his new friends by renovating and redecorating his Flatbush mansion, which he threw open in a series of receptions, summoning all the acquaintances he could remember, and extending a special welcome to the fully forgiven relatives who had so lately sought his restraint. Some attended through curiosity, others through duty; but all were suddenly charmed by the dawning grace and urbanity of the former hermit. He had, he asserted, accomplished most of his allotted work; and having just inherited some property from a half-forgotten European friend, was about to spend his remaining years in a brighter second youth which ease, care, and diet had made possible to him. Less and less was he seen at Red Hook, and more and more did he move in the society to which he was born. Policemen noted a tendency of the gangsters to congregate at the old stone church and dance-hall instead of at the basement flat in Parker Place, though the latter and its recent annexes still overflowed with noxious life.

Then two incidents occurred—wide enough apart, but both of intense interest in the case as Malone envisaged it. One was a quiet announcement in the *Eagle* of Robert Suydam's engagement to Miss Cornelia Gerritsen of Bayside, a young woman of excellent position, and distantly related to the elderly bridegroom-elect; whilst the other was a raid on the dance-hall church by city police, after a report that the face of a kidnapped child had been seen for a second at one of the basement windows. Malone had participated in this raid, and studied the place with much care when inside. Nothing was found—in fact, the building was entirely deserted when visited—but the sensitive Celt was vaguely disturbed by many things about the interior. There were crudely painted panels he did not like—panels which depicted sacred faces with peculiarly worldly and sardonic expressions, and which occasionally took liberties that even a layman's sense of decorum could scarcely countenance. Then, too, he did not relish the Greek inscription on the wall above the pulpit; an ancient incantation which he had once stumbled upon in Dublin college days, and which read, literally translated,

O friend and companion of night, thou who rejoices in the baying of dogs and spilt blood, who wanderest in the midst of shades among the tombs, who longest for blood and bringest terror to mortals, Gorgo, Marmo, thousand-faced moon, look favourably on our sacrifices!

When he read this he shuddered, and thought vaguely of the cracked bass organ notes he fancied he had heard beneath the church on certain nights. He shuddered again at the rust around the rim of a metal basin which stood on the altar, and paused nervously when his nostrils seemed to detect a curious and ghastly stench from somewhere in the neighbourhood. That organ memory haunted him, and he explored the basement with particular assiduity before he left. The place was very hateful to him; yet after all, were the blasphemous panels and inscriptions more than mere crudities perpetrated by the ignorant?

By the time of Suydam's wedding the kidnapping epidemic had become a popular newspaper scandal. Most of the victims were young children of the lowest classes, but the increasing number of disappearances had worked up a sentiment of the strongest fury. Journals clamoured for action from the police, and once more the Butler Street station sent its men over Red Hook for clues, discoveries, and criminals. Malone was glad to be on the trail again, and took pride in a raid on one of Suydam's Parker Place houses. There, indeed, no stolen child was found, despite the tales of screams and the red sash picked up in the areaway; but the paintings and rough inscriptions on the peeling walls of most of the rooms, and the primitive chemical laboratory in the attic, all helped to convince the detective that he was on the track of something tremendous. The paintings were appalling—hideous monsters of every shape and size, and parodies on human outlines which cannot be described. The writing was in red,

and varied from Arabic to Greek, Roman, and Hebrew letters. Malone could not read much of it, but what he did deci-
pher was portentous and cabalistic enough. One frequently
repeated motto was in a sort of Hebraised Hellenistic Greek,
and suggested the most terrible daemon evocations of the
Alexandrian decadence:

HEL • HELOYM • SOTHER • EMMANVEL •
SABAOTH • AGLA • TETRAGRAMMATON •
AGYROS • OTHEOS • ISCHYROS •
ATHANATOS • IEHOVA • VA • ADONAI •
SADAY • HOMOVSION • MESSIAS •
ESCHEREHEYE.

Circles and pentagrams loomed on every hand, and told
indubitably of the strange beliefs and aspirations of those who
dwelt so squalidly here. In the cellar, however, the strangest
thing was found—a pile of genuine gold ingots covered carelessly with a piece of burlap, and bearing upon their shining
surfaces the same weird hieroglyphics which also adorned the
walls. During the raid the police encountered only a passive
resistance from the squinting Orientals that swarmed from
every door. Finding nothing relevant, they had to leave all as
it was; but the precinct captain wrote Suydam a note advis-
ing him to look closely to the character of his tenants and
protégés in view of the growing public clamour.

V

Then came the June wedding and the great sensation.
Flatbush was gay for the hour about high noon, and pen-

nanted motors thronged the streets near the old Dutch church where an awning stretched from door to highway. No local event ever surpassed the Suydam-Gerritsen nuptials in tone and scale, and the party which escorted the bride and groom to the Cunard Pier was, if not exactly the smartest, at least a solid page from the Social Register. At five o'clock adieux were waved, and the ponderous liner edged away from the long pier, slowly turned its nose seaward, discarded its tug, and headed for the widening water spaces that led to old world wonders. By night the outer harbour was cleared, and late passengers watched the stars twinkling above an unpolluted ocean.

Whether the tramp steamer or the scream was first to gain attention, no one can say. Probably they were simultaneous, but it is of no use to calculate. The scream came from the Suydam stateroom, and the sailor who broke down the door could perhaps have told frightful things if he had not forthwith gone completely mad—as it is, he shrieked more loudly than the first victims, and thereafter ran simpering about the vessel till caught and put in irons. The ship's doctor who entered the stateroom and turned on the lights a moment later did not go mad, but told nobody what he saw till afterward, when he corresponded with Malone in Chepachet. It was murder—strangulation—but one need not say that the claw-mark on Mrs. Suydam's throat could not have come from her husband's or any other human hand, or that upon the white wall there flickered for an instant in hateful red a legend which, later copied from memory, seems to have been nothing less than the fearsome Chaldee letters of the word LILITH. One need not mention these things because they vanished so quickly—as for Suydam, one could at least bar others from the room until one knew what to think oneself. The doctor has distinctly assured Malone that he did not see IT. The open porthole, just before he turned on the lights, was clouded for a second with a certain phosphorescence, and for a moment there seemed to echo in the night outside the suggestion of a faint and hellish tittering; but no real outline met the eye. As proof, the doctor points to his continued sanity.

Then the tramp steamer claimed all attention. A boat put off, and a horde of swart, insolent ruffians in officers' dress swarmed aboard the temporarily halted Cunarder. They wanted Suydam or his body—they had known of his trip, and for certain reasons were sure he would die. The captain's deck was almost a pandemonium; for at the instant, between the doctor's report from the stateroom and the demands of the men from the tramp, not even the wisest and gravest seaman could think what to do. Suddenly the leader of the visiting mariners, an Arab with a hatefully negroid mouth, pulled forth a dirty, crumpled paper and handed it to the captain. It was signed by Robert Suydam, and bore the following odd message:

> *In case of sudden or unexplained accident or death on my part, please deliver me or my body unquestioningly into the hands of the bearer and his associates. Everything, for me, and perhaps for you, depends on absolute compliance. Explanations can come later—do not fail me now.*
>
> ROBERT SUYDAM

Captain and doctor looked at each other, and the latter whispered something to the former. Finally they nodded rather helplessly and led the way to the Suydam stateroom.

The doctor directed the captain's glance away as he unlocked the door and admitted the strange seaman, nor did he breathe easily till they filed out with their burden after an unaccountably long period of preparation. It was wrapped in bedding from the berths, and the doctor was glad that the outlines were not very revealing. Somehow the men got the thing over the side and away to their tramp steamer without uncovering it. The Cunarder started again, and the doctor and a ship's undertaker sought out the Suydam stateroom to perform what last services they could. Once more the physician was forced to reticence and even to mendacity, for a hellish thing had happened. When the undertaker asked him why he had drained off all of Mrs. Suydam's blood, he neglected to affirm that he had not done so; nor did he point to the vacant bottle-spaces on the rack, or to the odour in the sink which showed the hasty disposition of the bottles' original contents. The pockets of those men—if men they were—had bulged damnably when they left the ship. Two hours later, and the world knew by radio all that it ought to know of the horrible affair.

VI

That same June evening, without having heard a word from the sea, Malone was desperately busy among the alleys of Red Hook. A sudden stir seemed to permeate the place, and as if apprised by "grape-vine telegraph" of something singular, the denizens clustered expectantly around the dance-hall church and the houses in Parker Place. Three children had just disappeared—blue-eyed Norwegians from the streets toward Gowanus—and there were rumours of a mob forming among the sturdy Vikings of that section. Malone had for weeks been urging his colleagues to attempt a general cleanup; and at last, moved by conditions more obvious to their common sense than the conjectures of a Dublin dreamer, they had agreed upon a final stroke. The unrest and menace of this evening had been the deciding factor, and just about midnight a raiding party recruited from three stations descended upon Parker Place and its environs. Doors were battered in, stragglers arrested, and candle-lighted rooms forced to disgorge unbelievable throngs of mixed foreigners in figured robes, mitres, and other inexplicable devices. Much was lost in the melee, for objects were thrown hastily down unexpected shafts, and betraying odours deadened by the sudden kindling of pungent incense. But spattered blood was everywhere, and Malone shuddered whenever he saw a brazier or altar from which the smoke was still rising.

He wanted to be in several places at once, and decided on Suydam's basement flat only after a messenger had reported the complete emptiness of the dilapidated dance-hall church. The flat, he thought, must hold some clue to a cult of which the occult scholar had so obviously become the centre and leader; and it was with real expectancy that he ransacked the musty rooms, noted their vaguely charnel odour, and examined the curious books, instruments, gold ingots, and glass-stoppered bottles scattered carelessly here and there. Once a lean, black-and-white cat edged between his feet and tripped him, overturning at the same time a beaker half full of red liquid. The shock was severe, and to this day Malone is not certain of what he saw; but in dreams he still pictures that cat as it scuttled away with certain monstrous alterations and peculiarities. Then came the locked cellar door, and the search for something to break it down. A heavy stool stood near, and its tough seat was more than enough for the antique panels. A crack formed and enlarged, and the whole door gave way—but from the *other side*; whence poured a howling tumult of ice-cold wind with all the stenches of the bottomless pit, and whence reached a sucking force not of earth or heaven, which, coiling sentiently about the paralysed detective, dragged him through the aperture and down unmeasured spaces filled with whispers and wails, and gusts of mocking laughter.

Of course it was a dream. All the specialists have told him so, and he has nothing to prove the contrary. Indeed, he would rather have it thus; for then the sight of old brick slums and dark foreign faces would not eat so deeply into his soul. But at the time it was all horribly real, and nothing can ever efface the memory of those nighted crypts, those titan arcades, and those half-formed shapes of hell that strode gigantically in silence holding half-eaten things whose still surviving portions screamed for mercy or laughed with madness. Odours of incense and corruption joined in sickening concert, and the black air was alive with the cloudy, semivisible bulk of shapeless elemental things with eyes. Somewhere dark sticky water was lapping at onyx piers, and once the shivery tinkle of raucous little bells pealed out to greet the insane titter of a naked phosphorescent thing which swam into sight, scrambled ashore, and climbed up to squat leeringly on a carved golden pedestal in the background.

Avenues of limitless night seemed to radiate in every direction, till one might fancy that here lay the root of a contagion destined to sicken and swallow cities, and engulf nations in the foetor of hybrid pestilence. Here cosmic sin had entered, and festered by unhallowed rites had commenced the grinning march of death that was to rot us all to fungous abnormalities too hideous for the grave's holding. Satan here held his Babylonish court, and in the blood of stainless childhood the leprous limbs of phosphorescent Lilith were laved. Incubi and succubae howled praise to Hecate, and headless moon-calves bleated to the Magna Mater. Goats leaped to the sound of thin accursed flutes, and Ægypans chased endlessly after misshapen fauns over rocks twisted like swollen toads. Moloch and Ashtaroth were not absent; for in this quintessence of all damnation the bounds of consciousness were let down, and man's fancy lay open to vistas of every realm of horror and every forbidden dimension that evil had power to mould. The world and Nature were helpless against such assaults from unsealed wells of night, nor could any sign or prayer check the Walpurgis-riot of horror which had come when a sage with the hateful key had stumbled on a horde with the locked and brimming coffer of transmitted daemon-lore.

Suddenly a ray of physical light shot through these phantasms, and Malone heard the sound of oars amidst the blasphemies of things that should be dead. A boat with a lantern in its prow darted into sight, made fast to an iron ring in the slimy stone pier, and vomited forth several dark men bearing a long burden swathed in bedding. They took it to the naked phosphorescent thing on the carved golden pedestal, and the thing tittered and pawed at the bedding. Then they unswathed it, and propped upright before the pedestal the gangrenous corpse of a corpulent old man with stubbly beard and unkempt white hair. The phosphorescent thing tittered again, and the men produced bottles from their pockets and anointed its feet with red, whilst they afterward gave the bottles to the thing to drink from.

All at once, from an arcaded avenue leading endlessly

away, there came the daemoniac rattle and wheeze of a blasphemous organ, choking and rumbling out the mockeries of hell in a cracked, sardonic bass. In an instant every moving entity was electrified; and forming at once into a ceremonial procession, the nightmare horde slithered away in quest of the sound—goat, satyr, and Ægypan, incubus, succubus and lemur, twisted toad and shapeless elemental, dog-faced howler and silent strutter in darkness—all led by the abominable naked phosphorescent thing that had squatted on the carved golden throne, and that now strode insolently, bearing in its arms the glassy-eyed corpse of the corpulent old man. The strange dark men danced in the rear, and the whole column skipped and leaped with Dionysiac fury. Malone staggered after them a few steps, delirious and hazy, and doubtful of his place in this or in any world. Then he turned, faltered, and sank down on the cold damp stone, gasping and shivering as the daemon organ croaked on, and the howling and drumming and tinkling of the mad procession grew fainter and fainter.

Vaguely he was conscious of chanted horrors and shocking croakings afar off. Now and then a wail or whine of ceremonial devotion would float to him through the black arcade, whilst eventually there rose the dreadful Greek incantation whose text he had read above the pulpit of that dance-hall church.

"*O friend and companion of night, thou who rejoicest in the baying of dogs* (here a hideous howl burst forth) *and spilt blood* (here nameless sounds vied with morbid shriekings) *who wanderest in the midst of shades among the tombs* (here a whistling sigh occurred), *who longest for blood and bringest terror to mortals* (short, sharp cries from myriad throats), *Cargo* (repeated as response), *Mormo* (repeated with ecstasy), *thousand-faced moon* (sighs and flute notes), *look favourably on our sacrifices!"*

As the chant closed, a general shout went up, and hissing sounds nearly drowned the croaking of the cracked bass organ. Then a gasp as from many throats, and a babel of barked and bleated words—"Lilith, Great Lilith, behold the Bridegroom!" More cries, a clamour of rioting, and the sharp, clicking footfalls of a running figure. The footfalls approached, and Malone raised himself to his elbow to look.

The luminosity of the crypt, lately diminished, had now slightly increased; and in that devil-light there appeared the fleeting form of that which should not flee or feel or breathe—the glassy-eyed, gangrenous corpse of the corpulent old man, now needing no support, but animated by some infernal sorcery of the rite just closed. After it raced the naked, tittering, phosphorescent thing that belonged on the carven pedestal, and still farther behind panted the dark men, and all the dread crew of sentient loathsomeness. The corpse was gaining on its pursuers, and seemed bent on a definite object, straining with every rotting muscle toward the carved golden pedestal, whose necromantic importance was evidently so great. Another moment and it had reached its goal, whilst the trailing throng laboured on with more frantic speed. But they were too late, for in one final spurt of strength which ripped tendon from tendon and sent its noisome bulk floundering to the floor in a state of jellyfish dissolution, the staring corpse which had been Robert Suydam achieved its object and its triumph. The push had been tremendous, but the force had held out; and as the pusher collapsed to a muddy blotch of corruption, the pedestal he had pushed tottered, tipped, and finally careened from its onyx base into the thick waters below, sending up a parting gleam of carven gold as it sank heavily to undreamable gulfs of lower Tartarus. In that instant, too, the whole scene of horror faded to nothingness before Malone's eyes; and he fainted amidst a thunderous crash which seemed to blot out all the evil universe.

VII

Malone's dream in full before he knew of Suydam's death and transfer at sea, was curiously supplemented by some odd realities of the case; though that is no reason why anyone should believe it. The three old houses in Parker Place, doubtless long rotten with decay in its most insidious form, collapsed without visible cause while half the raiders and most of the prisoners were inside; and of both the greater number were instantly killed. Only in the basements and cellars was there much saving of life, and Malone was lucky to have been deep below the house of Robert Suydam. For he really was there, as no one is disposed to deny. They found him unconscious by the edge of a night-black pool, with a grotesquely horrible jumble of decay and bone, identifiable through dental work as the body of Suydam, a few feet away. The case was plain, for it was hither that the smugglers' underground canal led; and the men who took Suydam from the ship had brought him home. They themselves were never found, or at least never identified; and the ship's doctor is not yet satisfied with the simple certitudes of the police.

Suydam was evidently a leader in extensive man-smuggling operations, for the canal to his house was but one of several subterranean channels and tunnels in the neighbourhood. There was a tunnel from this house to a crypt beneath the dance-hall church; a crypt accessible from the church only through a narrow secret passage in the north wall, and in whose chambers some singular and terrible things were discovered. The croaking organ was there, as well as a vast arched chapel with wooden benches and a strangely figured altar. The walls were lined with small cells, in seventeen of which—hideous to relate—solitary prisoners in a state of complete idiocy were found chained, including four mothers with infants of disturbingly strange appearance. These infants died soon after exposure to the light; a circumstance which the doctors thought rather merciful. Nobody but Malone, among those who inspected them, remembered the sombre question of old Delrio: "*An sint unquam daemones incubi et succubae, et an ex tali congressu proles enascia quea?*"

Before the canals were filled up they were thoroughly dredged, and yielded forth a sensational array of sawed and split bones of all sizes. The kidnapping epidemic, very clearly, had been traced home; though only two of the surviving prisoners could by any legal thread be connected with it. These men are now in prison, since they failed of conviction as accessories in the actual murders. The carved golden pedestal or throne so often mentioned by Malone as of primary occult importance was never brought to light, though at one place under the Suydam house the canal was observed to sink into a well too deep for dredging. It was choked up at the mouth and cemented over when the cellars of the new houses were made, but Malone often speculates on what lies beneath. The police, satisfied that they had shattered a dangerous gang of maniacs and man-smugglers, turned over to the Federal authorities the unconvicted Kurds, who before their deportation were conclusively found to belong to the Yezidi clan of devil-worshippers. The tramp ship and its crew remain an elusive mystery, though cynical detectives are once more ready to combat its smuggling and rum-running ventures. Malone thinks these detectives show a sadly limited perspective in their lack of wonder at the myriad unexplainable details, and the suggestive obscurity of the whole case; though he is just as critical of the newspapers, which saw only a morbid sensation and gloated over a minor sadist cult which they might have proclaimed a horror from the universe's very heart. But he is content to rest silent in Chepachet, calming his nervous system and praying that time may gradually transfer his terrible experience from the realm of present reality to that of picturesque and semi-mythical remoteness.

Robert Suydam sleeps beside his bride in Greenwood Cemetery. No funeral was held over the strangely released bones, and relatives are grateful for the swift oblivion which overtook the case as a whole. The scholar's connection with the Red Hook horrors, indeed, was never emblazoned by legal proof; since his death forestalled the inquiry he would otherwise have faced. His own end is not much mentioned, and the Suydams hope that posterity may recall him only as a gentle recluse who dabbled in harmless magic and folklore.

As for Red Hook—it is always the same. Suydam came and went; a terror gathered and faded; but the evil spirit of darkness and squalor broods on amongst the mongrels in the old brick houses, and prowling bands still parade on unknown errands past windows where lights and twisted faces unaccountably appear and disappear. Age-old horror is a hydra with a thousand heads, and the cults of darkness are rooted in blasphemies deeper than the well of Democritus. The soul of the beast is omnipresent and triumphant, and Red Hook's legions of blear-eyed, pockmarked youths still chant and curse and howl as they file from abyss to abyss, none knows whence or whither, pushed on by blind laws of biology which they may never understand. As of old, more people enter Red Hook than leave it on the landward side, and there are already rumours of new canals running underground to certain centres of traffic in liquor and less mentionable things.

The dance-hall church is now mostly a dance hall, and queer faces have appeared at night at the windows. Lately a policeman expressed the belief that the filled-up crypt has been dug out again, and for no simple explainable purpose. Who are we to combat poisons older than history and mankind? Apes danced in Asia to those horrors, and the cancer lurks secure and spreading where furtiveness hides in rows of decaying brick.

Malone does not shudder without cause—for only the other day an officer overheard a swarthy squinting hag teaching a small child some whispered patois in the shadow of an areaway. He listened, and thought it very strange when he heard her repeat over and over again,

"O friend and companion of night, thou who rejoicest in the baying of dogs and spilt blood, who wanderest in the midst of shades among the tombs, who longest for blood and bringest terror to mortals, Gorgo, Mormo, thousand-faced moon, look favourably on our sacrifices!"

ONLY THE DEAD
KNOW BROOKLYN

BY THOMAS WOLFE

Brooklyn Subway

(Originally published in 1935)

D ere's no guy livin' dat knows Brooklyn t'roo an'
t'roo, because it'd take a guy a lifetime just to find
his way aroun' duh f—— town.

So like I say, I'm waitin' for my train t' come when I sees
dis big guy standin' deh—dis is duh foist I eveh see of him.
Well, he's lookin' wild, y'know, an' I can see dat he's had
plenty, but still he's holdin' it; he talks good an' is walkin'
straight enough. So den, dis big guy steps up to a little guy
dat's standin' deh, an' says, "How d'yuh get t' Eighteent'
Avenoo an' Sixty-sevent' Street?" he says.

"Jesus! Yuh got me, chief," duh little guy says to him. "I
ain't been heah long myself. Where is duh place?" he says.
"Out in duh Flatbush section somewhere?"

"Nah," duh big guy says. "It's out in Bensonhoist. But I
was neveh deh befoeh. How d'yuh get deh?"

"Jesus," duh little guy says, scratchin' his head, y'know—
yuh could see duh little guy didn't know his way about—"yuh
got me, chief. I neveh hoid of it. Do any of youse guys know
where it is?" he says to me.

"Sure," I says. "It's out in Bensonhoist. Yuh take duh Fourt'
Avenoo express, get off at Fifty-nint' Street, change to a Sea
Beach local deh, get off at Eighteent' Avenoo an' Sixty-toid,

an' den walk down foeh blocks. Dat's all yuh got to do," I says.

"G'wan!" some wise guy dat I neveh seen befoeh pipes up. "Whatcha talkin' about?" he says—oh, he was wise, y'know. "Duh guy is crazy! I tell yuh what yuh do," he says to duh big guy. "Yuh change to duh West End line at Toity-sixt'," he tells him. "Get off at Noo Utrecht and Sixteent' Avenoo," he says. "Walk two blocks oveh, foeh blocks up," he says, "an' you'll be right deh." Oh, a *wise* guy, y'know.

"Oh, yeah?" I says. "Who told *you* so much?" He got me sore because he was so wise about it. "How long you been livin' heah?" I says.

"All my life," he says. "I was bawn in Williamsboig," he says. "An' I can tell you t'ings about dis town you neveh hoid of," he says.

"Yeah?" I says.

"Yeah," he says.

"Well, den, you can tell me t'ings about dis town dat nobody else has eveh hoid of, either. Maybe you make it all up yoehself at night," I says, "befoeh you go to sleep—like cuttin' out papeh dolls, or somp'n."

"Oh, yeah?" he says. "You're pretty wise, ain't yuh?"

"Oh, I don't know," I says. "Duh boids ain't usin' my head for Lincoln's statue yet," I says. "But I'm wise enough to know a phony when I see one."

"Yeah?" he says. "A wise guy, huh? Well, you're so wise dat someone's goin' t'bust yuh one right on duh snoot some day," he says. "Dat's how wise *you* are."

Well, my train was comin', or I'da smacked him den and dere: but when I seen duh train was comin', all I said was, "All right, mug! I'm sorry I can't stay to take keh of you, but I'll be seein' yuh sometime, I hope, out in duh cemetery." So den I says to duh big guy, who'd been standin' deh all duh time, "You come wit me," I says. So when we gets onto duh train I says to him, "Where yuh goin' out in Bensonhoist?" I says. "What number are yuh lookin' for?" I says. *You* know—I t'ought if he told me duh address I might be able to help him out.

"Oh," he says, "I'm not lookin' for no one. I don't know no one out deh."

"Then whatcha goin' out deh for?" I says.

"Oh," duh guy says, "I'm just goin' out to see duh place," he says. "I like duh sound of duh name—Bensonhoist, y'know—so I t'ought I'd go out an' have a look at it."

"Whatcha tryin' t'hand me?" I says. "Whatcha tryin' t'do—kid me?" *You* know, I t'ought duh guy was bein' wise wit me.

"No," he says, "I'm tellin' yuh duh troot. I like to go out an' take a look at places wit nice names like dat. I like to go out an' look at all kinds of places," he says.

"How'd yuh know deh was such a place," I says, "if yuh neveh been deh befoeh?"

"Oh," he says, "I got a map."

"A *map?*" I says.

"Sure," he says, "I got a map dat tells me about all dese places. I take it wit me every time I come out heah," he says.

And Jesus! Wit dat, he pulls it out of his pocket, an' so help me, but he's *got* it—he's tellin' duh troot—a big map of duh whole f—— place with all duh different pahts mahked out. You know Canarsie an' East Noo Yawk an' Flatbush, Bensonhoist, Sout' Brooklyn, duh Heights, Bay Ridge, Greenpernt—duh whole goddam layout, he's got it right deh on duh map.

"You been to any of dose places?" I says.

"Sure," he says, "I been to most of 'em. I was down in Red Hook just last night," he says.

"Jesus! Red Hook!" I says. "Whatcha do down deh?"

"Oh," he says, "nuttin' much. I just walked aroun'. I went into a coupla places an' had a drink," he says, "but most of the time I just walked aroun'."

"Just walked aroun'?" I says.

"Sure," he says, "just lookin' at t'ings, y'know."

"Where'd yuh go?" I asts him.

"Oh," he says, "I don't know duh name of duh place, but I could find it on my map," he says. "One time I was walkin' across some big fields where deh ain't no houses," he says, "but I could see ships oveh deh all lighted up. Dey was loadin'. So I walks across duh fields," he says, "to where duh ships are."

"Sure," I says, "I know where you was. You was down to duh Erie Basin."

"Yeah," he says, "I guess dat was it. Dey had some of dose big elevators an' cranes an' dey was loadin' ships, an' I could see some ships in dry dock all lighted up; so I walks across duh fields to where dey are," he says.

"Den what did yuh do?" I says.

"Oh," he says, "nuttin' much. I came on back across duh fields after a while an' went into a coupla places an' had a drink."

"Didn't nuttin' happen while yuh was in dere?" I says.

"No," he says. "Nuttin' much. A coupla guys was drunk in one of duh places an' stahted a fight, but dey bounced 'em out," he says, "an' den one of duh guys stahted to come back again, but duh bartender gets his baseball bat out from under duh counteh; so duh guy goes on."

"Jesus!" I said. "Red Hook!"

"Sure," he says. "Dat's where it was, all right."

"Well, you keep outa deh," I says. "You stay away from deh."

"Why?" he says. "What's wrong wit it?"

"Oh," I says, "it's a good place to stay away from, dat's all. It's a good place to keep out of."

"Why?" he says. "Why is it?"

Jesus! Whatcha gonna do wit a guy as dumb as that? I saw it wasn't no use to try to tell him nuttin'—he wouldn't know what I was talkin' about; so I just says to him, "Oh, nuttin'. Yuh might get lost down deh, dat's all."

"Lost?" he says. "No, I wouldn't get lost. I got a map," he says.

A map! Red Hook! Jesus!

So den duh guy begins to ast me all kinds of nutty questions: how big was Brooklyn, an' could I find my way aroun' in it, an' how long would it take a guy to know duh place.

"Listen!" I says. "You get dat idea outa yoeh head right now," I says. "You ain't neveh gonna get to know Brooklyn," I says. "Not in a hunderd yeahs. I been livin' heah all my life," I says, "an' I don't even know all deh is to know about it, so how do you expect to know duh town," I says, "when you don't even live heah?"

"Yes," he says, "but I got a map to help me find my way about."

"Map or no map," I says, "yuh ain't gonna get to know Brooklyn wit no map," I says.

"Can you swim?" he says, just like dat. Jesus! By dat time, y'know, I begun to see dat duh guy was some kind of nut. He'd had plenty to drink, of course, but he had dat crazy look in his eye I didn't like. "Can you swim?" he says.

"Sure," I says. "Can't you?"

"No," he says. "Not more'n a stroke or two. I neveh loined good."

"Well, it's easy," I says. "All yuh need is a little confidence. Duh way I loined, me older bruddeh pitched me off duh dock one day when I was eight yeahs old, cloes an' all. 'You'll swim,' he says. 'You'll swim all right—or drown.' An' believe me, I *swam!* When yuh know yuh got to, you'll do it. Duh only t'ing yuh need is confidence. An' once you've loined," I says, "you've got nuttin' else to worry about. You'll neveh forget it. It's somp'n dat stays wit yuh as long as yuh live."

"Can yuh swim good?" he says.

"Like a fish," I tells him. "I'm a regulah fish in duh wateh," I says. "I loined to swim right off duh docks with all duh oddeh kids," I says.

"What would you do if yuh saw a man drownin'?" duh guy says.

"Do? Why, I'd jump in an' pull him out," I says. "Dat's what I'd do."

"Did yuh eveh see a man drown?" he says.

"Sure," I says. "I see two guys—bot' times at Coney Island. Dey got out too far, an' neider one could swim. Dey drowned befoeh any one could get to 'em."

"What becomes of people after dey've drowned out heah?" he says.

"Drowned out where?" I says.

"Out heah in Brooklyn."

"I don't know whatcha mean," I says. "Neveh hoid of no one drownin' heah in Brooklyn, unless you mean a swimmin' pool. Yuh can't drown in Brooklyn," I says. "Yuh gotta drown somewhere else—in duh ocean, where dere's wateh."

"Drownin'," duh guy says, lookin' at his map. "Drownin'." Jesus! I could see by den he was some kind of nut; he had dat crazy expression in his eyes when he looked at you, an' I didn't know what he might do. So we was comin' to a station, an' it wasn't my stop, but I got off anyway, an' waited for duh next train.

"Well, so long, chief," I says. "Take it easy, now."

"Drownin'," duh guy says, lookin' at his map. "Drownin'."

Jesus! I've t'ought about dat guy a t'ousand times since den an' wondered what eveh happened to 'm goin' out to look at Bensonhoist because he liked duh name! Walkin' aroun' t'roo Red Hook by himself at night an' lookin' at his map! How many people did I see get drowned out heah in Brooklyn! How long would it take a guy wit a good map to know all deh was to know about Brooklyn!

Jesus! What a nut *he* was! I wondeh what evah happened to 'im, anyway! I wondeh if someone knocked him on duh head or if he's still wanderin' aroun' in duh subway in duh middle of duh night wit his little map! Duh poor guy! Say, I've got to laugh, at dat, when I t'ink about him! Maybe he's found out by now dat he'll neveh live long enough to know duh whole of Brooklyn! It'd take a guy a lifetime to know Brooklyn t'roo an' t'roo. An' even den, yuh wouldn't know it all.

BOROUGH OF CEMETERIES

BY IRWIN SHAW

Brownsville

(Originally published in 1938)

D uring the cocktail hour, in Brownsville, the cab drivers gather in Lammanawitz's Bar and Grill and drink beer and talk about the world and watch the sun set slowly over the elevated tracks in the direction of Prospect Park.

"Mungo?" they say. "Mungo? He got a fish for a arm. A mackerel. He will pitch Brooklyn right into the first division of the International League."

"I saw the Mayor today. His Honor, himself. The Little Flower. What this country needs . . ."

"Pinky, I want that you should trust me for a glass of beer."

Pinky wiped the wet dull expanse of the bar. "Look, Elias. It is against the law of the State of New York," he said, nervously, "to sell intoxicating liquors on credit."

"One glass of beer. Intoxicatin'!" Elias's lips curled. "Who yuh think I am, Snow White?"

"Do you want me to lose my license?" Pinky asked plaintively.

"I stay up nights worryin' Pinky might lose his license. My wife hears me cryin' in my sleep," Elias said. "One beer, J. P. Morgan."

Regretfully, Pinky drew the beer, with a big head, and

sighed as he marked it down in the book. "The last one," he said, "positively the last one. As God is my witness."

"Yeah," Elias said. "Keep yer mouth closed." He drank the beer in one gulp, with his eyes shut. "My God," he said quietly, his eyes still shut, as he put the glass down. "Fer a lousy dime," he said to the room in general, "yuh get somethin' like that! Fer a lousy dime! Brooklyn is a wonderful place."

"Brooklyn stinks," said another driver, down the bar. "The borough of cemeteries. This is a first class place for graveyards."

"My friend Palangio," Elias said. "Il Doochay Palangio. Yuh don't like Brooklyn, go back to Italy. They give yuh a gun, yuh get shot in the behind in Africa." The rest of the drivers laughed and Elias grinned at his own wit. "I seen in the movies. Go back t' Italy, wit' the fat girls. Who'll buy me a beer?"

Complete silence fell over the bar, like taps over an army camp.

"My friends," Elias said bitterly.

"Brooklyn is a wonderful place," Palangio said.

"All day long," Elias said, reflectively rubbing his broken nose, "I push a hack. Eleven hours on the street. I now have the sum of three dollars and fifty cents in my pocket."

Pinky came right over. "Now, Elias," he said, "there is the small matter of one beer. If I'd knew you had the money . . ."

Elias impatiently brushed Pinky's hand off the bar. "There is somebody callin' for a beer down there, Pinky," he said. "Attend yer business."

"I think," Pinky grumbled, retreating, "that a man oughta pay his rightful debts."

"He thinks. Pinky thinks," Elias announced. But his

heart was not with Pinky. He turned his back to the bar and leaned on his frayed elbows and looked sadly up at the tin ceiling. "Three dollars and fifty cents," he said softly. "An' I can't buy a beer."

"Whatsamatta?" Palangio asked. "Yuh got a lock on yuh pocket?"

"Two dollars an' seventy-fi' cents to the Company," Elias said. "An' seventy-fi' cents to my lousy wife so she don't make me sleep in the park. The lousy Company. Every day for a year I give 'em two dollars an' seventy-fi' cents an' then I own the hack. After a year yuh might as well sell that crate to Japan to put in bombs. Th' only way yuh can get it to move is t' drop it. I signed a contract. I need a nurse. Who wants t' buy me a beer?"

"I signed th' same contract," Palangio said. A look of pain came over his dark face. "It got seven months more to go. Nobody shoulda learned me how to write my name."

"If you slobs would only join th' union," said a little Irishman across from the beer spigots.

"Geary," Elias said. "The Irish hero. Tell us how you fought th' English in th' battle of Belfast."

"O.K., O.K.," Geary said, pushing his cap back excitably from his red hair. "You guys wanna push a hack sixteen hours a day for beans, don' let me stop yuh."

"Join a union, get yer hair parted down the middle by the cops," Elias said. "That is my experience."

"O.K., boys." Geary pushed his beer a little to make it foam. "Property-owners. Can't pay for a glass a beer at five o'clock in th' afternoon. What's the use a' talkin' t' yuh? Lemme have a beer, Pinky."

"Geary, you're a red," Elias said. "A red bastidd."

"A Communist," Palangio said.

"I want a beer," Geary said loudly.

"Times're bad," Elias said. "That's what's th' trouble."

"Sure." Geary drained half his new glass. "Sure."

"Back in 1928," Elias said, "I averaged sixty bucks a week."

"On New Year's Eve, 1927," Palangio murmured, "I made thirty-six dollars and forty cents."

"Money was flowin'," Elias remembered.

Palangio sighed, rubbing his beard bristles with the back of his hand. "I wore silk shirts. With stripes. They cost five bucks a piece. I had four girls in 1928. My God!"

"This ain't 1928," Geary said.

"Th' smart guy," Elias said. "He's tellin' us somethin'. This ain't 1928, he says. Join th' union, we get 1928 back."

"Why the hell should I waste my time?" Geary asked himself in disgust. He drank in silence.

"Pinky!" Palangio called. "Pinky! Two beers for me and my friend Elias."

Elias moved, with a wide smile, up the bar, next to Palangio. "We are brothers in misery, Angelo," he said. "Me and th' Wop. We both signed th' contract."

They drank together and sighed together.

"I had th' biggest pigeon flight in Brownsville," Elias said softly. "One hundred and twelve pairs of pedigreed pigeons. I'd send 'em up like fireworks, every afternoon. You oughta've seen 'em wheelin' aroun' an' aroun' over th' roofs. I'm a pigeon fancier." He finished his glass. "I got fifteen pigeons left. Every time I bring home less than seventy-five cents, my wife cooks one for supper. A pedigreed pigeon. My lousy wife."

"Two beers," Palangio said. He and Elias drank with grave satisfaction.

"Now," Elias said, "if only I didn't have to go home to my lousy wife. I married her in 1929. A lot of things've changed since 1929." He sighed. "What's a woman?" he asked. "A woman is a trap."

"You shoulda seen what I seen today," Palangio said. "My third fare. On Eastern Parkway. I watched her walk all th' way acrost Nostrand Avenue, while I was waitin' on the light. A hundred-and-thirty-pound girl. Blonde. Swingin' her hips like orchester music. With one of those little straw hats on top of her head, with the vegetables on it. You never saw nothin' like it. I held onto the wheel like I was drownin'. Talkin' about traps! She went to the St. George Hotel."

Elias shook his head. "The tragedy of my life," he said, "is I was married young."

"Two beers," Palangio said.

"Angelo Palangio," Elias said, "yer name reminds me of music."

"A guy met her in front of the St. George. A big fat guy. Smilin' like he just seen Santa Claus. A big fat guy. Some guys . . ."

"Some guys . . ." Elias mourned. "I gotta go home to Annie. She yells at me from six to twelve, regular. Who's goin' to pay the grocer? Who's goin' to pay the gas company?" He looked steadily at his beer for a moment and downed it. "I'm a man who married at the age a' eighteen."

"We need somethin' to drink," Palangio said.

"Buy us two whiskies," Elias said. "What the hell good is beer?"

"Two Calverts," Palangio called. "The best for me and my friend Elias Pinsker. "

"Two gentlemen," Elias said, "who both signed th' contract."

"Two dumb slobs," said Geary.

"Th' union man," Elias lifted his glass. "To th' union!" He downed the whisky straight. "Th' hero of th' Irish Army."

"Pinky," Palangio shouted. "Fill 'em up to the top."

"Angelo Palangio," Elias murmured gratefully.

Palangio soberly counted the money out for the drinks. "Now," he said, "the Company can jump in Flushing Bay. I am down to two bucks even."

"Nice," Geary said sarcastically. "Smart. You don't pay 'em one day, they take yer cab. After payin' them regular for five months. Buy another drink."

Palangio slowly picked up his glass and let the whisky slide down his throat in a smooth amber stream. "Don't talk like that, Geary," he said. "I don't want to hear nothin' about taxicabs. I am busy drinkin' with friends."

"You dumb Wop," Geary said.

"That is no way to talk," Elias said, going over to Geary purposefully. He cocked his right hand and squinted at Geary. Geary backed off, his hands up. "I don't like to hear people call my friend a dumb Wop," Elias said.

"Get back," Geary shouted, "before I brain yuh."

Pinky ran up excitably. "Lissen, boys," he screamed, "do you want I should lose my license?"

"We are all friends," Palangio said. "Shake hands. Everybody shake hands. Everybody have a drink. I hereby treat everybody to a drink."

Elias lumbered back to Palangio's side. "I am sorry if I made a commotion. Some people can't talk like gentlemen."

"Everybody have a drink," Palangio insisted.

Elias took out three dollar bills and laid them deliberately on the bar. "Pass the bottle around. This is on Elias Pinsker."

"Put yer money away, Elias." Geary pushed his cap

around on his head with anger. "Who yuh think yuh are? Walter Chrysler?"

"The entertainment this afternoon is on me," Elias said inexorably. "There was a time I would stand drinks for twenty-five men. With a laugh, an' pass cigars out after it. Pass the bottle around, Pinky!"

The whisky flowed.

"Elias and me," Palangio said. "We are high class spenders."

"You guys oughta be fed by hand," Geary said. "Wards of the guvment."

"A man is entitled to some relaxation," Elias said. "Where's that bottle?"

"This is nice," Palangio said. "This is very nice."

"This is like the good old days," Elias said.

"I hate to go home." Palangio sighed. "I ain't even got a radio home."

"Pinky!" Elias called. "Turn on the radio for Angelo Palangio."

"One room," Palangio said. "As big as a toilet. That is where I live."

The radio played. It was soft and sweet and a rich male voice sang "I Married an Angel."

"When I get home," Elias remembered, "Annie will kill a pedigreed pigeon for supper. My lousy wife. An' after supper I push the hack five more hours and I go home and Annie yells some more and I get up tomorrow and push the hack some more." He poured himself another drink. "That is a life for a dog," he said. "For a Airedale."

"In Italy," Palangio said, "they got donkeys don't work as hard as us."

"If the donkeys were as bad off as you," Geary yelled, "they'd have sense enough to organize."

"I want to be a executive at a desk." Elias leaned both elbows on the bar and held his chin in his huge gnarled hands. "A long distance away from Brownsville. Wit' two thousand pigeons. In California. An' I should be a bachelor. Geary, can yuh organize *that*? Hey, Geary?"

"You're a workin' man," Geary said, "an' you're goin' to be a workin' man all yer life."

"Geary," Elias said. "You red bastidd, Geary."

"All my life," Palangio wept, "I am goin' to push a hack up an' down Brooklyn, fifteen, sixteen hours a day an' pay th' Company forever an' go home and sleep in a room no bigger'n a toilet. Without a radio. Jesus!"

"We are victims of circumstance," Elias said.

"All my life," Palangio cried, "tied to that crate!"

Elias pounded the bar once with his fist. "Th' hell with it! Palangio!" he said. "Get into that goddamn wagon of yours."

"What do yuh want me to do?" Palangio asked in wonder.

"We'll fix 'em," Elias shouted. "We'll fix those hacks. We'll fix that Company! Get into yer cab, Angelo. I'll drive mine, we'll have a chicken fight."

"You drunken slobs!" Geary yelled. "Yuh can't do that!"

"Yeah," Palangio said eagerly, thinking it over. "Yeah. We'll show 'em. Two dollars and seventy-fi' cents a day for life. Yeah. We'll fix 'em. Come on, Elias!"

Elias and Palangio walked gravely out to their cars. Everybody else followed them.

"Look what they're doin'!" Geary screamed. "Not a brain between the both of them! What good'll it do to ruin the cabs?"

"Shut up," Elias said, getting into his cab. "We oughta done this five months ago. Hey, Angelo," he called, leaning out of his cab. "Are yuh ready? Hey, Il Doochay!"

"Contact!" Angelo shouted, starting his motor. "Boom! Boom!"

The two cars spurted at each other, in second, head-on. As they hit, glass broke and a fender flew off and the cars skidded wildly and the metal noise echoed and re-echoed like artillery fire off the buildings.

Elias stuck his head out of his cab. "Are yuh hurt?" he called. "Hey, Il Doochay!"

"Contact!" Palangio called from behind his broken windshield. "The Dawn Patrol!"

"I can't watch this," Geary moaned. "Two workin' men." He went back into Lammanawitz's Bar and Grill.

The two cabs slammed together again and people came running from all directions.

"How're yuh?" Elias asked, wiping the blood off his face.

"Onward!" Palangio stuck his hand out in salute. "Sons of Italy!"

Again and again the cabs tore into each other.

"Knights of the Round Table," Palangio announced.

"Knights of Lammanawitz's Round Table," Elias agreed, pulling at the choke to get the wheezing motor to turn over once more.

For the last time they came together. Both cars flew off the ground at the impact and Elias's toppled on its side and slid with a harsh grating noise to the curb. One of the front wheels from Palangio's cab rolled calmly and decisively toward Pitkin Avenue. Elias crawled out of his cab before anyone could reach him. He stood up, swaying, covered with blood, pulling at loose ends of his torn sweater. He shook hands soberly with Palangio and looked around him with satisfaction at the torn fenders and broken glass and scattered headlights and twisted steel. "Th' lousy

Company," he said. "That does it. I am now goin' to inform 'em of th' accident."

He and Palangio entered the Bar and Grill, followed by a hundred men, women, and children. Elias dialed the number deliberately.

"Hullo," he said, "hullo, Charlie? Lissen, Charlie, if yuh send a wreckin' car down to Lammanawitz's Bar and Grill, yuh will find two of yer automobiles. Yuh lousy Charlie." He hung up carefully.

"All right, Palangio," he said.

"Yuh bet," Palangio answered.

"Now we oughta go to the movies," Elias said.

"That's right," Palangio nodded seriously.

"Yuh oughta be shot," Geary shouted.

"They're playin' Simone Simon," Elias announced to the crowd. "Let's go see Simone Simon."

Walking steadily, arm in arm, like two gentlemen, Elias and Angelo Palangio went down the street, through the lengthening shadows, toward Simone Simon.

PART II

New School Brooklyn

TUGBOAT SYNDROME

BY JONATHAN LETHEM

Carroll Gardens

(Originally published in 1999)

ontext is everything. Dress me up and see. I'm a carnival barker, an auctioneer, a downtown performance artist, a speaker in tongues, a senator drunk on filibuster. My mouth won't quit, though mostly I whisper or subvocalize like I'm reading aloud, my Adam's apple bobbing, jaw muscle beating like a miniature heart under my cheek, the noise suppressed, the words escaping silently, mere ghosts of themselves, husks empty of breath and tone. In this diminished form the words rush out of the cornucopia of my brain to course over the surface of the world, tickling reality like fingers on piano keys. Caressing, nudging. They're an invisible army on a peacekeeping mission, a peaceable horde. They mean no harm. They placate, interpret, massage. Everywhere they're smoothing down imperfections, putting hairs in place, putting ducks in a row, replacing divots. Counting and polishing the silver. Patting old ladies gently on the behind, eliciting a giggle. Only—here's the rub—when they find too much perfection, when the surface is already buffed smooth, the ducks already orderly, the old ladies complacent, then my little army rebels, breaks into the stores. Reality needs a prick here and there, the carpet needs a flaw. My words begin plucking at threads nervously, seeking purchase, a weak point, a vulnerable ear. That's when it comes, the urge to shout in the church, the nursery, the crowded movie house. It's an itch at first. Inconsequential. But that itch is soon a torrent behind a straining dam. Noah's flood. That itch is my whole life. Here it comes now. Cover your ears. Build an ark. I've got Tourette's.

"Eat me!" I scream.

I grew up in the library of St. Vincent's Home for Boys in downtown Brooklyn, on a street which serves as the off-ramp to the Brooklyn Bridge. There the Home faced eight lanes of traffic, lined by Brooklyn's central sorting annex for the post office, a building that hummed and blinked all through the night, its gates groaning open to admit trucks bearing mountains of those mysterious items called letters; by the Burton Trade School for Automechanics, where hardened students attempting to set their lives dully straight spilled out twice a day for sandwich-and-beer breaks, overwhelming the cramped bodega next door; by a granite bust of Lafayette, indicating his point of entry into the Battle of Brooklyn; by a car lot surrounded by a high fence topped with wide curls of barbed wire and wind-whipped fluorescent flags, and by a red-brick Quaker meetinghouse that had presumably been there when the rest was farmland. In short, this jumble of stuff at the clotted entrance to the ancient, battered borough was officially Nowhere, a place strenuously ignored in passing through to Somewhere Else. Until rescued by Frank Minna I lived, as I said, in the library.

I set out to read every book in that tomblike library, every miserable dead donation ever indexed and forgotten there— a mark of my profound fear and boredom at St. Vincent's as well as an early sign of my Tourettic compulsions for counting, processing and inspection. Huddled there in the windowsill, turning dry pages and watching dust motes pinball through beams of sunlight, I sought signs of my odd dawning self in Theodore Dreiser, Kenneth Roberts, J.B. Priestley and back issues of *Popular Mechanics* and failed, couldn't find the language of myself. I was closer on Saturday mornings—Daffy Duck especially gave me something, if I could bear to imagine growing up a dynamited, beak-shattered duck. Art Carney on *The Honeymooners* gave me something too, in the way he jerked his neck, when we were allowed to stay up to see him. But it was Minna who brought me the language, Minna and Court Street that let me speak.

We four were selected because we were the four white boys at St. Vincent's. I was surely undersold goods, a twitcher and nosepicker retrieved from the library instead of the schoolyard, probably a retard, certainly a regrettable, inferior offering. Mr. Kassel was a teacher who knew Frank Minna from the neighborhood, and his invitation to Minna to borrow us for the afternoon was a first glimpse of the halo of favors and favoritism that extended around Minna—"knowing somebody" as a life condition. Minna was our exact reverse, we who knew no one and benefited nothing from it when we did.

Minna had asked for white boys to suit his clients' presumed prejudice—and his own certain ones. But he didn't show any particular tenderness that first day, a sweltering August weekday afternoon after classes, streets like black chewing gum, slow-creeping cars like badly projected science-class slides in the haze. Though he seemed a man to us, Minna was probably twenty-five. He was gangly except for a tiny potbelly in his pocket-T, and his hair was combed into a smooth pompadour, a Brooklyn hairstyle that stood outside time, projecting from some distant Frank Sinatra past. He opened the rear of his dented, graffitied van and told us to get inside, then slammed and padlocked the doors without explanation, without asking our names.

We four gaped at one another, giddy and astonished at this escape, not knowing what it meant, not really needing to know. The others, Tony, Gilbert and Danny, were willing to be grouped with me, to pretend I fit with them, if that was what it took to be plucked up by the outside world and seated in the dark on a dirty steel truck bed vibrating its way to somewhere that wasn't St. Vincent's. Of course I was vibrating too, vibrating before Minna rounded us up, vibrating inside always and straining to keep it from showing. I didn't kiss the other three boys, but I wanted to. Instead I made a kissing, chirping sound, like a bird's peep, over and over: "Chrip, chrip, chrip."

Tony told me to shut the fuck up, but his heart wasn't in it, not this day, in the midst of life's unfolding mystery. For Tony, especially, this was his destiny coming to find him. He saw more in Minna from the first because he'd prepared himself to see it. Tony Vermonte was famous at St. Vincent's for the confidence he exuded, confidence that a mistake had been made, that he didn't belong in the Home. He was Italian, better than the rest of us, who didn't know what we were. His father was either a mobster or a cop—Tony saw no contradiction in this, so we didn't either. The Italians would return for him, in one guise or another, and that was what he'd taken Minna for.

Tony was famous for other things as well. He had lived outside the Home and then come back. A Quaker family had taken Tony in, intending to give him a permanent home. He'd announced his contempt even as he packed his clothes: They weren't Italian. Still, he lived with them for a few months. They installed him at Brooklyn Friends, a private school a few blocks away, and on his way home most days he'd come and hang on the St. Vincent's fence and tell stories of the private-school girls he'd felt up and sometimes penetrated, the faggy private-school boys who swam and played soccer but were easily humiliated in fistfights. Then one day his foster parents found prodigious Tony in bed with one girl too many: their own sixteen-year-old daughter. Or so the story went; there was only one source. Anyway, he was reinstalled at St. Vincent's, where he fell easily into his old routine of beating up and befriending me on alternating afternoons.

Gilbert Coney was Tony's right hand, a stocky boy just passing for tough—he would have beamed at you for calling him a thug. But he was tolerant of me, and we had a couple of secrets. On a Home for Boys visit to the Museum of Natural History, Gilbert and I had split from the group and returned to the room dominated by an enormous plastic blue whale suspended from the ceiling, which had been the focus of the official visit. But underneath the whale was a gallery of murky dioramas of undersea life, lit so you had to press close to the glass to find the wonders tucked deep in the corners. In one a sperm whale fought a giant squid. In another a killer whale pierced a floor of ice. Gilbert and I wandered hypnotized, and when a class of third graders was led away we found we had the giant hall to ourselves. Gilbert showed me his discovery: a small brass door beside the penguin diorama had been left unlocked. When he opened it we saw that it led both behind and into the penguin scene.

"Get in, Lionel," said Gilbert.

If I'd not wanted to, it would have been bullying, but I wanted to desperately. Every minute the hall remained empty was precious. The lip of the doorway was knee-high. I clambered in and opened the flap in the ocean-blue painted boards that made the side wall of the diorama, then slipped into the picture. The ocean floor was a smooth bowl of painted plaster. I scooted down the grade on my bended knees, looking out at a flabbergasted Gilbert on the other side of the glass. Swimming penguins were mounted on rods extending straight from the far wall, and others were suspended in the plastic waves of ocean surface that now made a low ceiling over my head. I caressed the nearest penguin, one mounted low, shown diving in pursuit of a fish, patted its head, stroked its gullet as though helping it swallow a dry pill. Gilbert guffawed, thinking I was performing comedy for him, when in fact I'd been overwhelmed by a tender, touchy impulse toward the stiff, poignant penguin. Now it became imperative that I touch *all* the penguins, or all I could, anyway—some were inaccessible to me, on the other side of the barrier of the ocean's surface, standing on ice floes. Shuffling on my knees I made the rounds, affectionately tagging each swimming bird before I made my escape back through the brass door. Gilbert was impressed, I could tell. I was now a kid who'd do anything, do crazy things. He was right and wrong, of course— once I'd touched the first penguin I had no choice.

Somehow this led to a series of confidences. I was crazy but also easily intimidated, which made me Gilbert's idea of a safe repository for his crazy feelings. Gilbert was a precocious masturbator, and looking for some triangulation between his own experiments and schoolyard lore. Did I do it? How often? One hand or two? Close my eyes? Ever rub against the mattress? I took his inquiries seriously, but I didn't really have the information he needed, not yet. My stupidity made Gilbert grouchy at first, and he spent a week or two glowering to let me know what galactic measures of pain awaited if I ratted him out. Then he came back, more urgent than ever. Try it and I'll watch, he said. It's not so hard. I obeyed, as I had in the museum, but the results weren't as good. I couldn't treat myself with the tenderness I'd lavished on the penguins, at least not in front of Gilbert. He became grouchy again, and after two or three go-arounds the subject was permanently dropped.

Tourette's teaches you what people will ignore and forget, teaches you to see the mechanism people employ to tuck away the incongruous, the disruptive—it teaches you because you're the one lobbing the incongruous and disruptive their way. Once I sat on a bus a few rows ahead of a man with a belching tic—long, groaning, almost vomitous-sounding noises, the kind a fifth grader learns to make by swallowing a bellyful of air, then forgets by high school when charming girls becomes more vital than freaking them out. This man's compulsion was terribly specific: he sat at the back of the bus, and only when every head faced forward did he give out with his digestive simulacra. Then, every sixth or seventh time, he'd mix in a messy farting sound. He was a miserable-looking black man in his sixties. Despite the peek-a-boo brilliance of his timing, it was clear to anyone he was the source, and so the other riders coughed reprovingly, quit giving him the satisfaction of looking. Of course, our not glancing back freed him to run together great uninterrupted phrases of his ripest noise. To all but me he was just an antisocial jerk fishing for attention. But I saw that it was unmistakably a compulsion, a tic—Tourette's—and I knew those other passengers would barely recall it a few minutes after stepping off to their destinations. Despite how that maniacal croaking filled the auditorium of the bus, the concertgoers were plainly engaged in the task of forgetting the music. Consensual reality is both fragile and elastic, and it heals like the skin of a bubble. The belching man ruptured it so quickly and completely that I could watch the wound instantly seal.

Similarly, I doubt the other boys directly recalled my bouts of kissing. That tic was too much for us all. Nine months or so after touching the penguins I had begun to overflow with reaching, tapping, grabbing and kissing urges. Those compulsions emerged first, while language was still trapped like a roiling ocean under a calm floe of ice, the way I'd been trapped in the underwater half of the penguin display. I'd begun reaching for door frames, kneeling to grab at skittering loosened sneaker laces (a recent fashion among the toughest boys at St. Vincent's, unfortunately for me), incessantly tapping the metal-pipe legs of the schoolroom desks and chairs and, worst, grabbing and kissing my fellow boys. I grew terrified of myself then and burrowed deeper into the library, but I was forced out for classes or meals. Then it would happen. I'd lunge at someone and kiss their cheek or neck or forehead, whatever I hit. After, compulsion expelled, I could try to explain, defend myself or flee. I kissed Greg Toon and Edwin Torres, whose eyes I'd never dared meet. I kissed Leshawn Montrose, who'd broken Mr. Voccaro's arm with a chair. I kissed Tony Vermonte and Gilbert Coney and tried to kiss Danny Fantl. I kissed my own counterparts, other invisible boys working the margins at St. Vincent's. "It's a game!" I'd say, pleadingly. "It's a game." Since the most inexplicable things in our lives were games, with their ancient embedded rituals, British Bulldog, Ringolevio and Scully, it seemed possible I might persuade them this was another one, the Kissing Game. Just as important, I might persuade myself. "It's a game," I'd say desperately, as tears of pain ran down my face. Leshawn Montrose cracked my head against a porcelain water fountain; Greg Toon and Edwin Torres generously only shucked me off onto the floor. Tony Vermonte twisted my arm behind my back and forced me against a wall. "It's a game," I breathed. He released me and shook his head, full of contempt and pity. Danny Fantl saw my move coming and faked me out, then vanished down a stairwell. Gilbert stood and glared, deeply unnerved due to our private history. "A game," I reassured him.

Meantime beneath that frozen shell a sea of language was reaching full boil. It became harder and harder not to notice that when a television pitchman said *to last the rest of a lifetime* my brain went *to rest the lust of a loaftomb*, that when I heard "Alfred Hitchcock" I silently replied "Altered Houseclock," that when I sat reading Booth Tarkington in the library, my throat and jaw worked behind my clenched lips, desperately fitting the syllables of the prose to the rhythms of "Rapper's Delight," which was then playing every fifteen or twenty minutes out on the yard.

I found other outlets, other obsessions. The pale thirteen-year-old Mr. Kassel pulled out of the library and offered to Minna was prone to floor-tapping, whistling, tongue clicking, rapid head turns and wall stroking, anything but the direct utterances for which my Tourette's brain most yearned. Language bubbled inside me now but it felt too dangerous to let out. Speech was intention, and I couldn't let anyone else or myself know how intentional my craziness felt. Pratfalls, antics, those were accidental lunacy, and so forgivable. Practically speaking, it was one thing to stroke Leshawn Montrose's arm, or even to kiss him, another entirely to walk up and call him Shefawn Mongoose or Fuckyou Moonprose. So, though I collected words, treasured them like a drooling sadistic captor, melting them down, filing off their edges, before release I translated them into physical performance, manic choreography.

My body was an overwound watch spring, one which could easily drive a vast factory mechanism like the one in *Modern Times*, which we watched that year in the basement of the Brooklyn Public Library on Fourth Avenue. I took Chaplin as a model: obviously blazing with aggression, he'd managed to keep his trap shut and so had skirted danger and been regarded as cute. I needn't exactly strain for a motto: silence, golden, get it? Got it. Hone your timing instead, burnish those physical routines, your idiot wall stroking and lace chasing, until they're funny in a flickering black-and-white way, until your enemies don policemen's caps and begin tripping over themselves, until doe-eyed women swoon. So I kept my tongue wound in my teeth, ignored the pulsing in my cheek, the throbbing in my gullet, persistently swallowed language back like vomit. It burned as hotly.

We rode a mile or two before Minna's van halted, engine guttering to a stop. Then he let us out of the back and we found ourselves in a gated warehouse yard under the shadow of the Brooklyn-Queens Expressway, in a ruined industrial zone. Minna led us to a large truck, a detached twelve-wheel trailer with no cab in evidence, then rolled up the back to reveal a load of identical cardboard crates, a hundred, two hundred, maybe more.

"Couple you boys get up inside," said Minna distractedly. Tony and Danny had the guile to immediately leap into the truck, where they could work shaded from the sun. "You're just gonna run this stuff inside, that's all. Hand shit off, move it up to the front of the truck, get it in. Straight shot, you got it?" He pointed to the warehouse. We all nodded, and I peeped. It went unnoticed.

Minna opened the big panel doors of the warehouse and showed us where to set the crates. We started quickly, then wilted in the heat. Tony and Danny massed the crates at the lip of the truck while Gilbert and I made the first dozen runs, then the older boys ceded their advantage and began to help us drag them across the blazing yard. Minna never touched a crate; he spent the whole time in the office of the warehouse, a cluttered room full of desks, file cabinets, tacked-up notes and pornographic calendars and a stacked tower of orange traffic cones, visible to us through an interior window, smoking cigarettes and jawing on the telephone, apparently not listening for replies. Every time I glanced through the window his mouth was moving, but the door was closed, and he was inaudible behind the glass. At some point another man appeared, from where I wasn't sure, and stood in the yard wiping his forehead as though he were the one laboring. Minna came out, the two stepped inside the office, the other man disappeared. We moved the last of the crates inside, Minna rolled the gate of the truck and locked the warehouse, pointed us back to his van, but paused before shutting us into the back.

"Hot day, huh?" he said, looking at us directly for what might have been the first time.

Bathed in sweat, we nodded, afraid to speak.

"You monkeys thirsty? Because personally I'm dying out here."

Minna drove us to Smith Street, a few blocks from St. Vincent's, and pulled over in front of a bodega, then bought us pop-top cans of Miller, and sat with us in the back of the van, drinking. It was my first beer.

"Names," said Minna, pointing at Tony, our obvious leader. We said our first names, starting with Tony. Minna didn't offer his own, only drained his beer and nodded. I began tapping the truck panel beside me.

Physical exertion over, astonishment at our deliverance from St. Vincent's receding, my symptoms found their opening again.

"You probably ought to know, Lionel's a freak," said Tony, his voice vibrant with self-regard. He jerked his thumb in my direction.

"Yeah, well, you're all freaks, if you don't mind me pointing it out," said Minna. "No parents—or am I mixed up?"

Silence.

"Finish your beer," said Minna, tossing his can past us, into the back of the van.

And that was the end of our first job for Frank Minna.

But Minna rounded us up again the next week, brought us to that same desolate yard, and this time he was friendlier. The task was identical, almost to the number of boxes, and we performed it in the same trepidatious silence. I felt a violent hatred burning off Tony in my and Gilbert's direction, as though he thought we were in the process of screwing up his Italian rescue. Danny was exempt and oblivious. Still, we'd begun to function as a team—demanding physical work contained its own truths, and we explored them despite ourselves.

Over beers Minna said, "You like this work?"

One of us said *sure*.

"You know what you're doing?" Minna grinned at us, waiting. The question was confusing. "You know what kind of work this is?"

"What, moving boxes?" said Tony.

"Right, moving. Moving work. That's what you call it when you work for me. Here, look." He stood to get into his pocket, pulled out a roll of twenties and a small stack of white cards. He stared at the roll for a minute, then peeled off four twenties and handed one to each of us. It was my first twenty dollars. Then he offered us each a card. It read: *L & L Movers. Gerard & Frank Minna.* And a phone number.

"You're Gerard or Frank?" said Tony.

"Minna, Frank." Like *Bond, James.* He ran his hand through his hair. "So you're a moving company, get it? Doing moving work." This seemed a very important point: that we call it *moving.* I couldn't imagine what else to call it.

"Who's Gerard?" said Tony. Gilbert and I, even Danny, watched Minna carefully. Tony was questioning him on behalf of us all.

"My brother."

"Older or younger?"

"Older."

Tony thought for a minute. "Who's L & L?"

"Just the name, L & L. Two Ls. Name of the company."

"Yeah, but what's it mean?"

"What do you need it to mean, Fruitloop—Living Loud? Loving Ladies? Laughing at you Losers?"

"What, it doesn't mean anything?" said Tony.

"I didn't say that, did I?"

"Least Lonely," I suggested.

"There you go," said Minna, waving his can of beer at me. "L & L Movers, Least Lonely."

Tony, Danny and Gilbert all stared at me, uncertain how I'd gained this freshet of approval.

"Liking Lionel," I heard myself say.

"Minna, that's an Italian name?" said Tony. This was on his own behalf, obviously. It was time to get to the point. The rest of us could all go fuck ourselves.

"What are you, the census?" said Minna. "Cub reporter? What's your full name, Jimmy Olsen?"

"Lois Lane," I said.

"Tony Vermonte," said Tony, ignoring me.

"Vermont-ee," repeated Minna. "That's what, like a New England thing, right? You a Red Sox fan?"

"Yankees," said Tony, confused and defensive. The Yankees were champions now, the Red Sox their hapless, eternal victims, vanquished most recently by Bucky Dent's famous home run. We'd all watched it on television.

"Luckylent," I said, remembering. "Duckybent."

Minna erupted with laughter. "Yeah, Ducky fucking Bent! That's good. Don't look now, it's Ducky Bent."

"Lexluthor," I said, reaching out to touch Minna's shoulder. He only stared at my hand, didn't move away. "Lunchylooper, Laughyluck—"

"All right, Loopy," said Minna. "Enough already."

"Loopylip—" I was desperate for a way to stop. My hand went on tapping Minna's shoulder.

"Let it go," said Minna, and now he returned my shoulder taps, once, hard. "Don't tug the boat."

To tugboat was to try Minna's patience. Any time you pushed your luck, said too much, overstayed a welcome or overestimated the usefulness of a given method or approach you were guilty of having tugged the boat. *Tugboating* was most of all a dysfunction of wits and storytellers, and a universal one: anybody who thought themselves funny would likely tug a boat here or there. Knowing when a joke or verbal gambit was right at its limit, quitting before the boat had been tugged, that was art.

Years before the word *Tourette's* was familiar to any of us, Minna had me diagnosed: Terminal Tugboater.

Distributing eighty dollars and those four business cards was all Minna had to do to instate the four of us as the junior staff of L & L Movers. Twenty dollars and a beer remained our usual pay. Minna would gather us sporadically, on a day's notice, or no notice at all—the latter possibility became incentive, once we'd begun high school, for us to return to St. Vincent's directly after classes and lounge in the schoolyard, pretending not to listen for the distinctive grumble of his van's motor. The jobs varied enormously. We'd load merchandise, like the cartons in the trailer, in and out of storefront basement grates all up and down Court Street, borderline shady activity that it seemed wholesalers ought to be handling themselves, transactions sealed with a shared cigar in the back of the shop. Or we'd bustle apartment loads of furniture in and out of brownstone walk-ups, legitimate moving jobs, where fretting couples worried we weren't old or expert enough to handle their belongings—Minna would hush them, remind them of the cost of distractions: "The meter's running." We put sofas through third-story windows with a makeshift cinch and pulley, Tony and Minna on the roof, Gilbert and Danny in the window to receive, me on the ground with the guide ropes. A massive factory building under the Manhattan Bridge, owned by an important unseen friend of Minna's, had been damaged in a fire, and we moved the inhabitants for free, as some sort of settlement or concession. The terms were obscure, but Minna was terrifically urgent about it, seething at any delay—the only meter running now was Minna's credibility with his friend-client. Once we emptied an entire electronics showroom into Minna's truck, pulling unboxed stereos off shelves and out of window displays, disconnecting the wires from lit, blinking amplifiers, eventually even taking the phone off the desk—it would have seemed a sort of brazen burglary had Minna not been standing on the sidewalk in front, drinking beer and telling jokes with the man who'd unpadlocked the shop gates for us as we filed past with the goods. Everywhere Minna connived and cajoled and dropped names, winking at us to make us complicit, and everywhere Minna's clients stared at us boys, some wondering if we'd palm a valuable when they weren't looking, some trying to figure the angle, perhaps hoping to catch a hint of disloyalty, an edge over Minna they'd save for when they needed it. We palmed nothing, revealed no disloyalty. Instead we stared back, tried to make them flinch. And we listened, gathered information. Minna was teaching us, when he meant to and when he didn't.

It changed us as a group. We developed a certain collective ego, a presence apart at the Home. We grew less embattled from within, more from without: non-white boys sensed in our privilege a hint of their future deprivations and punished us for it. Age had begun to heighten those distinctions anyway. So Tony, Gilbert, Danny and myself smoothed out our old antipathies and circled the wagons. We stuck up for one another, at the Home and at Sarah J. Hale, our local high school.

There at Sarah J.: the St. Vincent's Boys were disguised, blended with the larger population, a pretty rough crowd despite their presumably having parents and siblings and telephones and bedroom doors with locks and a thousand other unimaginable advantages. There we mixed with girls for the first time—what mixing was possible with the brutal, strapping black girls of Sarah J., gangs of whom laid after-school ambushes for any white boy daring enough to have flirted, even made eye-contact, with one inside the building. The girls were claimed by boyfriends too sophisticated to bother with school, who rode by for them at lunch hour in cars throbbing with amplified basslines and sometimes boasting bullet-riddled doors, and their only use for us was as a dartboard for throwing lit cigarette butts. Yes, relations between the sexes were strained at Sarah J., and I doubt any of us four, even Tony, so much as copped a feel from the girls we were schooled with there.

Minna's Court Street was the old Brooklyn, a placid ageless surface alive underneath with talk, with deals and casual insults, a neighborhood political machine with pizzeria and butcher-shop bosses and unwritten rules everywhere. All was talk except for what mattered most, which were unspoken understandings. The barbershop, where he took us for identical haircuts that cost three dollars each, except even that fee was waived for Minna—no one had to wonder why the price of a haircut hadn't gone up since 1966, nor why six old barbers were working out of the same ancient storefront; the barbershop was a retirement home, a social club and front for a backroom poker game. The barbers were taken care of because this was Brooklyn, where people *looked out*. Why would the prices go up, when nobody walked in who wasn't part of this conspiracy, this trust?—though if you spoke of it you'd surely meet with confused denials, or laughter and a too-hard cuff on the cheek. Another exemplary mystery was the "arcade," a giant storefront containing three pinball machines and six or seven video games, Asteroids, Frogger, Centipede, and a cashier who'd change dollars to quarters and accept hundred-dollar bills folded into lists of numbers, names of horses and football teams. The curb in front of the arcade was lined with Vespas. They sat without anything more than a bicycle lock for protection, a taunt to vandals. A block away, on Smith, they would have been stripped, but here they were pristine, a curbside showroom. It didn't need explaining—this was Court Street. And Court Street, where it passed through Carroll Gardens and Cobble Hill, was the only Brooklyn, really—north was Brooklyn Heights, secretly a part of Manhattan, south was the harbor, and the rest, everything east of the Gowanus Canal, apart from small outposts of civilization in Park Slope and Windsor Terrace, was an unspeakable barbarian tumult.

Sometimes he needed just one of us. He'd appear at the Home in his Impala instead of the van, request someone specific, then spirit them away to the bruised consternation of those left behind. Tony was in and out of Minna's graces, his ambition and pride costing him as much as he won, but he was unmistakably our leader and Minna's right hand. He wore his private errands with Minna like Purple Hearts, but refused to report on their content to the rest of us. Danny, athletic, silent and tall, became Minna's greyhound, sent on private deliveries and rendezvous, and given early driving lessons in a vacant Red Hook lot, as though Minna were grooming him for work as an international spy, or Kato for a new Green Hornet. Gilbert, all bullish determination, was pegged for the grunt work, sitting in double-parked cars, repairing a load of ruptured cartons with strapping tape, and repainting the van, whose graffitied exterior some of Minna's neighbors had apparently found objectionable. And I was an extra set of eyes and ears and opinions. Minna would drag me along to backrooms and offices and barbershop negotiations, then debrief me afterwards. What did I think of that guy? Shitting or not? A moron or retard? A shark or a mook? Minna encouraged me to have a take on everything, and to spit it out, as though he thought my verbal disgorgings were only commentary not yet anchored to subject matter. And he adored my echolalia. He thought I was doing impressions.

Needless to say, it wasn't commentary and impressions, but my verbal Tourette's flowering at last. Like Court Street, I seethed behind the scenes with language and conspiracies, inversions of logic, sudden jerks and jabs of insult. Now Minna had begun to draw me out. With his encouragement I freed myself to ape the rhythm of his overheard dialogues, his complaints and endearments, his for-the-sake-of arguments. And Minna loved my effect on his clients and associates, the way I'd unnerve them, disrupt some schmooze with an utterance, a head jerk, a husky "*eatme!*" I was his special effect, a running joke embodied. They'd look up startled and he'd wave his hand knowingly, counting money, not even bothering to look at me. "Don't mind him, he can't help it," he'd say. "Kid's shot out of a cannon." Or: "He likes to get a little nutty sometimes." Then he'd wink at me, acknowledge our conspiracy. I was evidence of life's unpredictability and rudeness and poignancy, a scale model of his own nutty heart. In this way Minna licensed my speech, and speech, it turned out, liberated me from the overflowing disaster of my

Tourettic self, turned out to be the tic that satisfied where others didn't, the scratch that briefly stilled the itch.

"You ever listen to yourself, Lionel?" Minna would say later, shaking his head. "You really are shot out of a fucking cannon."

"*Scott Out Of The Canyon!* I don't know why, I just—*fuckitup!*—I just can't stop."

"You're a freak show, that's why. Human freak show, and it's free. Free to the public."

"Freefreak!" I tapped his shoulder.

"That's what I said: a free human freak show."

"Makes you think you're Italian?" said Minna one day, as we all rode together in his Impala.

"What do I look like to you?" said Tony.

"I was thinking maybe Greek," said Minna. "I used to know this Greek guy went around knocking up the Italian girls down Union Street, until a couple their older brothers took him out under the bridge. You remind me of him, you know? Got that dusky tinge. I'd say half Greek. Or maybe Puerto Rican."

"Fuck you."

"Probably know all your parents. We're not talking the international jet set here—bunch of teen mothers, probably live in a five-mile radius, need to know the goddamn truth."

We learned to negotiate the labyrinth of Minna's weird prejudices blind, and blindly. Hippies, for instance, were dangerous and odd, also sort of sad in their utopian wrongness. ("Your parents must of been hippies," he'd tell me. "That's why you came out the superfreak you are.") Homosexual men were harmless reminders of the impulse Minna was sure lurked in all of us—and "half a fag," was more shameful than a whole one. Certain baseball players were half a fag. So were most rock stars and anyone who'd been in the Armed Services but not in a war. The Arabic population of Atlantic Avenue was as unfathomable as the Indian tribes that had held our land before Columbus. "Classic" minorities—Irish, Jews, Poles, Italians, Greeks and Puerto Ricans were the clay of life itself, funny in their essence, while blacks and Asians of all types were soberly snubbed, unfunny. But bone-stupidity, mental illness and familial or sexual anxiety—these were the bolts of electricity that made the clay walk, the animating forces that rendered human life amusing. It was a form of racism, not respect, that restricted blacks and Asians from ever being stupid like a Mick or Polack. If you weren't funny you didn't quite exist. And it was usually better to be fully stupid, impotent, lazy, greedy or freakish than to seek to dodge your destiny, or layer it underneath pathetic guises of vanity or calm.

Though Gerard Minna's name was printed on the business card, we met him only twice, and never on a moving job. The first time was Christmas day, at Minna's mother's apartment.

Carlotta Minna was an *old stove*. That was the Brooklyn term for it, according to Minna. She was a cook who worked in her own apartment, making plates of sautéed squid and stuffed peppers and jars of tripe soup which were purchased at her door by a constant parade of buyers, mostly neighborhood women with too much housework and single men, young or elderly, bocce players who'd take her plates to the park with them, racing bettors who'd eat her food standing up outside the OTB, butchers and contractors who'd sit on crates in the backs of their shops and wolf her cutlets, folding them with their fingers like waffles. She truly worked an old stove, too, a tiny enamel four-burner that was crusted with ancient sauces and on which three or four pots invariably bubbled. The whole kitchen glowed with heat like a kiln. Mrs. Minna herself seemed to have been baked, her whole face dark and furrowed like the edges of an overdone calzone. We never arrived without nudging aside some buyers from her door, nor without packing off with plateloads of food. When we were in her presence Minna bubbled himself, with talk, all directed at his mother, banking cheery insults off anyone else in the apartment, delivery boys, customers known and unknown, tasting everything she had cooking and making suggestions on every dish, poking and pinching every raw ingredient or ball of unfinished dough and also his mother herself, her earlobes and chin, wiping flour off her dark arms with his open hand. And she never once uttered a word.

That Christmas Minna had us all up to his mother's to eat at her table, first nudging aside sauce-glazed stirring spoons and baby-food jars of spices to clear spots for our plates. Minna stood at the stove, sampling her broth, and Mrs. Minna hovered over us as we devoured her meatballs, running her floury fingers over the backs of our chairs, then gently touching our heads, the napes of our necks. We pretended not to notice, ashamed to show that we drank in her nurturance as eagerly as her meat sauce. We splashed, gobbled, kneed one another under the table. Privately, I polished the handle of my spoon, quietly aping the motions of her fingers on my nape, and fought not to twist in my seat and jump at her. All the while she went on caressing with hands that would have horrified us if we'd looked close.

Minna spotted her and said, "This is exciting for you, Ma? I got all of motherless Brooklyn up here for you. Merry Christmas."

Minna's mother only produced a sort of high, keening sigh. We stuck to the food.

"*Motherless Brooklyn*," repeated a voice we didn't know.

It was Minna's brother, Gerard. He'd come in without our noticing. A fleshier, taller Minna. His eyes and hair were as dark, his mouth as wry, lips deep-indented at the corners. He wore a brown-and-tan leather coat, which he left buttoned, his hands pushed into the fake patch pockets.

"So this is your little moving company," he said.

"Hey, Gerard," said Minna.

"Christmas, Frank," said Gerard Minna absently, not looking at his brother. Instead he was making short work of the four of us, his hard gaze snapping us each in two like bolt cutters on inferior padlocks. It didn't take long before he was done with us forever—that was how it felt.

"Yeah, Christmas to you," said Minna. "Where you been?"

"Upstate," said Gerard.

"What, with Ralph and them?" I detected something new in Minna's voice, a yearning, sycophantic strain.

"More or less."

"What, just for the holidays you're gonna go talkative on me? Between you and Ma it's like the Cloisters up here."

"I brought you a present." He handed Minna a white legal envelope, stuffed fat. Minna began to tear at the end, and Gerard said in a voice low and full of ancient sibling authority: "Put it away."

Now we understood we'd all been staring. All except Mrs. Minna, who was at her stove, piling together a cornucopic holiday plate for her older son.

"Make it to go, Mother."

She moaned again, closed her eyes.

"I'll be back," said Gerard. He put his hands on her, much as Minna did. "I've got a few people to see today. I'll be back tonight. Enjoy your little orphan party."

He took the foil-wrapped plate and was gone.

Minna said: "What're you staring at? Eat your food!" He stuffed the white envelope into his jacket. Then he cuffed us, the bulging gold ring on his middle finger clipping our crowns in the same place his mother had fondled.

One day in April, five months after that Christmas meal, Minna drove up with all his windows thoroughly smashed, the van transformed into a blinding crystalline sculpture, a mirrorball on wheels, reflecting the sun. It was plainly the work of a man with a hammer or crowbar and no fear of interruption. Minna appeared not to have noticed; he ferried us out to a job without mentioning it. On our way back to the Home, as we rumbled over the cobblestones of Hoyt Street, Tony nodded at the windshield, which sagged in its frame like a beaded curtain, and said: "So what happened?"

"What happened to what?" It was a Minna game, forcing us to be literal when we'd been trained by him to talk in glances, in three-corner shots.

"Somebody fucked up your van."

Minna shrugged, excessively casual. "I parked it on that block of Pacific Street."

We didn't know what he was talking about.

"These guys around that block had this thing about how I was uglifying the neighborhood." A few weeks after Gilbert's paint job the van had been covered again with graffiti, vast ballooning font and an overlay of stringy tags. Something made Minna's van a born target, the flat battered sides like a windowless subway car, a homely public surface crying for spray paint where private cars were inviolate. "They told me not to park it around there anymore."

Minna lifted both hands from the wheel to gesture his indifference. We weren't totally convinced.

"Someone's sending a message," said Tony.

"What's that?" said Minna.

"I just said it's a message," said Tony.

"Yeah, but what are you trying to say?" said Minna.

"*Fuckitmessage,*" I suggested impulsively.

"You know what I mean," said Tony defiantly, ignoring me.

"Yeah, maybe," said Minna. "But put it in your own words." I could feel his anger unfolding, smooth as a fresh deck of cards.

"*Put it in your fuckitall!*" I was like a toddler devising a tantrum to keep his parents from fighting.

But Minna wasn't distractable. "Quiet, Freakshow," he said, never taking his eyes from Tony. "Tell me what you said," he told Tony again.

"Nothing," said Tony. "Damn." He was backpedaling.

Minna pulled the van to the curb at a fire hydrant on the corner of Bergen and Hoyt. Outside, a couple of black men sat on a stoop, drinking from a bag. They squinted at us.

"Tell me what you said," Minna insisted.

He and Tony stared at one another, and the rest of us melted back. I swallowed away a few variations.

"Just, you know, somebody's sending you a message." Tony smirked.

This clearly infuriated Minna. He and Tony suddenly spoke a private language in which *message* signified heavily. "You think you know a thing," he said.

"All I'm saying is I can see what they did to your truck, Frank." Tony scuffed his feet in the layer of tiny cubes of safety glass that had peeled away from the limp window and lay scattered on the floor of the van.

"That's not all you said, Dickweed."

Dickweed: it was different from any insult Minna had bestowed on us before. Bitter as it sounded—*dickweed.* Our little organization was losing its innocence, although I couldn't have explained how or why.

"I can't help what I see," said Tony. "Somebody put a hit on your windows."

"Think you're a regular little wiseguy, don't you?"

Tony stared at him.

"You want to be Scarface?"

Tony didn't give his answer, but we knew what it was. *Scarface* had opened a month before and Al Pacino was ascendant, a personal colossus astride Tony's world, blocking out the sky.

"See, the thing about Scarface," said Minna, "is before he got to be Scarface he was *Scabface.* Nobody ever considers that. You have to want to be Scabface first."

For a second I thought Minna was going to hit Tony, damage his face to make the point. Tony seemed to be waiting for it too. Then Minna's fury leaked away.

"Out," he said. He waved his hand, a Caesar gesturing to the heavens through the roof of his refitted postal van.

"What?" said Tony. "Right here?"

"Out," he said again, equably. "Walk home, you muffin asses."

We sat gaping, though his meaning was clear enough. We weren't more than five or six blocks from the Home, anyway. But we hadn't been paid, hadn't gone for beers or slices or a bag of hot, clingy zeppole. I could taste the disappointment— the flavor of powdered sugar's absence. Tony slid open the door, dislodging more glass, and we obediently filed out of the van and onto the sidewalk, into the day's glare, the suddenly formless afternoon.

Minna drove off, leaving us there to bob together awkwardly before the drinkers on the stoop. They shook their heads at us, stupid-looking white boys a block from the projects. But we were in no danger there, nor were we dangerous ourselves. There was something so primally humiliating in our ejection that Hoyt Street itself seemed to ridicule us, the humble row of brownstones and sleeping bodegas. We were inexcusable to ourselves. Others clotted street corners, not us, not anymore. We rode with Minna. The effect was deliberate: Minna knew the value of the gift he'd withdrawn.

"Muffin ass," I said forcefully, measuring the shape of the words in my mouth, auditioning them for tic-richness. Then I sneezed, induced by the sunlight.

Gilbert and Danny looked at me with disgust, Tony with something worse.

"Shut up," he said. There was cold fury in his teeth-clenched smile.

"Tellmetodoit, muffinass," I croaked.

"Be quiet now," warned Tony. He plucked a piece of wood from the gutter and took a step towards me.

Gilbert and Danny drifted away from us warily. I would have followed them, but Tony had me cornered against a parked car. The men on the stoop stretched back on their elbows, slurped their malt liquor thoughtfully.

"Dickweed," I said. I tried to mask it in another sneeze, which made something in my neck pop. I twitched and spoke again. *"Dickweed! Dicketywood!"* I was trapped in a loop of self, stuck refining a verbal tic to free myself from its grip. Certainly I didn't mean to be defying Tony. Yet *dickweed* was

the name Minna had called him, and I was throwing it in his face.

Tony held the stick he'd found, a discarded scrap of lattice with clumps of plaster stuck to it. I stared, anticipating my own pain like I'd anticipated Tony's, at Minna's hand, a minute before. Instead Tony moved close, stick at his side, and grabbed my collar.

"Open your mouth again," he said.

I grabbed Tony back, my hands exploring the neck of his T-shirt, fingers running inside it like an anxious, fumbling lover. Then, struggling not to speak, I pursed my lips, jerked my head to the side and kissed his knuckles where they gripped my collar.

Gilbert and Danny had started up Hoyt Street in the direction of the Home. "C'mon, Tony," said Gilbert, tilting his head. Tony ignored them. He scraped his stick in the gutter and came up with a smear of dog shit, mustard yellow and pungent.

"Open," he said.

Gilbert and Danny slinked away, heads bowed. The street was brightly, absurdly empty. Nobody but the men on the stoop, impassive witnesses. I jerked my head as Tony jabbed with his stick, and he only managed to paint my cheek. I could smell it though, powdered sugar's opposite, married to my face.

"Eat me!" I shouted. Falling back against the car behind me, I turned my head again and again, twitching away, enshrining the moment in ticceography. The stain followed me, adamant, on fire.

Our witnesses crinkled their paper bags, offered ruminative sighs.

Tony dropped his stick and turned away. He'd disgusted himself, couldn't meet my eye. About to speak, he thought better of it, instead jogged to catch Gilbert and Danny as they shrugged away up Hoyt Street, leaving the scene.

We didn't see Minna again until five weeks later, Sunday morning at the Home's yard, late May. He had his brother Gerard with him; it was the second time we'd laid eyes on him.

None of us had seen Frank in the intervening weeks, though I know the others, like myself, had each wandered down Court Street, nosed at a few of his usual haunts, the barbershop, the arcade. He wasn't in them. It meant nothing, it meant everything. He might never reappear, but if he turned up and didn't speak of it we wouldn't think twice. We didn't speak of it to one another, but a pensiveness hung over us, tinged with orphan's melancholy, our resignation to permanent injury. A part of each of us still stood astonished on the corner of Hoyt and Bergen, where we'd been ejected from Minna's van.

A horn honked, the Impala's, not the van's. Then the brothers got out and came to the cyclone fence and waited for us to gather. Tony and Danny were playing basketball, Gilbert ardently picking his nose on the sidelines. That's how I picture it, anyway. I wasn't in the yard when they drove up. Gilbert had to come inside and pull me out of the library, to which I'd mostly retreated since Tony's attack. I was wedged into a windowsill seat when Gilbert found me, immersed in a novel by Allen Drury.

Frank and Gerard were dressed too warmly for that morning, Frank in his bomber jacket, Gerard in his patchwork leather coat. The back seat of the Impala was loaded with shopping bags packed with what looked like Frank's clothes and a pair of old leather suitcases. They stood at the

fence, Frank bouncing nervously on his toes, Gerard hanging
on the mesh, fingers dangling through, doing nothing to conceal his impatience with his brother, an impatience shading
into disgust.

Frank smirked, raised his eyebrows, shook his head.
Danny held his basketball between forearm and hip; Minna
nodded at it, mimed a set shot, dropped his hand at the wrist
and made a delicate *o* with his mouth to signify the *swish* that
would result.

Then, idiotically, he bounced a pretend pass to Gerard.
His brother didn't seem to notice. Minna shook his head,
then wheeled, aimed two trigger fingers through the fence,
and grit his teeth for *rat-tat-tat*, a little imaginary schoolyard
massacre. We could only gape. It was as though somebody
had taken Minna's voice away. And Minna *was* his voice—
didn't he know? His eyes said yes, he did. They looked panicked, like they'd been caged in the body of a mime.

Gerard gazed off emptily into the yard, ignoring the show.
Minna made a few more faces, wincing, chuckling silently,
shaking off some invisible annoyance by twitching his cheek.
I fought to keep from mirroring him.

Then he cleared his throat. "I'm, ah, going out of town
for a while," he said at last.

We waited for more. Minna just nodded and squinted
and grinned his close-mouthed grin at us as though he were
acknowledging applause.

"Upstate?" said Tony.

Minna coughed in his fist. "Oh yeah. Place my brother
goes. He thinks we ought to get a little country air."

"When are you coming back?" said Tony.

"Ah, coming back," said Minna. "You got an unknown
there, Scarface. Unknown factors."

We must have gaped at him, because he added, "I wouldn't wait underwater, if that's what you had in mind."

We were in our second year of high school. Till now I'd counted my future in afternoons, but with Minna leaving, a door of years swung open. And Minna wouldn't be there to tell us what to think of Minna's not being there, to give it a name.

"All right, Frank," said Gerard, turning his back to the fence. "Motherless Brooklyn appreciates your support. I think we better get on the road."

"My brother's in a hurry," said Frank. "He's seeing ghosts everywhere."

"Yeah, I'm looking right at one," said Gerard, though in fact he wasn't looking at anyone, only the car.

Minna tilted his head at us, at his brother, to say *you know.* And *sorry.*

Then he pulled a book out of his pocket, a small paperback. I don't think I'd ever seen a book in his hands before. "Here," he said to me. He dropped it on the pavement and nudged it under the fence with the toe of his shoe. "Take a look," he said. "Turns out you're not the only freak in the show."

I picked it up. *Understanding Tourette's Syndrome* was the title. It was the first time I'd seen the words.

"Meaning to get that to you," he said. "But I've been sort of busy."

I reached for him through the fence and tapped his shoulder, once, twice, let my hand fall, then raised it again and let fly a staccato burst of Tourettic caresses.

"Eatme, Minnaweed," I said under my breath.

"You're a laugh and a half, Freakshow," said Minna, his face completely grim.

"Great," said Gerard, taking Minna by the arm. "Let's get out of here."

Tony had been searching every day after school, I suspect. It was three days later that he found it and led us others there, to the edge of the Brooklyn-Queens Expressway at the end of Baltic. The van was diminished, sagged to its rims, tires melted. The explosion had cleared the windows of their crumbled panes of safety glass, which now lay in a spilled penumbra of grains on the sidewalk and street, together with flakes of traumatized paint and smudges of ash, a photographic map of force. The panels of the truck were layered, graffiti still evident in bone-white outline, all else, Gilbert's shoddy coat of enamel and the manufacturer's ancient green, now chalky black, and delicate like sunburned skin. It was like an X ray of the van that had been before.

We circled it, strangely reverent, afraid to touch, and then I ran away, toward Court Street, before anything could come out of my mouth.

THE ALL-NIGHT
BODEGA OF SOULS

BY COLSON WHITEHEAD

Fort Greene

(Originally published in 2001)

At the all-night bodega of souls the crackheads promenade, jigger and shimmy, trade palsies in fitful games of one-upmanship, count coins beneath the corrugated tin of the yellow canopy. The bodega never closes. At midnight the night man removes the brick from the front door and transactions proceed through bulletproof plastic. He takes requests. He strains to hear the crackheads. When he withdraws into the recesses of his mercantile domain to retrieve malt liquor and potato chips of anonymous manufacture, protein shakes if that's all the customer can keep down, the crackheads etch nonsense slogans and their names into the plastic with keys or dimes, halfhearted dispatches from underground. They look over their shoulders for 5-0; if they pooled their resources they could come up with two dozen warrants and summonses among them, surely. They taunt the night man for no reason, reason enough. They deprecate his sensory apparatus. Yo, you deaf? I wanted one St. Ides and two O.E.s, motherfucker, not two St. Ides, shit. I wanted those Lays chips you got right there, not that plantain shit, shit, you blind? They talk through the bulletproof plastic about the state of the economy. What you want another ten cent? Day before yesterday it was a dollar ninety-five, now you trying to tell me it's another ten cent? My boy was down here two hours ago, nigger, he got the same shit and it wasn't no ten cent more. You Dominican niggers try to rip a nigger off. If the night man is too tired to grant this impromptu haggling session the attention it deserves, he'll let the guy off the hook and hear his name cursed by the man to the other crackheads down the line. If he feels like standing his ground, he'll turn the revolving bulletproof box around so that the man sees his insufficient coin there on the yellowed plastic, a museum exhibit on ghetto commerce. He can come up with that dime or he can leave. Cigarettes and condoms may be purchased singly. The new demand for Phillies cigars is accounted for. The night man runs back and forth. Even a request for simple orange juice from this crowd, at this time of night, gathers licentious aspect. These people take ordinary items from his uncle's shelves and convert them into criminal accessories. The same faces night after night. Crackheads and drug dealers and here's that guy for three Coronas.

J. Sutter on deadline queues up with crackheads in the sinister A.M. His fingers hurt from late employment at the tiny buttons of J.'s microcassette recorder, where they teased shrill idiocy from metallic spools. On the tape the actor and pinup expounded on Tantric sex and the Dalai Lama, from a white table poolside at a hotel in Los Angeles. That day, a year ago, J. sipped a margarita and squinted at his notes in the bleaching sunlight. He felt himself getting soft and overripe in the sunlight just like everything else in the state, his brain splitting and spilling juices. Brody Mills had just finished a stint at a court-appointed substance abuse rehabilitation facility. "Four weeks of seriously getting my head together," as he described it that day, and a year later in J.'s apartment through diminutive technology. He tapped ash on the coarse tile of the hotel Sun Deck Lounge, eschewing for reasons of his own the elegant ashtray proximate his hand. "I'm clean for the first time in years and it feels so great," he said, while eyeing and coveting J.'s frothy blue margarita like a Bedlam fiend.

Brody Mills dispensed rehearsed penance as the viscount of the studio publicity mechanism nodded and smiled and tapped Brody's tanned forearm when he wandered too close to the demilitarized zone between their agreed-upon orchestrations and the facts themselves. His implosion had announced itself for months, first as nameless ectoplasm in blind items of gossip pages, then as bold-faced and named instigator in a brawl at a Manhattan after-hours club, finally no longer omen but event itself, as Brody Mills was cast against type in a hooded sweatshirt and detectives led him into the precinct at the top of the nightly news. On every channel. He was Wednesday's scandal, he took a wrong turn after an afternoon spent with his surgeon-sculpted proboscis deep in cocaine anthill, slapped his longtime model girlfriend around, and bit the arresting officer on the ass when he came to investigate the noise complaint delivered to 911 by fellow residents of the upscale downtown co-op. The judge gave the actor and heartthrob probation and ordered a mandatory stay in rehab. J. was one of ten journalists scheduled for poolside chats that day, one of pop's own parole review board. Brody certainly looked better than in his now infamous mugshot: the goatee shreds in a Beverly Hills sink; the black halos around his eyes trod away by step after step (numbering twelve in total) of self-awakening. J. was there to force the man to his mark, the X of tape where the public wanted him to stand, centered beneath the cleansing spotlight of contrition. Brody moved obediently. "Fame came so quickly," he conceded, "I never had a chance to grow up."

When J. got to that part of the tape, a few days later, when he was back in the civilized regions of Brooklyn, that quotation insisted on itself as an obvious and natural segue for a recap of Brody's early career. He grew up before the public's eyes but the child remained inside him. It was obvious, blunt, and ready for copy.

The magazine called him up, asked J. if he wanted to fly to L.A. to interview the actor and idol on his release from rehabilitation. J. flew out, interviewed this nipple-pierced Lazarus and filed the piece on time. But Fellini died. The great director Federico Fellini was dead in Italy and the managing editor wanted to run a package on the man's demise: capsule reviews of his key movies rated by one to four stars for video store convenience; brief statements by leading American directors (no one too art housey) who were influenced by his work; and an essay on his impact on the world of film, the peculiar economy of postwar Italian life and how it produced idiosyncratic and beautiful art, this essay prepared months before when the man first checked into the hospital, just in case. There's a protocol for such things. J.'s piece on the Confessions of Brody Mills, Actor and Superstar, was pushed back a week to make room for the package, and then another week, and then no one cared and a kill fee (full) arrived in the mail. That was a year ago.

Then this morning J. got a call rousing him from a dream, one of the agitated type that he gets only when the noon light gushes full and accusatory on his face through the bedroom window. Brody was in trouble again, falling naturally to mischief just as he did in the show that made him famous, the Fox television program *Quaker's Dozen*, a situation comedy concerning twelve orphans of different ethnic backgrounds and the hip preacher who is their guardian. (When one of the child actors wanted to leave the show, or was eliminated by the producers' caprices, they were "adopted" at the end of the season, a truly successful adaptation in the Darwinian jungle hell of modern entertainment, rarely a dry eye in the house when this stunt was performed, and seismic, Neilsen-wise.) Brody arrested yet again, and on the eve of the pre-miere of his new action film, yet. Will neighbors ever refrain from calling the police over loud noises that disturb the early morning metropolitan calm? When the constables arrived at the Paramount Hotel this morning and knocked down the door, Brody Mills was as naked as a babe (or the famous bare-ass scene in *Ten Miles*, the first film he made after he was adopted from the hip priest's orphanage) and arguing with invisible critics and studio executives (for the unseen goblins he harangued must have surely been critics and studio exec-utives) while the paraphernalia of narcotics abuse lay in plain sight and the hotel reservoir of pay-per-view pornography inundated the well-appointed suite at high volume. "It took half a dozen of New York's Finest to restrain him," the mag-azine editor related to J. from the AP wire, and would J. mind fixing up his piece from last year, two thousand words if pos-sible, buck a word and by tomorrow noon?

J. put down the phone and went back to sleep. Paid twice for basically the same thing: he slept unperturbed by hector-ing afternoon light, tranquilized by the thought of taking money off the troubled celeb. He woke and mulled over, guz-zling coffee, the talk show disaster on his TV screen. At five he strolled to Fort Greene Park for what he reckoned might be a pleasant hour of meditation but he bored quickly with the pavement and pitbulls and wilted condoms and beat it home after five minutes. His thoughts did not touch on the assignment for more than a few moments through the evening. Pop a few details into the original fifteen-hundred-word piece, no sweat, snatching lollipops from a baby, the tikes have no grip yet, he could get up early and do that easy. He ordered Chinese food and watched television until eleven o'clock, when the faint angel of professionalism perched on his shoulder, implored in a whisper, and he went to check the file. Place the X rays up to the light and see exactly where the fractures were, what needed mending tomorrow so to speak. When he called up the file he found gibberish, a glyphic conspiracy of pixelated symbols he didn't even know how to muster from his keys, it was a language from a cranky sect deep within the motherboard. He couldn't explain it. He had fifteen hundred words of shit when he called up the file *B. Mills Repentance Spiel*.

But he still had the interview tape in his income tax receipt drawer, and he had coffee beans. J. knocked back a pot of coffee and transcribed once again the actor and teen scream's confessional peregrinations. J. fastforwarded past his own voice; he loathed the sound of his voice through the tiny speaker, it was amplified and remastered by the machine so that it contained a quality of earnestness and sincerity that he did not truly possess. Since Brody Mills never answered any of his questions, preferring instead a Dada discourse, it did not matter that J. did not hear his questions. But two and a half hours into his reconstructions, J.'s fingers were rebellious from rewinding and fastforwarding, and his stomach and heart convulsed with the coffee bean's harassment. He was so jazzed up that he needed to calm down if he was going to get, what, two hours sleep maybe and be fresh for the morning's foray to the happy hunting grounds of hackery. And that meant an expedition to the only establishment open at this time of night. He must make his descent.

There was a time that whenever he suited up for a late night bodega run, J. would take the necessary bills and leave his wallet behind. Crackheads begging for change, knuckle-heads out on the prowl: best to make a strategic withdrawal. But nothing ever happened and he stopped. More dreadful than becoming a participant in the city's most popular street theater (the mugging on darkened corner, a spectacle tourists from all over the globe line up to get to see, easier to get than Broadway tickets) are the black windows in all the buildings. Surely, he thinks when he sees them, he cannot be the only one awake at this hour, he is not alone. But in all the build-ings and brownstones the neighbors sleep. The decent folk forsake these hours. Blue TV flicker in some windows tells him there are a few like him awake at this time, not many. Always the same windows too, he's noticed, scattered and well dispersed from block to block so as to adumbrate this nocturnal isolation to best effect. He waves at one blue dancer. No response. It's a four-block walk to the trading post with only two sketchy parts: the blind turn from Carlton to Lafayette (who knows what kind of scene he'll stumble into rounding that building's blade); and that block where street-lights stare blindly, handicapped by vandalism and city neglect, where shadows confab to trade samizdat decrying illumination. But nothing has ever happened on the walk. Two blocks down he sees the huddled messes group outside the bodega. He takes a deep breath and sallies forth.

The freaks come out at night.

He gets in line behind the crackhead who sometime dons a subway worker's reflective orange vest, a souvenir he picked up somewhere in the tunnels. This character likes to tell passersby he needs a token to get home, the orange vest intended to provide evidence of solid citizenship; why he'd need a token if he worked for the Metropolitan Transit Authority has apparently never occurred to the man. J. sizes up the group before him, they are travelers who have come a long way, certainly troubadours finally come to this neck of the woods: The most popular entertainment troupe in all of ShabbyLand, the Freebase Players. Yayo the Clown, his face rouged by dried blood and nose swollen after a recent third fracture, stands in his gay gray attire—he prefers to play the dignified gentleman raconteur down on his luck, happy to share a comedic tale of woe for some change. Those dynamic men on the flying trapeze, Gordy and Morty, who zoom on leave from gravity through alkaloid extracted from cocoa leaves, death defying, without a net worth, falling to earth only at dawn, when this team is too exhausted to perform any trick except attempting sleep while wired to the limits of human endurance. And of course the elders, Ma and Pa, married for twenty years, half that on the pipe, God bless 'em, keeping vigil over the dirty garbage bags containing the cherished props of their act, deposit bottles and broken toasters. And at the fringes of this group, mingling with the celebrities, are assorted teenagers just ducking around the corner for supplies, some malt liquor and Newports, identifiable by their baggy jeans and beepers and youthful joie de vivre, so refreshing beneath the timer-controlled beam of the streetlight.

The line progresses slowly. Tonight everybody hassles the night man, they denounce the service at this establishment. But there are no questionable characters hanging around who fall outside the usual disrepute of the crowd, so J. starts thinking about the article, he leaves this corner and is conveyed to its double on Grub Street. Then J. sees him.

J. sees him zigzagging down the street, stymieing any snipers of euthanasic bent who might be roosting on the

Brooklyn rooftops, an out-of-control prop plane in for an uneasy landing. Tony darts here to finger the coin slot of a pay phone, diddling around in luckless pursuit of change, scrambles there to see if that glint (bottle top) is a dime or *mirabile dictu* a quarter. J. sees Tony, the ghoul's fingers wiggling in the air like crab's legs over wharf bottom detritus. Tony lopes down the avenue, scanning and panning, and J. knows that with Yayo the Clown's meticulous and agonized counting of pennies (always that same deficient sum, the limited number of pockets in which to search), there is no way J. will get clear before Tony lands at the bodega.

J. is the only mark in the ragged assembly on the corner; Tony will not approach the malt liquor boys, contusions have taught him better, and the crackheads are his comrade connoisseurs of the pipe and competitors for change, outside the game. During the day the street has enough traffic that J. is not always discovered as the object of Tony's salvage operation. During the day Tony is a puppy; at night he's a damned barnacle, strung out on an odyssey for the next piece of rock and there's no shaking him. J. and Tony have a relationship at this point, going back to when J. first moved to Brooklyn and had a pocket full of change. Tony looked more craving than hungry, but he needed the change more than J., fuck it, J. was in a good mood. Tony smiled and memorized the sucker's stupid face. The act wed them as mark and con man, till zip code do you part. That first contribution was a binding contract (everyone at the bodega now would attest to its legality) although J. hadn't bothered to read all those subclauses, the fine print he couldn't see in the bright and easy light of that aimless afternoon. They have a relationship, with rules. During the day "Sorry, man," will dispatch Tony to the next mark down the street, that bohemian homesteader of these Brooklyn badlands, the goofy white dude with the goatee. Plenty of marks on the afternoon street, such is the bounty of the neighborhood. Another rule: Tony won't beg for change if J.'s escorting a lady; he'll tip a nonexistent hat, but that's it. At night, though, times are tough, and tonight J.'s the only sap around.

Tony's evidently having a bad night. All sorts of tectonic mayhem afoot in Tony's face this eve: his troubled visage bursts with subcutaneous lumps of calcified ooze and porous eruptions trickling a clear fluid. The hair he managed to grow last week and was quite proud of (they talked about it while J. walked briskly for the subway, forbidden turf for the shambling man; the subway cops had beat him up once, or so Tony claimed) has evacuated in patches, exposing old and angry scabby flesh. Tony arrives just after J. asks the man behind the bulletproof glass for three Coronas. He assumes his hovering remora position and says, "Hey, Mickey Mouse man, you having a good night?"

"All right," J. responds, glancing at Tony and then staring dead into the store. J. was wearing a freebie T-shirt from Disney that first day Tony hit him up for cash. Remembering and filing his clients' distinguishing characteristics helps the crackhead keep his various pitches in order.

"That's good, that's good," Tony says, nodding to comrades down the line, who pantomime back things seen. "Say, listen, listen, could you spare a few dollars for some food? I haven't eaten all day, man, and I'm hungry." Holding his stomach urchinwise.

"We'll see," J. says. This is one night he should have left his wallet behind. In a few moments J. will open his wallet and Tony will take a big thirsty peek at the cash. Can't really say he doesn't have any cash when there's a sheaf of twenties in there.

"Sure am hungry," Tony says, nonchalant.

"Maybe," J. says. He withdraws a five, holding his wallet close. He thinks of soldiers in trenches cupping their cigarette tips so that the Kaiser's goons won't see the flame and draw a bead. The night man returns with three Coronas and rings it up, cue now for J. to slide the money into the bulletproof box and spin it around for approval. The night man slips his agile fingers into the register and drops the change and the bottles into the box, slides it around, transaction complete.

Tony bobs happily next to him. J. stuffs the dollar twenty-five into his jeans and withdraws from the crackhead bazaar. "Hey, brotherman, how about that change?" Tony murmurs.

"Sorry, man," J. says. Cradles beer to his chest and strides.

Tony's head rocks back and forth and he pulls up next to J. "But you said so."

Semantics now. "I said maybe. Can't help you out tonight." He just got two checks in yesterday, so giving the man a quarter is no big deal. Tony can have the change and smoke himself to death, no big deal, it's spare change. But J. has that article due, he's been transcribing word for word a Hollywood junkie's incoherent speeches and he's had enough of junkies tonight. Coffee curdling in him, deadline creeping: he's in servitude to one druggie tonight and that leaves him with empty pockets for this neighborhood nuisance. "See ya later," J. says.

They're the same age, J. found out one day. Tony trotted next to him, like he is now, halfheartedly rapping about needing some Similac for his baby, a ploy Tony used the first few months after their original meeting but eventually dropped when he realized that he didn't come off as a dutiful daddy (no one glows that maniacally with the joys of paternity).

Tony said, "How old do you think I am?" and J. guessed forty-five. Tony grinned broken teeth and giggled, "I'm twenty-nine! Twenty-nine years old! Today's my birthday!" And with that he cackled away down the block.

Tony is not giving up so easily tonight. He's hurting for a little something. Tony says, stepping closer than J. would like, "You want some LPs? 'Cause I know a Guy that got some. You like that old funk? I could hook you up." Switching tactics tonight. He knows a Guy, a Guy who J. has learned is a truly enterprising individual. Over the years this Guy, with Tony as the middle man, has been able to furnish stereos ("Real cheap!"), VCRs of the finest Japanese craftsmanship ("Videos too! You like porno?"), sticky weed ("I saw you walking with that dread last week. Maybe he wants some smoke."), and women ("The night guy at the old people home pays me five bucks to get a woman for him—I could hook you up!"). The Guy Tony knew was a true entrepreneur. Perhaps one day J. will ask if the Guy has a line on devices that make receipts, but not tonight. Nor is he interested in a bunch of old records that the Guy robbed from someone's house.

"No thanks," J. says.

"I haven't eaten all day, man, please."

"No."

"What do you mean no? I see you every day, mother-fucker, and now you can't even help a nigger out with some money to eat. That's terrible." A boil splits on Tony's face and drips. "Can't even help a nigger out with a sandwich. I saw you got plenty of money on you."

"No." They're on the block of broken streetlights. Tony's mother lives on this block. Tony's pointed it out to J. before; it's a nice old brownstone in the middle of the block. Family discord: Tony lives a few streets away in a vacant lot shack. Or he used to. The habitation burned down a few weeks ago and Tony pointed to a glistening pink burn on his arm for proof. A problem with the wiring no doubt.

"You got money for alcohol but I can't eat," Tony says. As if this suppurating shade wanted the money for food, strung out like he was. No one on the street but them and all the windows dark. Tony takes the advantage of his opponent and leans up and whispers, "I'm so hungry I might have to take it then, I'm so hungry," and the threat sits there in J.'s ear. There was that night when J. was heading for the subway to make it to a book party in Manhattan and he saw Tony prowling around, cussing. His clothes were inside out and blood seeped from a gash above his eye. When he saw J. he asked him if he'd seen these three knuckleheads walking around anywhere. J. replied he hadn't and Tony said that he got into a beef with them and they beat him up and made him take off his clothes and put them on inside out. Or maybe they made him put his clothes on inside out and then beat him up. At any rate, he was looking for them and he had something: he pulled up his shirt and pointed to the long carving knife tucked into his belt. He was going to cut them when he found them. J. told him to calm down and get himself cleaned up. He wasn't going to cut anybody. Tony considered this possibility, nodded and agreed. He pulled his shirt down over the knife. Then he asked J. for some change.

J. doesn't respond to the threat. They walk in silence for a few feet, and they leave the threat on the pavement behind them. They move into the next streetlight's circle and Tony says, "Hey, you know I wouldn't do that. I ain't like those other crazy niggers they got up in here. But I gotta eat. What do you want me to do?"

"Can't help you, man." If he gave into the crackhead now, it would look as if he was giving in to the threat, even with Tony's withdrawal of it. A principle involved: he doesn't want to be punked out. There's one more block before he gets to his house and he doesn't want Tony there when he gets to his front door.

"You want me to sing for my supper?" Tony asks. "You want me to sing for my supper? I'll sing for my supper." He spits a gremlin of phlegm to the pavement and scratches his foot across the sidewalk like a pitcher taming his mound for a pitch. Then he jumps up and down and sings from his singed throat, "This old hammer killed John Henry but it won't kill me! This old hammer killed John Henry but it won't kill me!" J. looks back at the crackhead. Tony's eyes bulge out with the strain of producing that gross racket. "This old hammer killed John Henry but it won't kill me!" And here, J. thinks, this is the essential difference between this neighborhood and those of Brody Mills's orbit. No one here will call the police about the noise. They hear gunshots and arguments in the middle of the night and they might creep to the window to see what's going on but they won't call the police. They'll pray they don't hear a rape, something that will force them to get involved, or consider getting involved, but the people behind the black windows will not call the police at this. "This old hammer killed John Henry but it won't kill me!" It's up to J. He has no more resistance. He pulls out the change from the five dollars and gives it to the crackhead. Without touching the man's palm. Who knows what the guy wipes his ass with.

"You like that song?" Tony asks.

"You won," J. responds. Yards between them now, the distance between the mark and the expert con.

J. hears Tony yell, "Hey, brotherman, brotherman, wait a minute!"

J. turns, knowing from the volume of the man's voice that there are distances, old distances, between them. Tony jabs his finger at him and says, "You're a solid brother, Mickey Mouse, you're a solid citizen." He bows and scampers away in the direction of a building without a door, a building with secret steps and codes.

At his desk J. sips his first Corona and looks down at his notes. He calculates what he'll get done before he's dampened enough to fall asleep. He considers how much sleep he'll get and through the calculus of doggerel arrives at how many words per hour he has to produce by noon. He presses a button and listens to the lying junkie. Only variety of junkie awake at this hour.

THE ONLY GOOD JUDGE

BY CAROLYN WHEAT

Brooklyn Heights

(Originally published in 2001)

What do you say to a naked judge?

I said yes. Averting my eyes from the too, too solid judicial flesh.

I mean, the steam room is a place for relaxation, a place where you close your eyes and inhale the scent of eucalyptus and let go the frustrations of the day—most of which were caused by judges in the first place—so the last thing you want to do while taking a *schvitz* is accept a case on appeal, for God's sake, but there was the Dragon Lady, looking not a whit less authoritative for the absence of black robes, or indeed, the absence of any other clothing including a towel.

She'd been a formidable opponent as a trial judge, and we at the defense bar breathed a sigh of relief when she went upstairs to the appellate bench. The Dragon Lady was one of the great plea-coercers of her time; she could strike fear and terror into the hearts of the most hardened criminals and have them begging for that seventeen-to-life she'd offered only yesterday.

Yes, I said she "offered." I know, you think it's the district attorney who makes plea offers while the judge sits passively on the bench. You think judges are neutral parties with no stake in the outcome, no interest in whether the defendant pleads out or goes to trial.

You've been watching too much *Law & Order*. The Dragon Lady made Jack McCoy look like a soft-on-crime liberal. She routinely rejected plea bargains on the ground that the DA wasn't being tough enough. She demanded and got a bureau chief in her courtroom to justify any reduction in the maximum sentence.

So what was she doing asking me, as a personal favor, to handle a case on appeal? I almost fell off the steam room bench. I was limp as a noodle well past *al dente*, and I'd been hoping to slide out the door without having to acknowledge the presence of my naked nemesis parked on the opposite bench like a leather-tanned Buddha. It seemed the health club equivalent of subway manners: you don't notice them, they won't notice you, and the city functions on the lubrication of mutual indifference.

But she broke the invisible wall between us. She named my name and asked a favor, and I was so nonplussed I said yes and I said "Your Honor" and three other women in the steam room shot me startled open-eyed glances as if to say, who are you to shatter our illusion of invisibility? If you two know one another and talk to one another, then you must be able to see us in all our nakedness and that Changes Everything in this steam room.

They left, abruptly and without finishing the sweating process that was beginning to reduce me to dehydrated delirium. I murmured something and groped my way to the door. I left the Dragon Lady, who'd been there twice as long as I had, yet showed no signs of needing a respite; like a giant iguana, she sat in heavy-lidded torpor, basking in the glow of the coals in the corner of the room. She lifted a wooden ladle and poured water on the hot rocks to raise more steam.

I stumbled to the shower and put it on cold, visualizing

myself rolling in Swedish snow, pure and cold and crystalline.

The frigid water shocked me into realizing what I'd just done.

A favor for the Dragon Lady.

Since when did she solicit representation for convicted felons?

Four days later, she was dead.

My old Legal Aid buddy Pat Flaherty told me, in his characteristic way. He always said the only good judge was a dead judge, so when he greeted me in Part 32 with the words, "The Dragon Lady just became a good judge," I knew what he meant.

"Wow. I was talking to her the other day." I shook my head and lowered my voice to a whisper. "Heart attack?"

A sense of mortality swept over me. The woman had looked healthy enough in a reptilian way. I'd noticed her sagging breasts and compared them to my own, which, while no longer as perky as they'd once been, didn't actually reach my navel.

But give me ten years.

"No," Flaherty said, an uneasy grin crossing his freckled face. "She was killed by a burglar."

"Shot?"

"Yeah. Died instantly, they said on the radio."

"Jesus." At a loss for words—and, believe it or not, considering how much I'd resented the old boot when she was alive, annoyed at Flaherty for making light of the murder.

Good judge. It's one thing to say that about a ninety-year-old pill who dies in his sleep, but a woman like the DL, cut down in what would be considered the prime of her life if she were a man and her tits didn't sag—that verged on the obscene.

The big question among the Brooklyn defense bar: Should we or should we not go to the funeral?

We'd all hated her. We'd all admired her, in a way. I loved the fact that she used to wear a Wonder Woman T-shirt under her black robe. She was tough and smart and sarcastic and powerful and she'd been all that when I was still in high school.

But she'd also been one hell of an asset to the prosecution, a judge who thought her duty was to fill as many jail cells as possible and to move her calendar with a speed that gave short shrift to due process of law.

In the end, I opted to skip the actual funeral, held in accordance with Jewish custom the day after the medical examiner released the body, but I slipped into the back row of Part 49 for the courthouse memorial service two weeks later.

What the hell, I was in the building anyway.

I was in the building to meet Darnell Patterson, the client she'd stuck me with. It had taken me two weeks to get him down from Dannemora, where he was serving twenty years for selling crack.

Twenty years. The mind boggled, especially since he wasn't really convicted of the actual sale, just possession of a sale-weight quantity, meaning that someone in the DA's office thought the amount he had in his pocket was too much to be for his personal use. Since he'd been convicted before, he was nailed as a three-time loser and given a persistent felony jacket.

"It's like they punishing me for thinking ahead," he said in a plaintive voice. "I mean, I ain't no dealer. I don't be selling no shit, on account if I do, the dudes on the corner gonna bust my head wide open. I just like to buy a goodly amount so's I don't have to go out there in the street and buy no more anytime soon. I likes a hefty stash; I likes to save a little for a rainy day, you hear what I'm saying?"

"Yeah," I said. "You're the industrious ant and all the other users are grasshoppers. The law rewards the grasshoppers because they bought a two-day supply, whereas you, the frugal one, stocked up."

"You got that right," he said with a broad smile. "I think you and me's gonna get along fine, counselor. You just tell that to the pelican court and they'll knock down my sentence."

It was conservative economics applied to narcotics addiction. Maybe I could get an affidavit from Alan Greenspan on the economic consequences of punishing people for saving instead of spending. I could hear my argument before the appellate court:

"Your Honors, all my client did was to invest in commodities. He wanted a hedge against inflation, so he bought in quantity, not for resale, but to insure himself against higher prices and to minimize the number of street buys he had to make, thus reducing his chances of being caught. Punishing him with additional time for his prudence is like punishing someone for saving instead of running up bills and declaring bankruptcy."

The more I thought about it, the more I liked it. The appellate judges—"pelicans" in defendantese—had heard it all. They were unlikely to buy the "mandatory sentences suck" argument and they had no interest in hearing the drug laws attacked as draconian, and they sure as hell didn't give a damn about my client's lousy childhood. Supply-side economics had the advantage of novelty.

When I walked out of the ninth-floor pens, I still had no idea why I'd been asked to take Darnell's case. The sentence was a travesty, of course, far outweighing whatever harm to society this man had done, but what was new or unusual about that? And why had the Dragon Lady, of all people, taken such an interest in a low-level crack case?

With her dead, I'd probably never know.

I had no inkling of a connection between the case and her untimely death.

It took the second murder for the connection to become apparent.

The deceased was a district attorney we called the Terminator; that quality of mercy that droppeth as a gentle rain from heaven was completely absent from his makeup. So once again, there were few tears shed among us defense types, and, in truth, a lot of really bad jokes made the rounds, considering how Paul French died.

He fell out a window in the tall office building behind Borough Hall, the same building that housed the Brooklyn DA's office, but not the actual floor the trial bureau was on. Which, in retrospect, should have told us something. What was he doing there? Had he fallen, or was he pushed? And had the Dragon Lady really died at the hands of a clumsy burglar who picked her house at random, or was somebody out to eliminate the harshest prosecutors and judges in the borough of Brooklyn?

His own office called it suicide. Word went around that he was upset when someone else was promoted to bureau chief over him.

Bullshit, was what I thought. I knew Paul French, tried cases against him and was proud to say we were even—three wins for him, three for me—which in the prosecution-stacked arithmetic of the criminal courts put me way ahead as far as lawyering was concerned. And I knew that while he might have enjoyed cracking the whip for a while as bureau chief, it was the courtroom he loved. It was beating the opponent, rubbing her nose in his victory, tussling in front of the judge, and selling his case to the jury that got his heart started in the morning. He might have gotten pissed off if someone else got a job he thought should have been his, but no way would that have pushed him out a tenth-story window.

The suicide story was bogus, a fact that was confirmed for me when two cops rang the bell of my Court Street office and said they wanted to discuss Paul French. I invited them in, poured them coffee—Estate Java, wasted on cops used to drinking crankcase oil at the station house—and congratulated them on not buying the cover story. The man was murdered; the only question was which of the fifty thousand or so defendants he'd sent up the river could legitimately take the credit.

The larger and older of the cops opened his notebook and said, "You represented a Jorge Aguilar in September of 1995, is that right, counselor?"

It took a minute to translate his fractured pronunciation. It took another minute to recall the case; 1995 might as well have been twenty years ago, I'd represented so many other clients in so many other cases.

"Jorge, yeah," I said, conjuring up a vision of a cocky, swaggering kid in gang colors who'd boasted he could "do twenty years standing on his head." Despite his complete lack of remorse and absence of redeeming qualities, I'd felt sorry for him. In twenty years, he'd be broken and almost docile, still illiterate and unemployable, and he'd probably commit another crime within a year just so he could get back to his nice, safe prison. He could do twenty years, all right. He just couldn't do anything else.

It took all of thirty seconds for me to disabuse them of the notion that Jorge's case killed Paul French. "Look," I pointed out, "the whole family rejoiced when the kid went upstate. It meant they could keep a television set for more than a week. And he was no gang leader; the real gang-bangers barely tolerated him. So I don't think—"

"What about Richie Toricelli, then?" The older cop leaned forward in my visitor's chair and I had the feeling he was getting to the real point of his interrogation.

"Now we're talking. Toricelli I could see killing Paul French. I'm not sure I see him pushing anyone out a window, though. I'd have expected Richie to use his sawed-off shotgun instead. He liked to see people bleed."

The younger cop gave me one of those "how can you defend those people" looks.

"I was appointed," I said in reply to the unspoken criticism. Which was no answer at all. I wouldn't have been appointed if I hadn't put myself on a list of available attorneys, and I wouldn't have done that if I hadn't been committed with every fiber of my being to criminal defense work.

I'd long since stopped asking myself why I did it. I did it, and I did it the best way I knew how, and I let others work up a philosophy of the job.

Some cases were easier to justify than others. Richie Toricelli's was one of the tough ones.

And if you thought he was a dead loss to society, you ought to meet his mother.

"Tell you the truth," I said, only half-kidding, "I'd sure like to know where Rose Toricelli was when French took his dive."

"She was in the drunk tank over on Gold Street," the younger cop said, a look of grim amusement on his brown face. "Nice alibi, only about fifty people and ten pieces of offi-cial paperwork put her there."

"Pretty convenient," I said, hearing the echo of the Church Lady in my head.

"Counselor, you know something you're not telling us?"

I dropped my eyes. A slight blush crept into my cheeks. I hated admitting this.

"I changed my phone number after Richie went in," I said. "For a year, I lived in fear that Rose Toricelli would find some way to get to me. She didn't just blame Paul French for Richie's conviction, she blamed me too."

The older cop cut me a look. Skeptical Irish blue eyes under bushy white eyebrows over a red-tinged nose. I got the message: *You're gonna do a man's job, you need a man's balls. Afraid of an old lady doesn't cut it.*

It pissed me off. This guy didn't know Richie's ma. "You look at her, you see a pathetic old woman who thinks her scurvy son is some kind of saint; I look at her and I see some-one who wants me dead and who could very easily convince herself that shooting me is the best way to tell the world her boy is innocent."

"Did she ever make threats? And did you report any of this?"

"Only in the courthouse the day they took Richie away. And, no," I said, anger creeping into my voice, "I didn't report it. I know what cops think about defense lawyers who get threats. You think we ask for it. And I didn't want to look like a wimp who couldn't handle a little old lady with a grudge."

What really chilled me weren't Rose Toricelli's threats to do damage to the sentencing judge, to Paul French, to me—that was standard stuff in the criminal courts. What really had my blood frozen were the words she said to her son as they shuffled him, cuffed and stunned like a cow on his way to becoming beefsteak:

"You show them, Richie. You show them you're innocent. It would serve them right if you hung yourself in there."

For a year after that, I waited for the news that Richie's body had been discovered hanging from the bars. Doing what Mamma wanted, like he always did.

But as far as I knew, he was still alive, still serving his time, which gave him an iron-bar-clad alibi for French's death, so why were the cops even bringing it up?

The question nagged at me even after the cops left. I turned to my computer, supplementing the information I pulled up with a few phone calls, and discovered something very interesting indeed.

Once upon a time, Richie Toricelli's cellmate had been Hector Dominguez.

You remember the case. It made all the papers and even gave birth to a joke or two on *Letterman*. Funny guy, that Hector.

He'd kidnapped his son, claiming the boy's mother was making him sick. A devout believer in Santeria, he accused his ex of working roots, casting spells, that sapped the boy's strength. He said God told him to save his little boy from a mother who had turned witch.

You can imagine how well that went over in the Dragon Lady's courtroom. She gaveled him quiet, had him bound and gagged because he wouldn't stop screaming at his sobbing wife. He hurled curses and threats throughout the trial, bringing down the wrath of his gods on the heads of everyone connected to the proceeding.

The day he was to be sentenced, they found the doll in his cell. Carved out of soap, it wore a crude robe of black

124 // Brooklyn Noir 2

nylon and sported a doll's wig the exact shade of the Dragon Lady's pageboy. Out of its heart, a hypodermic syringe protruded like a dagger.

Like I said, a lot of criminal defendants threaten the judge who sends them upstate, but a voodoo doll was unique, even in the annals of Brooklyn justice. The *Post* put it on the front page; the *News* thundered editorially about laxness in the Brooklyn House of Detention; *Newsday* did a very clever cartoon I'd taped to my office bulletin board; and the *Times* ignored the whole thing because it didn't happen in Bosnia.

I really wasn't in the courtroom when Dominguez was sentenced because I wanted to see the show. Unlike the two rows of reporters and most of the other lawyers present that day, I had business before the court. But I had to admit a certain curiosity about how the Dragon Lady was going to handle this one.

The lawyer asked her to recuse herself, saying she could hardly be objective under the circumstances. I could have told him to save his breath; the DL was never, under any circumstances, going to admit she couldn't do her job. She dismissed out of hand the notion that she'd taken the voodoo doll personally; it would play no part, she announced in ringing tones, in her sentencing.

Hector Dominguez was oddly compelling when he began to address the court. His English was so poor that an interpreter stood next to him in case he lapsed into his Dominican Spanish, but Hector waved away the help, determined to reach the judge in her own language.

"You Honor, I know it looking bad against me," he said in his halting way. "I just want to say I love my son with my whole heart. *Mi corazon* is hurt when my son get sick. I want her to stop making him sick. Please, You Honor, don't let that woman hurt my boy. He so little, he so pale, he so sick all the time and it all her fault, You Honor, all her doing with her spells and her evil ways."

The child's mother dabbed at her eyes with a tissue, shaking her head mournfully.

The DL gave Dominguez two years more than the District Attorney's office asked for, which was already two years more than the probation report recommended.

This, she insisted, had nothing to do with the doll, but was the appropriate sentence for a man who tried to convince a child that his loving mother was a witch.

Dominguez's last words to the DL consisted of a curse to the effect that she should someday know the pain he felt now, the pain of losing a child to evil.

The papers all commented on the irony of a man like Hector calling someone else evil. And Letterman milked his audience for laughs by holding up a voodoo doll in the image of a certain Washington lady.

But three years later, when the boy's mother was charged with attempted murder and the court shrinks talked about Munchausen's syndrome by proxy, the attitudes changed a bit. Now Hector was seen, not as a nut case who thought his wife was possessed, but as a father trying to protect his son and interpreting events he couldn't understand in the only context he knew, that of his spirit-based religion.

He was up for parole, and it was granted without much ado. He was free—but his little boy, six years old by now, lay in a coma, irreparably brain-damaged as a result of his mother's twisted ministrations.

By not listening to him, by treating him like a criminal instead of a concerned father, the Dragon Lady had prevented authorities from looking closely at the mother's conduct.

He had shared a jail cell with Richie Toricelli. That had to mean something—but what?

The theory hit me with the full force of a brainstorm: defendants on a train. Patricia Highsmith by way of Alfred Hitchcock.

What if Ma Toricelli, instead of killing the prosecutor who sent her precious Richie upstate, shot the Dragon Lady—who had no connection whatsoever to her or her son? And what if Dominguez, who had no reason to want Paul French dead, returned the favor by pushing French out the window? Each has an alibi for the murder they had a motive to commit, and no apparent reason to kill the person they actually murdered.

The more I thought about it, the more I liked it. I liked it so much I actually asked a cop for a favor. Which was how I ended up sifting through DD5s in the Eight-Four precinct as the winter sun turned the overcast clouds a dull pewter.

I learned nothing that hadn't been reported in the papers, and I was ready to pack it in, ready to admit that even if Ma Toricelli had done the deed, she'd covered her tracks pretty well, when one item caught my attention.

The neighbor across the street had seen a Jehovah's Witness ringing doorbells about twenty minutes prior to the crime. He knew the woman was a Witness because she carried a copy of the *Watchtower* in front of her like a shield.

This was a common enough sight in Brooklyn Heights, where the Witnesses owned a good bit of prime real estate, except for one little thing.

Jehovah's Witnesses traveled in pairs. Always.

One Jehovah's Witness just wasn't possible.

My heart pounded as I read the brief description of the bogus Witness: female, middle-aged, gray hair, gray coat, stout boots. Five feet nothing.

Ma Toricelli to a T.

I wasn't as lucky with the second set of detectives. I was told in no uncertain terms that nothing I had to say would get me a peek at the Paul French reports, so I left the precinct without any evidence that Hector Dominguez could have been in the municipal building when French took his dive.

Still, the idea had promise. I had no problem picturing Rose Toricelli firing a gun point-blank into the judge's mid-section and I was equally convinced that in return for the Dragon Lady's death, Hector Dominguez would have pushed five district attorneys out a window. But proving it was another matter.

I pondered these truths as I trudged down Court Street toward home. The sidewalks wore a new coat of powder, temporarily brightening the slush of melting gray snow. Dusk had arrived with winter suddenness, and only the snow-fogged streetlights lit the way. I was picking my way carefully in spite of well-treaded snow boots, my attention fixed on the depth of the chill puddle at the corner of Court and Atlantic Avenue, when the first shot zipped past my ear.

I didn't know it was a shot until the guy in the cigar store yelled at me to get down.

Get down where?

Get down why?

I honestly didn't hear it.

I couldn't even say it sounded like a car backfiring or a firecracker. And I didn't hear the second shot either, although this one I felt.

A sting, like a wasp or a hornet, and blood coursing down my cheek. A burning sensation and a really strong need to use a bathroom. I was ankle-deep in very cold water and couldn't decide whether to keep making my way across the street or run to the shelter of the cigar store. While I considered my options, a black SUV swerved around the corner, straight into the icy puddle, drenching me in dirty, frigid water.

That did it. I turned quickly, wrenching my knee, and hoisted myself onto the curb. I slid at once back into the puddle, landing hard on my backside. A couple of teenagers stopped to laugh, and I suppose it would have been funny if I hadn't been scared out of my mind. Limping and holding my bleeding cheek, I slipped and slid on my way to the amber-lighted cigar store on the corner.

Tobacco-hater that I am, I'd never been inside the cigar emporium before. The scent was overwhelming, but so was the warmth from the space heater on the floor.

The counterman met me at the door, a solicitous expression on his moon face. He was short, with a big bristling mustache and two chins. He reeked of cigar smoke, but I didn't mind at all when he put an arm around me and led me into the sanctuary of his store. He seated me on a folding chair and offered the only comfort he possessed. "Want a cigarillo, lady? On the house."

I started to laugh, but the laughter ended in tears of frustration and relief.

I was alive.

I was bleeding.

I'd been shot at.

The cops were on their way, the cigar man told me, and then he proudly added that he'd seen the shooter's car and had written down the license plate.

The cops, predictably enough, talked drive-by shooting and surmised that a gang member might have been walking nearby when the shots rang out. Since my attention was fully absorbed in not falling into the puddle, King Kong could have been behind me on the street and I wouldn't have noticed.

The second theory was the Atlantic Avenue hotbed-of-terrorism garbage that gets dragged out whenever anything happens on that ethnically charged thoroughfare. Just because Arab spice stores and Middle Eastern restaurants front the street, everything from a trash fire to littering gets blamed either on Arab extremists or anti-Arab extremists.

I have to admit, I was slow. Even I didn't think the shooting had anything to do with my visit to the Eight-Four precinct.

That didn't happen until the next day, when I learned that the car whose license plate the cigar man wrote down belonged to one Marcus Mitchell.

Marcus Mitchell had been royally screwed by Paul French in one of those monster drug prosecutions where everyone turned state's evidence except the lowest-level dealers. People who'd made millions cut deals that had the little guys serving major time for minor felonies, and Mitchell was a guy who had nothing with which to deal.

My own client gave up the guys above him and walked away with a bullet—that's one year and not even a year upstate, a year at Riker's, which meant his family could visit him and—let's be honest here—he could still run a good bit of his drug business from his cell. I know, that sucks, but French was only too happy to get the goods on the higher-ups and made the deal with open eyes. All I did was say yes.

All Marcus Mitchell did was keep his mouth shut, and he did that not out of stubbornness but out of sheer ignorance. He'd been the poor sap caught with a nice big bag of heroin, but the only thing he knew was that a guy named Willie handed it to him at the corner of Fulton and Franklin and told him not to come back until it was all sold.

For this, he got twenty to life. Released after three years on a technicality, but by that time his wife had left him, he'd lost his job, and his parents had died in shame. He had plenty of reason to want Paul French dead.

But why had he taken a potshot at me?

I had taken the day off work, called in shot. It was in the papers, so the judges bought it and told me to take all the time I needed to recuperate, then put my cases over a week. I sipped Tanzanian Peaberry while I felt the blood ooze into the gauze bandage on my cheek and reconsidered my theory.

It was still sound, except for two little things.

One: There were three, not two, defendants on a train.

Two: Ma Toricelli's chosen victim wasn't Paul French—it was the defense lawyer she blamed for her son's conviction. Me.

It went like this:

Ma Toricelli kills the Dragon Lady for Hector Dominguez.

Dominguez kills Paul French for Marcus Mitchell.

Marcus Mitchell tries to kill me for Ma Toricelli.

This time the cops listened. This time they questioned everyone in the building where Paul French died and found several witnesses who described Hector Dominguez to a T. Add that to the description of the bogus Witness, squeeze all three defendants until someone cracked, and the whole house of cards would tumble down.

I went to the arraignment. I was the victim, so I had a right to be there, and besides, I wanted to see firsthand the people who'd tried to end my life in an icy puddle.

When the time came for Ma Toricelli to plead for bail, she

thrust her chin forward and said, "She was supposed to be my boy's lawyer, but all she did was look down on him. She never did her job, Your Honor, not from the first day. She thought Richie was trash and she didn't care what happened to him."

I opened my mouth to respond, then realized it made no difference what I said. Even if I'd been the worst lawyer in the world, that didn't give Rose Toricelli the right to order my death. And I'd done a good job for Richie, a better job than the little sociopath deserved.

Perhaps my mental choice of words was what caught my attention.

If I really thought Richie was a sociopath, had I done my best for him? Or had I slacked off, let the prosecution get away with things I'd have fought harder if I'd truly believed my client innocent? It was a hard question. There were cases I'd handled better, but I honestly didn't see Richie getting off if Johnnie Cochran had been his lawyer. Still, my cellside manner could have been improved; I could have at least gone through the motions enough to convince Richie's mother that I was doing my best.

The letter came in due course, as we say in the trade. It was enclosed in a manila envelope with the name of a prominent Brooklyn law firm embossed in the left corner. I had no clue what was inside; I had no business pending with the firm and no reason to expect correspondence from them. I slit the thing open with my elegant black Frank Lloyd Wright letter opener, the one my dad gave me for Christmas two years ago.

Another letter with my name handwritten on the front, no address, no stamp, fell into my hands.

This one's return address was the Appellate Division, Second Department.

It was a message from beyond the grave.

Ms. Jameson:

I'm sure you have had reason to wonder why I asked you in particular to handle the case of Darnell Patterson on remand from this court.

Let us just say that I have had reason to regret the current fashion for mandatory minimum sentences and maximum jail time for defendants who commit nonviolent offenses. While I am not one to condone lawbreaking, I firmly believe in distinctions between those who are truly dangerous to society and those who are merely inconvenient.

Mr. Patterson would appear to fall into the latter category. I trust you will agree with me on this point and use your best efforts on his behalf.

You and I, Ms. Jameson, have seldom seen eye to eye, but those traits of yours that I most deplore, your tendency toward overzealousness and your refusal to "go through the motions" on even the most hopeless case, will prove to be just what Mr. Patterson needs in a lawyer.

I expect you will wonder what brought about my change of heart with respect to low-level narcotics cases.

I also expect you to live with your curiosity and make no effort to trace my change of heart to its roots. Suffice to say that it is a private family matter and therefore is nobody's business but my own.

Once again, I thank you for your attention to this matter.

There was no signature. The Dragon Lady had died before she could scrawl her name in her characteristic bold hand.

The compliments brought a traitorous tear to my eyes—especially since the words weren't true.

Mostly true. I was well-known in the Brooklyn court system as a fighter who didn't give up easily, who didn't back down in the face of threats from prosecutors or judges. The DL had been right to rely on me.

But Richie Toricelli hadn't been. I'd been so disgusted by his crimes, so turned off by his attitude, that I'd given less than my best to his defense. Ma Toricelli, for all her craziness, had a point. I'd phoned it in, done a half-baked job of presenting his alibi witnesses, given the jurors little reason to believe his story over that of the prosecution.

The irony was huge. The DL, of all people, sending me compliments on my fighting spirit while Ma Toricelli planned to kill me for rolling over and playing dead on her son's case. Me bailing on Richie and the Dragon Lady getting religion over a three-time loser who hoarded drugs like a squirrel saving up for winter.

The image of Hector Dominguez's voodoo doll swam before my eyes—the weapon protruding from its soap heart wasn't a knife, but a hypodermic. "May you lose a child to evil," he'd cursed, and perhaps she had. Perhaps reaching out to help Darnell Patterson was a way of atoning for that child. Perhaps she'd finally seen that justice needed a dose of mercy, like a drop of bitters in a cocktail.

I sat like a stone while the letter fluttered to the hardwood floor of my office.

Pat Flaherty had been right after all.

The Dragon Lady *had* become a good judge.

LUCK BE A LADY

BY MAGGIE ESTEP

Kensington

(Originally published in 2004)

Harry Sparrow'd had a run of luck so rotten you could smell it three blocks away. Harry felt like everywhere he set foot folks gave him the twice over and then some. Even doing hump things like his laundry and shopping. Used to be Old Elsa at the Laundorama on Caton Avenue always had a kind word for him, even sometimes let him use the special dryer at the end free of charge. Nowadays Elsa acted like Harry had Ebola. Lousy way to go. Blood pouring out of your eyes and mouth. Harry didn't like blood much. Or he guessed he didn't. He'd somehow made it through a lot of years living on the left side of the law without coming close to blood. Probably because Harry never carried a weapon. You took a fall with a weapon, it was Armed Robbery. Harry kept it to Breaking and Entering. He'd only ever done a little time. Jail not prison. Harry wanted to keep it that way.

Harry's luck took a turn for the better one night when he least expected it. The day had been lousy. The mercury hitting a hundred and staying there even though it was barely May. Harry hadn't wanted to be cooped up in his room that stank of baroque spices from his landlady Mrs. Desuj's cooking. So Harry had taken the F train to the A train to Aqueduct Racetrack to meet McCormick, a sometimes associate who swore he had a live tip from an apprentice jockey. McCormick was a small man who wore the same navy three-piece suit every day of the week. He had a history of mental illness and Harry took everything he said with a grain of salt. But Harry knew that sometimes McCormick's tips were live. So he kept an open mind about it. He tucked a C note in his sock and two twenties in the money clip given him by Susan, the last girl he'd dated. Susan had been arrested for forgery shortly after moving into Harry's room with him. Harry couldn't say he'd been sorry to see her go. She was pretty and fond of having sex in public places. Thing was, she had a mean streak. Even that would have been okay, but it was unpredictable. Harry would ask Susan to pass the sugar and she would snap. Start shouting at Harry and kicking him in the shins.

Harry and McCormick were at the rail in time for the first race. Harry glanced at the program. He was familiar with several of the horses running. He played a straight two dollar trifecta with an 18-1 shot over a 10-1 with the favorite to show. Miraculously, with just a sixteenth of a mile to go, the three horses in Harry's trifecta were running in the order he'd bet them. Harry felt the whole world opening up for him. The sky was wide and beautiful. Two strides shy of the wire, the second place horse stuck her nose in front of the 18-1 shot, ruining Harry's trifecta. Harry felt sick and headed home, leaving McCormick behind to chat up a floozy brunette with a skin condition.

On the train ride home, two kids got on with a boom box blaring an old Grandmaster Flash song. Harry had seen these kids before. They had a good act. People liked to give them money. The taller of the kids sat the boombox down in the middle of the floor as the shorter one started dancing like

Michael Jackson. The kid could dance. Everyone on the train could see it. Then the bigger kid got in on it. He moved well too. He did a few somersaults and a standing back flip. He picked up the smaller kid, twirled him above his head, and miscalculated. There was a horrible sound as the smaller kid's head smashed against the ceiling of the train. At first the tall kid tried to pretend everything was okay. But the smaller kid was just lying there on the floor. There was a nurse on the train car. She examined the small kid. Told him not to move. Harry knew a bad day was getting worse. Even when the kid eventually sat up and seemed okay. It was a day full of bad things.

So it was with some surprise that at 11:53 that night Harry Sparrow realized his luck had turned. At 10:15 he had walked down 17th Street. He was wearing dark clothing and noiseless rubber-soled shoes. He carried a black briefcase. He passed by the house he'd been eyeing and noted that the front stoop light was on but the rest of the brownstone was in darkness as it had been for many nights. He'd been careful in staking this place out. Had gotten an inside scoop from the maid who had once dated a friend of Harry's uncle. The Millers were upstate at their summer place for two weeks and they did not have an alarm. Harry approached from the backyard. The windows were locked. He put tape on the window then discretely cracked it. He reached his arm in, undid the window lock, and climbed in.

He didn't know much about the layout of the place. Only that the master bedroom was on the second floor, the safe behind an oil painting of a landscape. Jewelry and savings bonds in the safe. The Millers did not trust banks. They were the children of Holocaust survivors. Or so the maid had told the friend of Harry's uncle. Maybe it was wrong to rob the children of Holocaust survivors, but Harry's uncle had mentioned the Millers were unkind to their pet cat. Harry liked animals.

Harry had trained himself to see in the dark. He had a tiny beautiful flashlight in his briefcase, but so far he hadn't run into the kind of darkness he couldn't see through. Harry now made his way to the central staircase and went upstairs.

Harry had a big surprise waiting for him when he set foot in the master bedroom. It was a lavish bedroom. There was velvet and brocade. The ceilings soared and wore their 19th-century moldings intact. At the center of the room was an immense antique sleigh bed. On the bed sat a small woman with a gun. Just sitting in the dark like that with a gun. She was pointing the gun at Harry. Harry didn't like guns but he knew a little about them. He thought this one looked like a Raven .25.

"Hello, you must be the burglar," the girl said.

"Harry Sparrow, nice to meet you," Harry said. What else was he going to say? She was wildly attractive and she had a gun.

"We're in a quandary, aren't we?" the girl asked. She smiled. She had cute teeth. She also had very long brown hair and a face like a fox. She was petite but looked like she had some strength in her. Maybe she'd taken gymnastics as a child. Maybe even gone semi-pro with the gymnastics but wasn't quite good enough for the big leagues. Had enrolled in college studying some subject her heart wasn't really in. Her heart had been in the gymnastics. So there was a little bitterness there for one so young. But she could have been thirty. It was hard to tell. After college, she drifted a little. Now she was the house sitter for the Millers. Maybe the nanny? But the kids weren't here. Maybe she was pet sitting for the abused cat.

"A quandary. Yup," Harry said. Harry couldn't quite figure it. What made her wildly attractive. She was dressed in a pair of baggy navy gym shorts and a white tank top. She was close to flat-chested and her legs were short, albeit shapely. Mostly it had to do with her face and what was in her eyes. Mischief was in her eyes.

"Are you the house sitter?"

"Something like that," she said. Smiled a little, showing off the cute teeth.

"You're not what I expected," she added.

"You were expecting me?"

"I heard the window cracking downstairs. My pa's house got broke into once when I was ten. Same thing. The burglar cracked the glass. Pretty quiet about it, but I have overdeveloped auditory and visual senses. Always been that way. Some folks say it's a gift, but like all gifts it's a curse. I hear too much and I can't bear bright light."

She looked so tired when she said it. She was tired of hearing too much. Tired of the light hurting her eyes.

"Lucky I have my friend," she said, indicating the gun with her chin.

"I wish you'd stop pointing that at me, I don't like guns."

"An outlaw who doesn't like guns. You're a man of many faces, Harry Sparrow."

He liked the way she used his name.

"I don't believe in violence," Harry said.

"Ah yes, but the twenty-thousand-dollar question is, do you believe in love, Harry Sparrow?"

"You haven't told me your name," Harry said.

"Rebecca Church," the girl said.

Keeping an eye on the Raven .25, Harry sat down at the edge of the bed. He began asking the girl questions about herself. He asked did she like gymnastics.

"I hate sports," she said.

Harry said that sports were often detestable.

Rebecca was sitting cross-legged now. Her gym shorts were loose and Harry found himself staring at the place where gym short separated from inner thigh. Rebecca was not wearing underwear. Harry knew it couldn't be wise to stare at an armed girl's privates, but the more he struggled not to, the more he stared.

"You're staring," Rebecca said. Though she'd been resting the gun on her knee, she now picked it up and pointed it at Harry again. She made no effort to close her legs.

The gun was too close to Harry. It made him see double. It made his heart bump against his ribs. He reached over and touched Rebecca's cheek. Her eyes became smaller. He then ran one finger from her left knee up to her inner thigh. He let his finger rest there just where the gym shorts ended. The gun was inches from Harry's head. He put his mouth where his finger was resting. He repeatedly kissed that spot of thigh. He closed his eyes.

Harry Sparrow had always had a keen sense of self-preservation. That was all gone now. He started biting into Rebecca's upper thigh. He wanted to transplant himself inside of her.

Harry finally stopped biting the thigh, reached his fingers under the elastic waist of the gym shorts, and pulled them down to her knees. Rebecca kept holding the gun even as Harry yanked the tank top over her head. Harry let out a moan as he looked at her small body. The pubic hair a little unruly. It made Harry love her slightly, right then and there.

Rebecca rested the gun on her belly and moaned. Eventually, Harry reached for the gun. He got hold of it before Rebecca realized what was what. He didn't point it at her. Just held it.

"Get up," Harry said. All he wanted was to swallow her. Instead, he dressed her. She let him, like it was the most natural thing in the world. Harry retrieved her hairbrush from the bathroom and brushed her hair. She pouted. She put one hand down the front of her gym shorts and sucked the thumb of her other hand. Harry gave her the gun back.

Later on that night, Harry Sparrow learned that Rebecca Church was indeed the house sitter for the Millers. The Millers were friends of her second cousin Jim. Rebecca had been drifting from sublet to sublet since hitting town six months earlier. She'd been glad for a nice place to stay, but then found she didn't like the Millers. They'd seemed fine when she'd briefly met them the day they left on their trip, but once Rebecca had been in their house twenty-four hours, she disliked the Millers intensely. She disliked their magazines and their clothes that she saw hanging in their closets. The children's rooms were all wrong, decorated in banal pastels, as if all kids were supposed to like pastel. No kids Rebecca knew liked pastel.

By the time Harry Sparrow came to burglarize the place, Rebecca actively hated the Millers. Harry she liked. She didn't have second thoughts about helping Harry clean the place out.

"What about your cousin? Isn't this going to reflect badly on him?"

"I barely know him," Rebecca said, leaving it at that.

When Harry had a little trouble with the safe, Rebecca came and put her ear to it. She could hear things Harry could never hear. She could hear strangers' heartbeats on the subway. She could hear the small sounds insects made. She helped Harry get the safe open.

Once Harry had taken the jewelry and bonds and put them into the bag he'd had folded in his briefcase, Rebecca went to find Sally, the cat. She hadn't heard about the Millers's alleged cruelty to animals the way Harry had, but the food they had left for Sally contained by-products. Rebecca strongly disapproved of by-products so she decided to take the cat. As they left the house by the front door, Rebecca not even bothering to lock it behind her, Harry glanced at his watch. It was 11:53 p.m. on May 2 and Harry Sparrow's luck had turned.

Rebecca came with Harry to his furnished room in the attic of the Desuj's house on Friel Place. It was a stubby street just a few blocks from Prospect Park, but worlds away from some of the more upscale neighborhoods that hugged the park's perimeter. Humble frame houses were jammed together like teeth. The houses' inhabitants were working-class people from India, the Dominican Republic, and Guyana. Harry himself was from New Jersey. But no one minded.

"It's small," Rebecca said, after entering Harry's dismal attic room. She immediately turned off the lights and closed the lone window in spite of the thick heat.

"I've had a run of bad luck," Harry shrugged. He watched Rebecca make Sally the cat comfortable by offering her some of the nutritionally correct food they'd purchased in Park Slope. Once the cat started eating, Rebecca looked at Harry. She smiled a little and took off her tank top. Harry stared. She put her finger between her legs and stood there looking at Harry. Harry wondered if Mrs. Desuj was going to mind about the cat. He knew Indian people didn't think highly of cats. Cows were another story of course.

"How come you have a gun?" Harry asked Rebecca.

"I like to shoot things," Rebecca said.

This worried Harry a little but they could discuss it later. Rebecca came closer and put her hand down the front of Harry's trousers. Then she made a purring sound and kissed him. Harry looked at her lovely mischievous face and decided that not only had his luck changed, but he was now the luckiest man alive.

Harry had to do a lot of explaining and even break out the book of penal codes given him by a jailhouse lawyer, but he did finally convince Rebecca to leave the gun at home when they went out on jobs. Rebecca was attached to her gun even though she swore she'd only ever shot cans with it.

Harry and Rebecca worked well together. Rebecca could see in the dark even better than Harry and she was aces at the listening part of safe-cracking. Also, Harry knew that Rebecca was his luck.

It was a very lucrative month for Harry Sparrow and Rebecca Church. By September, they'd rented a nice two-bedroom down the block on the other side of Friel Place. The apartment had a tiny patch of backyard where Rebecca hung wind chimes and Sally the cat sunned herself.

By October, Rebecca got a little crazy. Oftentimes she didn't want to have sex with Harry because it was noisy. Harry bought her earplugs but she could still hear internal noise. Her sensitivity to light became acute and she wore Ray Charles–style glasses morning, noon, and even night. The world was too bright for her.

Harry Sparrow started feeling low.

December came. Friel Place was festive with holiday lights and plastic Santas. Even the Indian families had gotten fancy with lawn and window ornaments.

Harry and Rebecca started planning holiday-season burglaries. Harry felt it would bring them close again, maybe even temper Rebecca's hypersensitivities.

Harry and Rebecca staked out a slew of houses in Park Slope and Windsor Terrace. Christmas would be their big day. They had their sights on a lovely brownstone in Windsor Terrace. The occupants were obviously away. Newspapers and mail spilled from the box, and when early snow came, the walk went unshoveled. There was one light showing from the second floor but it was always on. The people were definitely away. Harry knew the place would be alarmed so he went for a brush-up course with Mac the Alarm Guy.

Harry and Rebecca set out in broad daylight on Christmas morning. It was a cold, overcast day and the streets were sleepy. Harry quickly picked the back door open. The alarm whined, threatening to start its full song unless someone disabled it pronto. The sound made Rebecca crouch to the floor and cup her hands over her ears. Harry left her crouching like that as he let his nose lead him to the alarm. He deactivated it in just a few seconds, mentally thanked Mac the Alarm Guy, and went back to find Rebecca. She wasn't there though. And somewhere upstairs there was music playing. Very soft piano music. Maybe it was French. There hadn't been music playing a few moments earlier. Had Rebecca gone upstairs and started playing records? She usually didn't want any music. It was all too brash for her ears. Even some of the soft country ballads and Chopin Nocturnes that Harry liked. But maybe she'd lost it so completely she was playing records on the job.

Suddenly, Harry had to take a leak. This was unusual. Harry had trained himself never to need to evacuate on a job. Some burglars liked that kind of thing. Taking people's stuff and pissing in their toilets too. Harry found this distasteful but he had to go pretty badly. He found a bathroom. He tried to pee. It wasn't coming though. He stood there with his johnson dangling. He thought about Rebecca. He thought about her fox face and her gymnast body and how for the first thirty-five days they had had sex at least three times a day and thereafter almost never. Because her ears got so bad. Harry was feeling a mix of frustrations. And he still couldn't pee. He wanted to call out to Rebecca to explain what the hold up was, but that would mean raising his voice, and Rebecca wouldn't like that.

Must have been twenty minutes that Harry stood there before giving up on peeing. He was in pain as he went upstairs to look for Rebecca. He had pain from not peeing and pain from Rebecca. But Rebecca Church was his luck and he went to find her.

What Harry saw up there in the high-ceilinged room at the top of the stairs was bewildering. There was trash everywhere. Spent containers of takeout food littered every surface. The furniture beneath the litter was expensive-looking but neglected. There were stains, dust bunnies, and even a pool of vomit. There was one hall light on and it dimly lit the scene. A man was sitting hunched in front of a big black piano, playing very softly. Rebecca was lying under the piano. Harry closed his eyes to put the hallucination away. When he looked again, it was all still there.

Harry wasn't sure how long he stood there, staring. Rebecca eventually noticed him. She yawned and smiled. When the man stopped playing, she introduced him to Harry. His name, it seemed, was Bernard. His dark hair hung over his eyes. Harry couldn't see what kind of look Bernard was giving him.

"I'm going to stay, Harry," Rebecca said, after making introductions.

"What do you mean, stay?"

"Stay here, with Bernard."

"What the hell are you talking about?" Harry heard his voice go up a notch. He sounded hysterical.

Rebecca said that Bernard played music so softly she could listen to it. And that's all she'd ever wanted. Harry had no idea that's what she'd wanted or he'd have tried to give it to her. But now it looked like it was too late. In the time it had taken Harry to try to pee in Bernard's toilet, Rebecca had evidently forged some sort of intimate relationship with the man. She clearly meant it. She was going to stay. Harry didn't know how long she'd stay or what Bernard thought about any of it, but Rebecca, Harry knew, always got her way. Bernard didn't look the type to protest anything, especially not Rebecca.

Rebecca was smiling as she told Harry how Bernard had a disease that gave him pain in his fingers. He'd been a con-cert pianist until the disease came when he turned forty. Now he stayed in his house eating from takeout containers and playing softly.

Bernard looked at Harry blankly as Rebecca reported all this. Harry wanted to bash his skull in.

When Harry showed no sign of leaving, Rebecca produced a gun from an ankle holster hidden below her pants. That got Harry mad. She had sworn she wouldn't bring the gun. She had broken a promise. Harry believed in keeping promises.

Harry said nothing more to Rebecca. He turned, leaving her and her gun with the dirty piano-playing lunatic.

Harry went home. He figured that was it. Back to the bad luck.

Five days later, Harry ran into McCormick. McCormick had a tip on a horse in the fourth, did Harry want to come to the track? It was cold and the sky was angry and Harry knew he would lose. But he went. Harry wanted to sit out the first race. Maiden three-year-olds going five and a half furlongs. Might as well pick numbers out of a hat, it was that unpredictable.

"Come on, Harry, what's got into you?" McCormick was egging him on.

Harry rolled his eyes, then looked from his program to the muscled and shining horses in the paddock. He picked out a trifecta. He went crazy. Put a 30-1 over a 6-1 over a 17-1. Miraculously, with less than a sixteenth of a mile to go, the three horses in Harry's trifecta were running in the order he'd bet them. He knew something would go wrong, though, so he looked away. Just walked away from the rail, leaving the crowd to gasp at a dramatic finish.

Harry's horses had come in. In the right order. The tri paid over ten thousand dollars. Harry had to go to the IRS window and have his picture taken and have his winnings reported to the government. That made him nervous, but the money was nice.

Most important, though, Harry realized his luck was still good. Rebecca Church had given him luck and let him keep it.

Harry Sparrow went home and fed Sally the cat. Rebecca hadn't even come back for the cat. But that was okay. Harry liked animals.

PART III

Cops & Robbers

BY THE DAWN'S EARLY LIGHT

BY LAWRENCE BLOCK

Sunset Park

(Originally published in 1984)

All this happened a long time ago.

Abe Beame was living in Gracie Mansion, though even he seemed to have trouble believing he was really the mayor of the city of New York. Ali was in his prime, and the Knicks still had a year or so left in Bradley and DeBusschere. I was still drinking in those days, of course, and at the time it seemed to be doing more for me than it was doing to me.

I had already left my wife and kids, my home in Syosset and the NYPD. I was living in the hotel on West Fifty-seventh Street where I still live, and I was doing most of my drinking around the comer in Jimmy Armstrong's saloon. Billie was the nighttime bartender. A Filipino youth named Dennis was behind the stick most days.

And Tommy Tillary was one of the regulars.

He was big, probably 6'2", full in the chest, big in the belly, too. He rarely showed up in a suit but always wore a jacket and tie, usually a navy or burgundy blazer with gray-flannel slacks or white duck pants in warmer weather. He had a loud voice that boomed from his barrel chest and a big, clean-shaven face that was innocent around the pouting mouth and knowing around the eyes. He was somewhere in his late forties and he drank a lot of top-shelf scotch. Chivas, as I remember it, but it could have been Johnnie Black. Whatever it was, his face was beginning to show it, with patches of permanent flush at the cheekbones and a tracery of broken capillaries across the bridge of the nose.

We were saloon friends. We didn't speak every time we ran into each other, but at the least we always acknowledged each other with a nod or a wave. He told a lot of dialect jokes and told them reasonably well, and I laughed at my share of them. Sometimes I was in a mood to reminisce about my days on the force, and when my stories were funny, his laugh was as loud as anyone's.

Sometimes he showed up alone, sometimes with male friends. About a third of the time, he was in the company of a short and curvy blonde named Carolyn. "Carolyn from the Caro-line" was the way he occasionally introduced her, and she did have a faint Southern accent that became more pronounced as the drink got to her.

Then, one morning, I picked up the *Daily News* and read that burglars had broken into a house on Colonial Road, in the Bay Ridge section of Brooklyn. They had stabbed to death the only occupant present, one Margaret Tillary. Her husband, Thomas J. Tillary, a salesman, was not at home at the time.

I hadn't known Tommy was a salesman or that he'd had a wife. He did wear a wide yellow-gold band on the appropriate finger, and it was clear that he wasn't married to Carolyn from the Caroline, and it now looked as though he was a widower. I felt vaguely sorry for him, vaguely sorry for the wife I'd never even known of, but that was the extent of it. I drank enough back then to avoid feeling any emotion very strongly.

And then, two or three nights later, I walked into Armstrong's and there was Carolyn. She didn't appear to be waiting for him or anyone else, nor did she look as though she'd just breezed in a few minutes ago. She had a stool by herself at the bar and she was drinking something dark from a low-ball glass.

I took a seat a few stools down from her. I ordered two double shots of bourbon, drank one and poured the other into the black coffee Billie brought me. I was sipping the coffee when a voice with a Piedmont softness said, "I forget your name."

I looked up.

"I believe we were introduced," she said, "but I don't recall your name."

"It's Matt," I said, "and you're right, Tommy introduced us. You're Carolyn."

"Carolyn Cheatham. Have you seen him?"

"Tommy? Not since it happened."

"Neither have I. Were you-all at the funeral?"

"No. When was it?"

"This afternoon. Neither was I. There. Whyn't you come sit next to me so's I don't have to shout. Please?"

She was drinking a sweet almond liqueur that she took on the rocks. It tastes like dessert, but it's as strong as whiskey.

"He told me not to come," she said. "To the funeral. He said it was a matter of respect for the dead." She picked up her glass and stared into it. I've never known what people hope to see there, though it's a gesture I've performed often enough myself.

"Respect," she said. "What's he care about respect? I would have just been part of the office crowd; we both work at Tannahill; far as anyone there knows, we're just friends. And all we ever were is friends, you know."

"Whatever you say."

"Oh, *shit*," she said. "I don't mean I wasn't fucking him,

for the Lord's sake. I mean it was just laughs and good times. He was married and he went home to Mama every night and that was jes' fine, because who in her right mind'd want Tommy Tillary around by the dawn's early light? Christ in the foothills, did I spill this or drink it?"

We agreed she was drinking them a little too fast. It was this fancy New York sweet-drink shit, she maintained, not like the bourbon she'd grown up on. You knew where you stood with bourbon.

I told her I was a bourbon drinker myself, and it pleased her to learn this. Alliances have been forged on thinner bonds than that, and ours served to propel us out of Armstrong's, with a stop down the block for a fifth of Maker's Mark—her choice—and a four-block walk to her apartment. There were exposed brick walls, I remember, and candles stuck in straw-wrapped bottles, and several travel posters from Sabena, the Belgian airline.

We did what grown-ups do when they find themselves alone together. We drank our fair share of the Maker's Mark and went to bed. She made a lot of enthusiastic noises and more than a few skillful moves, and afterward she cried some.

A little later, she dropped off to sleep. I was tired myself, but I put on my clothes and sent myself home. Because who in her right mind'd want Matt Scudder around by the dawn's early light?

Over the next couple of days, I wondered every time I entered Armstrong's if I'd run into her, and each time I was more relieved than disappointed when I didn't. I didn't encounter Tommy, either, and that, too, was a relief and in no sense disappointing.

Then, one morning, I picked up the *News* and read that

they'd arrested a pair of young Hispanics from Sunset Park for the Tillary burglary and homicide. The paper ran the usual photo—two skinny kids, their hair unruly, one of them trying to hide his face from the camera, the other smirking defiantly, and each of them handcuffed to a broad-shouldered, grim-faced Irishman in a suit. You didn't need the careful caption to tell the good guys from the bad guys.

Sometime in the middle of the afternoon, I went over to Armstrong's for a hamburger and drank a beer with it. The phone behind the bar rang and Dennis put down the glass he was wiping and answered it. "He was here a minute ago," he said. "I'll see if he stepped out." He covered the mouthpiece with his hand and looked quizzically at me. "Are you still here?" he asked. "Or did you slip away while my attention was diverted?"

"Who wants to know?"

"Tommy Tillary."

You never know what a woman will decide to tell a man or how a man will react to it. I didn't want to find out, but I was better off learning over the phone than face-to-face. I nodded and took the phone from Dennis.

I said, "Matt Scudder, Tommy. I was sorry to hear about your wife."

"Thanks, Matt. Jesus, it feels like it happened a year ago. It was what, a week?"

"At least they got the bastards."

There was a pause. Then he said, "Jesus. You haven't seen a paper, huh?"

"That's where I read about it. Two Spanish kids."

"You didn't happen to see this afternoon's *Post*."

"No. Why, what happened? They turn out to be clean?"

"The two spics. Clean? Shit, they're about as clean as the

room in the Times Square subway station. The cops hit their place and found stuff from my house everywhere they looked. Jewelry they had descriptions of, a stereo that I gave them the serial number, everything. Monogrammed shit. I mean, that's how clean they were, for Christ's sake."

"So?"

"They admitted the burglary but not the murder."

"That's common, Tommy."

"Lemme finish, huh? They admitted the burglary, but according to them it was a put-up job. According to them, I hired them to hit my place. They could keep whatever they got and I'd have everything out and arranged for them, and in return I got to clean up on the insurance by overreporting the loss."

"What did the loss amount to?"

"Shit, I don't know. There were twice as many things turned up in their apartment as I ever listed when I made out a report. There's things I missed a few days after I filed the report and others I didn't know were gone until the cops found them. You don't notice everything right away, at least I didn't, and on top of it, how could I think straight with Peg dead? You know?"

"It hardly sounds like an insurance setup."

"No, of course it wasn't. How the hell could it be? All I had was a standard homeowner's policy. It covered maybe a third of what I lost. According to them, the place was empty when they hit it. Peg was out."

"And?"

"And I set them up. They hit the place, they carted everything away, and I came home with Peg and stabbed her six, eight times, whatever it was, and left her there so it'd look like it happened in a burglary."

"How could the burglars testify that you stabbed your wife?"

"They couldn't. All they said was they didn't and she wasn't home when they were there, and that I hired them to do the burglary. The cops pieced the rest of it together."

"What did they do, take you downtown?"

"No. They came over to the house, it was early, I don't know what time. It was the first I knew that the spics were arrested, let alone that they were trying to do a job on me. They just wanted to talk, the cops, and at first I talked to them, and then I started to get the drift of what they were trying to put on to me. So I said I wasn't saying anything more without my lawyer present, and I called him, and he left half his breakfast on the table and came over in a hurry, and he wouldn't let me say a word."

"And the cops didn't take you in or book you?"

"No."

"Did they buy your story?"

"No way. I didn't really tell 'em a story, because Kaplan wouldn't let me say anything. They didn't drag me in, because they don't have a case yet, but Kaplan says they're gonna be building one if they can. They told me not to leave town. You believe it? My wife's dead, the *Post* headline says, 'Quiz Husband in Burglary Murder,' and what the hell do they think I'm gonna do? Am I going fishing for fucking trout in Montana? 'Don't leave town.' You see this shit on television, you think nobody in real life talks this way. Maybe television's where they get it from."

I waited for him to tell me what he wanted from me. I didn't have long to wait.

"Why I called," he said, "is Kaplan wants to hire a detective. He figured maybe these guys talked around the neighborhood, maybe they bragged to their friends, maybe there's a way to prove they did the killing. He says the cops won't concentrate on that end if they're too busy nailing the lid shut on me."

I explained that I didn't have any official standing, that I had no license and filed no reports.

"That's okay," he insisted. "I told Kaplan what I want is somebody I can trust, somebody who'll do the job for me. I don't think they're gonna have any kind of a case at all, Matt, but the longer this drags on, the worse it is for me. I want it cleared up, I want it in the papers that these Spanish assholes did it all and I had nothing to do with anything. You name a fair fee and I'll pay it, me to you, and it can be cash in your hand if you don't like checks. What do you say?"

He wanted somebody he could trust. Had Carolyn from the Caroline told him how trustworthy I was?

What did I say? I said yes.

I met Tommy Tillary and his lawyer in Drew Kaplan's office on Court Street, a few blocks from Brooklyn's Borough Hall. There was a Syrian restaurant next door and, at the corner, a grocery store specializing in Middle Eastern imports stood next to an antique shop overflowing with stripped-oak furniture and brass lamps and bedsteads. Kaplan's office ran to wood paneling and leather chairs and oak file cabinets. His name and the names of two partners were painted on the frosted-glass door in old-fashioned gold-and-black lettering. Kaplan himself looked conservatively up to date, with a three-piece striped suit that was better cut than mine. Tommy wore his burgundy blazer and gray-flannel trousers and loafers. Strain showed at the corners of his blue eyes and around his mouth. His complexion was off, too.

"All we want you to do," Kaplan said, "is find a key in one of their pants pockets, Herrera's or Cruz's, and trace it to a locker in Penn Station, and in the locker there's a footlong knife with their prints and her blood on it."

"Is that what it's going to take?"

He smiled. "It wouldn't hurt. No, actually, we're not in such bad shape. They got some shaky testimony from a pair of Latins who've been in and out of trouble since they got weaned to Tropicana. They got what looks to them like a good motive on Tommy's part."

"Which is?"

I was looking at Tommy when I asked. His eyes slipped away from mine. Kaplan said, "A marital triangle, a case of the shorts and a strong money motive. Margaret Tillary inherited a little over a quarter of a million dollars six or eight months ago. An aunt left a million two and it got cut up four ways. What they don't bother to notice is he loved his wife, and how many husbands cheat? What is it they say—ninety percent cheat and ten percent lie?"

"That's good odds."

"One of the killers, Angel Herrera, did some odd jobs at the Tillary house last March or April. Spring cleaning; he hauled stuff out of the basement and attic, a little donkey-work. According to Herrera, that's how Tommy knew him to contact him about the burglary. According to common sense, that's how Herrera and his buddy Cruz knew the house and what was in it and how to gain access."

"The case against Tommy sounds pretty thin."

"It is," Kaplan said. "The thing is, you go to court with something like this and you lose even if you win. For the rest of your life, everybody remembers you stood trial for murdering your wife, never mind that you won an acquittal.

"Besides," he said, "you never know which way a jury's going to jump. Tommy's alibi is he was with another lady at the time of the burglary. The woman's a colleague; they could see it as completely aboveboard, but who says they're going to? What they sometimes do, they decide they don't believe the alibi because it's his girlfriend lying for him, and at the same time they label him a scumbag for screwing around while his wife's getting killed."

"You keep it up," Tommy said, "I'll find myself guilty, the way you make it sound."

"Plus he's hard to get a sympathetic jury for. He's a big handsome guy, a sharp dresser, and you'd love him in a gin joint, but how much do you love him in a courtroom? He's a securities salesman, he's beautiful on the phone, and that means every clown who ever lost a hundred dollars on a stock tip or bought magazines over the phone is going to walk into the courtroom with a hard-on for him. I'm telling you, I want to stay the hell *out* of court. I'll *win* in court, I know that, or the worst that'll happen is I'll win on appeal, but who needs it? This is a case that shouldn't be in the first place, and I'd love to clear it up before they even go so far as presenting a bill to the grand jury."

"So from me you want—"

"Whatever you can find, Matt. Whatever discredits Cruz and Herrera. I don't know what's there to be found, but you were a cop and now you're private, and you can get down in the streets and nose around."

I nodded. I could do that. "One thing," I said. "Wouldn't you be better off with a Spanish-speaking detective? I know enough to buy a beer in a bodega, but I'm a long way from fluent."

Kaplan shook his head. "A personal relationship's worth

more than a dime's worth of '*Me llamo Matteo y ¿como está usted?*'"

"That's the truth," Tommy Tillary said. "Matt, I know I can count on you."

I wanted to tell him all he could count on was his fingers. I didn't really see what I could expect to uncover that wouldn't turn up in a regular police investigation. But I'd spent enough time carrying a shield to know not to push away money when somebody wants to give it to you. I felt comfortable taking a fee. The man was inheriting a quarter of a million, plus whatever insurance his wife had carried. If he was willing to spread some of it around, I was willing to take it.

So I went to Sunset Park and spent some time in the streets and some more time in the bars. Sunset Park is in Brooklyn, of course, on the borough's western edge, above Bay Ridge and south and west of Greenwood Cemetery. These days, there's a lot of brownstoning going on there, with young urban professionals renovating the old houses and gentrifying the neighborhood. Back then, the upwardly mobile young had not yet discovered Sunset Park, and the area was a mix of Latins and Scandinavians, most of the former Puerto Ricans, most of the latter Norwegians. The balance was gradually shifting from Europe to the islands, from light to dark, but this was a process that had been going on for ages and there was nothing hurried about it.

I talked to Herrera's landlord and Cruz's former employer and one of his recent girlfriends. I drank beer in bars and the back rooms of bodegas. I went to the local station house, I read the sheets on both of the burglars and drank coffee with the cops and picked up some of the stuff that doesn't get on the yellow sheets.

I found out that Miguelito Cruz had once killed a man in a tavern brawl over a woman. There were no charges pressed; a dozen witnesses reported that the dead man had gone after Cruz first with a broken bottle. Cruz had most likely been carrying the knife, but several witnesses insisted it had been tossed to him by an anonymous benefactor, and there hadn't been enough evidence to make a case of weapons possession, let alone homicide.

I learned that Herrera had three children living with their mother in Puerto Rico. He was divorced but wouldn't marry his current girlfriend because he regarded himself as married to his ex-wife in the eyes of God. He sent money to his children when he had any to send.

I learned other things. They didn't seem terribly consequential then and they've faded from memory altogether now, but I wrote them down in my pocket notebook as I learned them, and every day or so I duly reported my findings to Drew Kaplan. He always seemed pleased with what I told him.

I invariably managed a stop at Armstrong's before I called it a night. One night she was there, Carolyn Cheatham, drinking bourbon this time, her face frozen with stubborn old pain. It took her a blink or two to recognize me. Then tears started to form in the corners of her eyes, and she used the back of one hand to wipe them away.

I didn't approach her until she beckoned. She patted the stool beside hers and I eased myself onto it. I had coffee with bourbon in it and bought a refill for her. She was pretty drunk already, but that's never been enough reason to turn down a drink.

She talked about Tommy. He was being nice to her, she said. Calling up, sending flowers. But he wouldn't see her, because it wouldn't look right, not for a new widower, not for a man who'd been publicly accused of murder.

"He sends flowers with no card enclosed," she said. "He calls me from pay phones. The son of a bitch."

Billie called me aside. "I didn't want to put her out," he said, "a nice woman like that, shit-faced as she is. But I thought I was gonna have to. You'll see she gets home?"

I said I would.

I got her out of there and a cab came along and saved us the walk. At her place, I took the keys from her and unlocked the door. She half sat, half sprawled on the couch. I had to use the bathroom, and when I came back, her eyes were closed and she was snoring lightly.

I got her coat and shoes off, put her to bed, loosened her clothing, and covered her with a blanket. I was tired from all that and sat down on the couch for a minute, and I almost dozed off myself. Then I snapped awake and let myself out.

I went back to Sunset Park the next day. I learned that Cruz had been in trouble as a youth. With a gang of neighborhood kids, he used to go into the city and cruise Greenwich Village, looking for homosexuals to beat up. He'd had a dread of homosexuality, probably flowing as it generally does out of fear of a part of himself, and he stifled that dread by fag-bashing.

"He still doan' like them," a woman told me. She had glossy black hair and opaque eyes, and she was letting me pay for her rum and orange juice. "He's pretty, you know, an' they come on to him, an' he doan' like it."

I called that item in, along with a few others equally earthshaking. I bought myself a steak dinner at the Slate over on Tenth Avenue, then finished up at Armstrong's, not drinking very hard, just coasting along on bourbon and coffee.

Twice, the phone rang for me. Once, it was Tommy Tillary, telling me how much he appreciated what I was doing for him. It seemed to me that all I was doing was taking his money, but he had me believing that my loyalty and invaluable assistance were all he had to cling to.

The second call was from Carolyn. More praise. I was a gentleman, she assured me, and a hell of a fellow all around. And I should forget that she'd been bad-mouthing Tommy. Everything was going to be fine with them.

I took the next day off. I think I went to a movie, and it may have been *The Sting*, with Newman and Redford achieving vengeance through swindling.

The day after that, I did another tour of duty over in Brooklyn. And the day after that, I picked up the *News* first thing in the morning. The headline was nonspecific, something like KILL SUSPECT HANGS SELF IN CELL, but I knew it was my case before I turned to the story on page three.

Miguelito Cruz had torn his clothing into strips, knotted the strips together, stood his iron bedstead on its side, climbed onto it, looped his homemade rope around an overhead pipe, and jumped off the up-ended bedstead and into the next world.

That evening's six o'clock TV news had the rest of the story. Informed of his friend's death, Angel Herrera had recanted his original story and admitted that he and Cruz had conceived and executed the Tillary burglary on their own. It had been Miguelito who had stabbed the Tillary woman when she walked in on them. He'd picked up a kitchen knife while Herrera watched in horror. Miguelito always had a short temper, Herrera said, but they were friends, even cousins, and they had hatched their story to protect Miguelito. But now that he was dead, Herrera could admit what had really happened.

I was in Armstrong's that night, which was not remarkable. I had it in mind to get drunk, though I could not have told you why, and that *was* remarkable, if not unheard of. I got drunk a lot those days, but I rarely set out with that intention. I just wanted to feel a little better, a little more mellow, and somewhere along the way I'd wind up waxed.

I wasn't drinking particularly hard or fast, but I was working at it, and then somewhere around ten or eleven the door opened and I knew who it was before I turned around. Tommy Tillary, well dressed and freshly barbered, making his first appearance in Jimmy's place since his wife was killed.

"Hey, look who's here!" he called out and grinned that big grin. People rushed over to shake his hand. Billie was behind the stick, and he'd no sooner set one up on the house for our hero than Tommy insisted on buying a round for the bar. It was an expensive gesture—there must have been thirty or forty people in there—but I don't think he cared if there were three hundred or four hundred.

I stayed where I was, letting the others mob him, but he worked his way over to me and got an arm around my shoulders. "This is the man," he announced. "Best fucking detective ever wore out a pair of shoes. This man's money," he told Billie, "is no good at all tonight. He can't buy a drink; he can't buy a cup of coffee; if you went and put in pay toilets since I was last here, he can't use his own dime."

"The john's still free," Billie said, "but don't give the boss any ideas."

"Oh, don't tell me he didn't already think of it," Tommy said. "Matt, my boy, I love you. I was in a tight spot, I didn't want to walk out of my house, and you came through for me."

What the hell had I done? I hadn't hanged Miguelito Cruz or coaxed a confession out of Angel Herrera. I hadn't even set eyes on either man. But he was buying the drinks, and I had a thirst, so who was I to argue?

I don't know how long we stayed there. Curiously, my drinking slowed down even as Tommy's picked up speed. Carolyn, I noticed, was not present, nor did her name find its way into the conversation. I wondered if she would walk in— it was, after all, her neighborhood bar, and she was apt to drop in on her own. I wondered what would happen if she did.

I guess there were a lot of things I wondered about, and perhaps that's what put the brakes on my own drinking. I didn't want any gaps in my memory, any gray patches in my awareness.

After a while, Tommy was hustling me out of Armstrong's. "This is celebration time," he told me. "We don't want to sit in one place till we grow roots. We want to bop a little."

He had a car, and I just went along with him without paying too much attention to exactly where we were. We went to a noisy Greek club on the East Side, I think, where the waiters looked like Mob hit men. We went to a couple of trendy singles joints. We wound up somewhere in the Village, in a dark, beery cave.

It was quiet there, and conversation was possible, and I found myself asking him what I'd done that was so praiseworthy. One man had killed himself and another had confessed, and where was my role in either incident?

"The stuff you came up with," he said.

"What stuff? I should have brought back fingernail parings, you could have had someone work voodoo on them."

"About Cruz and the fairies."

"He was up for murder. He didn't kill himself because he was afraid they'd get him for fag-bashing when he was a juvenile offender."

Tommy took a sip of scotch. He said, "Couple days ago, huge black guy comes up to Cruz in the chow line. 'Wait'll you get up to Green Haven,' he tells him. 'Every blood there's gonna have you for a girlfriend. Doctor gonna have to cut you a brand-new asshole, time you get outa there.'"

I didn't say anything.

"Kaplan," he said. "Drew talked to somebody who talked to somebody, and that did it. Cruz took a good look at playin' drop the soap for half the jigs in captivity, next thing you know, the murderous little bastard was on air. And good riddance to him."

I couldn't seem to catch my breath. I worked on it while Tommy went to the bar for another round. I hadn't touched the drink in front of me, but I let him buy for both of us.

When he got back, I said, "Herrera."

"Changed his story. Made a full confession."

"And pinned the killing on Cruz."

"Why not? Cruz wasn't around to complain. Who knows which one of 'em did it, and for that matter, who cares? The thing is, you gave us the lever."

"For Cruz," I said. "To get him to kill himself."

"And for Herrera. Those kids of his in Santurce. Drew spoke to Herrera's lawyer and Herrera's lawyer spoke to Herrera, and the message was, 'Look, you're going up for burglary whatever you do, and probably for murder; but if you tell the right story, you'll draw shorter time, and on top of that, that nice Mr. Tillary's gonna let bygones be bygones and every month there's a nice check for your wife and kiddies back home in Puerto Rico.'"

At the bar, a couple of old men were reliving the Louis-Schmeling fight, the second one, where Louis punished the German champion. One of the old fellows was throwing roundhouse punches in the air, demonstrating.

I said, "Who killed your wife?"

"One or the other of them. If I had to bet, I'd say Cruz. He had those little beady eyes; you looked at him up close and you got that he was a killer."

"When did you look at him up close?"

"When they came and cleaned the house, the basement, and the attic. Not when they came and cleaned me out; that was the second time."

He smiled, but I kept looking at him until the smile lost its certainty. "That was Herrera who helped around the house," I said. "You never met Cruz."

"Cruz came along, gave him a hand."

"You never mentioned that before."

"Oh, sure I did, Matt. What difference does it make, anyway."

"Who killed her, Tommy?"

"Hey, let it alone, huh?"

"Answer the question."

"I already answered it."

"You killed her, didn't you?"

"What are you, crazy? Cruz killed her and Herrera swore to it, isn't that enough for you?"

"Tell me you didn't kill her."

"I didn't kill her."

"Tell me again."

"I didn't fucking kill her. What's the matter with you?"

"I don't believe you."

"Oh, Jesus," he said. He closed his eyes, put his head in his hands. He sighed and looked up and said, "You know, it's a funny thing with me. Over the telephone, I'm the best salesman you could ever imagine. I swear I could sell sand to the Arabs, I could sell ice in the winter, but face-to-face I'm no good at all. Why do you figure that is?"

"You tell me."

"I don't know. I used to think it was my face, the eyes and the mouth; I don't know. It's easy over the phone. I'm talking to a stranger, I don't know who he is or what he looks like, and he's not lookin' at me, and it's a cinch. Face-to-face, especially with someone I know, it's a different story." He looked at me. "If we were doin' this over the phone, you'd buy the whole thing."

"It's possible."

"It's fucking certain. Word for word, you'd buy the package. Suppose I was to tell you I did kill her, Matt. You couldn't prove anything. Look, the both of us walked in there, the place was a mess from the burglary, we got in an argument, tempers flared, something happened."

"You set up the burglary. You planned the whole thing, just the way Cruz and Herrera accused you of doing. And now you wriggled out of it."

"And you helped me—don't forget that part of it."

"I won't."

"And I wouldn't have gone away for it anyway, Matt. Not a chance. I'da beat it in court, only this way I don't have to go to court. Look, this is just the booze talkin', and we can forget it in the morning, right? I didn't kill her, you didn't accuse me, we're still buddies, everything's fine. Right?"

* * *

Blackouts are never there when you want them. I woke up the next day and remembered all of it, and I found myself wishing I didn't. He'd killed his wife and he was getting away with it. And I'd helped him. I'd taken his money, and in return I'd shown him how to set one man up for suicide and pressure another into making a false confession.

And what was I going to do about it?

I couldn't think of a thing. Any story I carried to the police would be speedily denied by Tommy and his lawyer, and all I had was the thinnest of hearsay evidence, my own client's own words when he and I both had a skinful of booze. I went over it for a few days, looking for ways to shake something loose, and there was nothing. I could maybe interest a newspaper reporter, maybe get Tommy some press coverage that wouldn't make him happy, but why? And to what purpose?

It rankled. But I would just have a couple of drinks, and then it wouldn't rankle so much.

Angel Herrera pleaded guilty to burglary, and in return, the Brooklyn D.A.'s Office dropped all homicide charges. He went Upstate to serve five to ten.

And then I got a call in the middle of the night. I'd been sleeping a couple of hours, but the phone woke me and I groped for it. It took me a minute to recognize the voice on the other end.

It was Carolyn Cheatham.

"I had to call you," she said, "on account of you're a bourbon man and a gentleman. I owed it to you to call you."

"What's the matter?"

"He ditched me," she said, "and he got me fired out of Tannahill and Company so he won't have to look at me around the office. Once he didn't need me to back up his story, he let go of me, and do you know he did it over the phone?"

"Carolyn—"

"It's all in the note," she said. "I'm leaving a note."

"Look, don't do anything yet," I said. I was out of bed, fumbling for my clothes. "I'll be right over. We'll talk about it."

"You can't stop me, Matt."

"I won't try to stop you. We'll talk first, and then you can do anything you want."

The phone clicked in my ear.

I threw my clothes on, rushed over there, hoping it would be pills, something that took its time. I broke a small pane of glass in the downstairs door and let myself in, then used an old credit card to slip the bolt of her spring lock.

The room smelled of cordite. She was on the couch she'd passed out on the last time I saw her. The gun was still in her hand, limp at her side, and there was a black-rimmed hole in her temple.

There was a note, too. An empty bottle of Maker's Mark stood on the coffee table, an empty glass beside it. The booze showed in her handwriting and in the sullen phrasing of the suicide note.

I read the note. I stood there for a few minutes, not for very long, and then I got a dish towel from the Pullman kitchen and wiped the bottle and the glass. I took another matching glass, rinsed it out and wiped it, and put it in the drainboard of the sink.

I stuffed the note in my pocket. I took the gun from her fingers, checked routinely for a pulse, then wrapped a sofa pillow around the gun to muffle its report. I fired one round into her chest, another into her open mouth.

I dropped the gun into a pocket and left.

* * *

They found the gun in Tommy Tillary's house, stuffed between the cushions of the living-room sofa, clean of prints inside and out. Ballistics got a perfect match. I'd aimed for soft tissue with the round shot into her chest, because bullets can fragment on impact with bone. That was one reason I'd fired the extra shots. The other was to rule out the possibility of suicide.

After the story made the papers, I picked up the phone and called Drew Kaplan. "I don't understand it," I said. "He was free and clear; why the hell did he kill the girl?"

"Ask him yourself," Kaplan said. He did not sound happy. "You want my opinion, he's a lunatic. I honestly didn't think he was. I figured maybe he killed his wife, maybe he didn't. Not my job to try him. But I didn't figure he was a homicidal maniac."

"It's certain he killed the girl?"

"Not much question. The gun's pretty strong evidence. Talk about finding somebody with the smoking pistol in his hand, here it was in Tommy's couch. The idiot."

"Funny he kept it."

"Maybe he had other people he wanted to shoot. Go figure a crazy man. No, the gun's evidence, and there was a phone tip—a man called in the shooting, reported a man running out of there, and gave a description that fitted Tommy pretty well. Even had him wearing that red blazer he wears, tacky thing makes him look like an usher at the Paramount."

"It sounds tough to square."

"Well, somebody else'll have to try to do it," Kaplan said. "I told him I can't defend him this time. What it amounts to, I wash my hands of him."

* * *

I thought of that when I read that Angel Herrera got out just the other day. He served all ten years because he was as good at getting into trouble inside the walls as he'd been on the outside.

Somebody killed Tommy Tillary with a homemade knife after he'd served two years and three months of a manslaughter stretch. I wondered at the time if that was Herrera getting even, and I don't suppose I'll ever know. Maybe the checks stopped going to Santurce and Herrera took it the wrong way. Or maybe Tommy said the wrong thing to somebody else and said it face-to-face instead of over the phone.

I don't think I'd do it that way now. I don't drink anymore and the impulse to play God seems to have evaporated with the booze.

But then, a lot of things have changed. Billie left Armstrong's not long after that, left New York, too; the last I heard, he was off drink himself, living in Sausalito and making candles. I ran into Dennis the other day in a bookstore on lower Fifth Avenue full of odd volumes on yoga and spiritualism and holistic healing. And Armstrong's is scheduled to close the end of next month. The lease is up for renewal, and I suppose the next you know, the old joint'll be another Korean fruit market.

I still light a candle now and then for Carolyn Cheatham and Miguelito Cruz. Not often. Just every once in a while.

THE BEST-FRIEND MURDER

BY DONALD E. WESTLAKE

Park Slope

(Originally published in 1959)

Detective Abraham Levine of Brooklyn's Forty-Third Precinct chewed on his pencil and glowered at the report he'd just written. He didn't like it, he didn't like it at all. It just didn't feel right, and the more he thought about it the stronger the feeling became.

Levine was a short and stocky man, baggily-dressed from plain pipe racks. His face was sensitive, topped by salt-and-pepper gray hair chopped short in a military crewcut. At fifty-three, he had twenty-four years of duty on the police force, and was halfway through the heart-attack age range, a fact that had been bothering him for some time now. Every time he was reminded of death, he thought worriedly about the aging heart pumping away inside his chest.

And in his job, the reminders of death came often. Natural death, accidental death, and violent death.

This one was a violent death, and to Levine it felt wrong somewhere. He and his partner, Jack Crawley, had taken the call just after lunch. It was from one of the patrolmen in Prospect Park, a patrolman named Tanner. A man giving his name as Larry Perkins had walked up to Tanner in the park and announced that he had just poisoned his best friend. Tanner went with him, found a dead body in the apartment Perkins had led him to, and called in. Levine and Crawley, having just walked into the station after lunch, were given the call. They turned around and walked back out again.

Crawley drove their car, an unmarked '56 Chevy, while Levine sat beside him and worried about death. At least this would be one of the neat ones. No knives or bombs or broken beer bottles. Just poison, that was all. The victim would look as though he were sleeping, unless it had been one of those poisons causing muscle spasms before death. But it would still be neater than a knife or a bomb or a broken beer bottle, and the victim wouldn't look quite so completely dead.

Crawley drove leisurely, without the siren. He was a big man in his forties, somewhat overweight, square-faced and heavy jowled, and he looked meaner than he actually was. The Chevy tooled up Eighth Avenue, the late spring sun shining on its hood. They were headed for an address on Garfield Place, the block between Eighth Avenue and Prospect Park West. They had to circle the block, because Garfield was a one-way street. That particular block on Garfield Place is a double row of chipped brownstones, the street running down between two rows of high stone stoops, the buildings cut and chopped inside into thousands of apartments, crannies and cubbyholes, niches and box-like caves, where the subway riders sleep at night. The subway to Manhattan is six blocks away, up at Grand Army Plaza, across the way from the main library.

At one P.M. on this Wednesday in late May, the sidewalks were deserted, the buildings had the look of long abandoned dwellings. Only the cars parked along the left side of the street indicated present occupancy.

The number they wanted was in the middle of the block, on the right-hand side. There was no parking allowed on that

side, so there was room directly in front of the address for
Crawley to stop the Chevy. He flipped the sun visor down,
with the official business card showing through the windshield, and followed Levine across the sidewalk and down the
two steps to the basement door, under the stoop. The door
was propped open with a battered garbage can. Levine and
Crawley walked inside. It was dim in there, after the bright
sunlight, and it took Levine's eyes a few seconds to get used
to the change. Then he made out the figures of two men
standing at the other end of the hallway, in front of a closed
door. One was the patrolman, Tanner, young, just over six
foot, with a square and impersonal face. The other was Larry
Perkins.

Levine and Crawley moved down the hallway to the two
men waiting for them. In the seven years they had been partners, they had established a division of labor that satisfied
them both. Crawley asked the questions, and Levine listened
to the answers. Now, Crawley introduced himself to Tanner,
who said, "This is Larry Perkins of 294 Fourth Street."

"Body in there?" asked Crawley, pointing at the closed
door.

"Yes, sir," said Tanner.

"Let's go inside," said Crawley. "You keep an eye on the
pigeon. See he doesn't fly away."

"I've got some stuff to go to the library," said Perkins suddenly. His voice was young and soft.

They stared at him. Crawley said, "It'll keep."

Levine looked at Perkins, trying to get to know him. It
was a technique he used, most of it unconsciously. First, he
tried to fit Perkins into a type or category, some sort of general stereotype. Then he would look for small and individual
ways in which Perkins differed from the general type, and he

would probably wind up with a surprisingly complete mental picture, which would also be surprisingly accurate.

The general stereotype was easy. Perkins, in his black wool sweater and belt-in-the-back khakis and scuffed brown loafers without socks, was "arty." What were they calling them this year? They were "hip" last year, but this year they were "beat." That was it. For a general stereotype, Larry Perkins was a beatnik. The individual differences would show up soon, in Perkins's talk and mannerisms and attitudes.

Crawley said again, "Let's go inside," and the four of them trooped into the room where the corpse lay.

The apartment was one large room, plus a closet-size kitchenette and an even smaller bathroom. A Murphy bed stood open, covered with zebra-striped material. The rest of the furniture consisted of a battered dresser, a couple of arm-chairs and lamps, and a record player sitting on a table beside a huge stack of long-playing records. Everything except the record player looked faded and worn and second-hand, including the thin maroon rug on the floor and the soiled flower-pattern wallpaper. Two windows looked out on a narrow cement enclosure and the back of another brownstone. It was a sunny day outside, but no sun managed to get down into this room.

In the middle of the room stood a card table, with a type-writer and two stacks of paper on it. Before the card table was a folding chair, and in the chair sat the dead man. He was slumped forward, his arms flung out and crumpling the stacks of paper, his head resting on the typewriter. His face was turned toward the door, and his eyes were closed, his facial muscles relaxed. It had been a peaceful death, at least, and Levine was grateful for that.

Crawley looked at the body, grunted, and turned to Perkins. "Okay," he said. "Tell us about it."

"I put the poison in his beer," said Perkins simply. He didn't talk like a beatnik at any rate. "He asked me to open a can of beer for him. When I poured it into a glass, I put the poison in, too. When he was dead, I went and talked to the patrolman here."

"And that's all there was to it?"

"That's all."

Levine asked, "Why did you kill him?"

Perkins looked over at Levine. "Because he was a pompous ass."

"Look at me," Crawley told him.

Perkins immediately looked away from Levine, but before he did so, Levine caught a flicker of emotion in the boy's eyes, what emotion he couldn't tell. Levine glanced around the room, at the faded furniture and the card table and the body, and at young Perkins, dressed like a beatnik but talking like the politest of polite young men, outwardly calm but hiding some strong emotion inside his eyes. What was it Levine had seen there? Terror? Rage? Or pleading?

"Tell us about this guy," said Crawley, motioning at the body. "His name, where you knew him from, the whole thing."

"His name is Al Gruber. He got out of the Army about eight months ago. He's living on his savings and the GI Bill. I mean, he *was*."

"He was a college student?"

"More or less. He was taking a few courses at Columbia, nights. He wasn't a full-time student."

Crawley said, "What was he, full-time?"

Perkins shrugged. "Not much of anything. A writer. An undiscovered writer. Like me."

Levine asked, "Did he make much money from his writing?"

"None," said Perkins. This time he didn't turn to look at Levine, but kept watching Crawley while he answered. "He got something accepted by one of the quarterlies once," he said, "but I don't think they ever published it. And they don't pay anything anyway."

"So he was broke?" asked Crawley.

"Very broke. I know the feeling well."

"You in the same boat?"

"Same life story completely," said Perkins. He glanced at the body of Al Gruber and said, "Well, almost. I write, too. And I don't get any money for it. And I'm living on the GI Bill and savings and a few home-typing jobs, and going to Columbia nights."

People came into the room then, the medical examiner and the boys from the lab, and Levine and Crawley, bracketing Perkins between them, waited and watched for a while. When they could see that the M.E. had completed his first examination, they left Perkins in Tanner's charge and went over to talk to him.

Crawley, as usual, asked the questions. "Hi, Doc," he said. "What's it look like to you?"

"Pretty straightforward case," said the M.E. "On the surface, anyway. Our man here was poisoned, felt the effects coming on, went to the typewriter to tell us who'd done it to him, and died. A used glass and a small medicine bottle were on the dresser. We'll check them out, but they almost certainly did the job."

"Did he manage to do any typing before he died?" asked Crawley.

The M.E. shook his head. "Not a word. The paper was in

the machine kind of crooked, as though he'd been in a hurry, but he just wasn't fast enough."

"He wasted his time," said Crawley. "The guy confessed right away."

"The one over there with the patrolman?"

"Uh huh."

"Seems odd, doesn't it?" said the M.E. "Take the trouble to poison someone, and then run out and confess to the first cop you see."

Crawley shrugged. "You can never figure," he said.

"I'll get the report to you soon's I can," said the M.E.

"Thanks, Doc. Come on, Abe, let's take our pigeon to his nest."

"Okay," said Levine, abstractedly. Already it felt wrong. It had been feeling wrong, vaguely, ever since he'd caught that glimpse of something in Perkins's eyes. And the feeling of wrongness was getting stronger by the minute, without getting any clearer.

They walked back to Tanner and Perkins, and Crawley said, "Okay, Perkins, let's go for a ride."

They walked back to Tanner.

"You're going to book me?" asked Perkins. He sounded oddly eager.

"Just come along," said Crawley. He didn't believe in answering extraneous questions.

"All right," said Perkins. He turned to Tanner. "Would you mind taking my books and records back to the library? They're due today. They're the ones on that chair. And there's a couple more over in the stack of Al's records."

"Sure," said Tanner. He was gazing at Perkins with a troubled look on his face, and Levine wondered if Tanner felt the same wrongness that was plaguing him.

"Let's go," said Crawley impatiently, and Perkins moved toward the door.

"I'll be right along," said Levine. As Crawley and Perkins left the apartment, Levine glanced at the titles of the books and record albums Perkins had wanted returned to the library. Two of the books were collections of Elizabethan plays, one was the New Arts Writing Annual, and the other two were books on criminology. The records were mainly folk songs, of the bloodier type.

Levine frowned and went over to Tanner. He asked, "What were you and Perkins talking about before we got here?"

Tanner's face was still creased in a puzzled frown. "The stupidity of the criminal mind," he said. "There's something goofy here, Lieutenant."

"You may be right," Levine told him. He walked on down the hall and joined the other two at the door.

All three got into the front seat of the Chevy, Crawley driving again and Perkins sitting in the middle. They rode in silence, Crawley busy driving, Perkins studying the complex array of the dashboard, with its extra knobs and switches and the mike hooked beneath the radio, and Levine trying to figure out what was wrong.

At the station, after booking, they brought him to a small office, one of the interrogation rooms. There was a bare and battered desk, plus four chairs. Crawley sat behind the desk, Perkins sat across the desk and facing him, Levine took the chair in a corner behind and to the left of Perkins, and a male stenographer, notebook in hand, filled the fourth chair, behind Crawley.

Crawley's first questions covered the same ground

already covered at Gruber's apartment, this time for the record. "Okay," said Crawley, when he'd brought them up to date. "You and Gruber were both doing the same kind of thing, living the same kind of life. You were both unpublished writers, both taking night courses at Columbia, both living on very little money."

"That's right," said Perkins.

"How long you known each other?"

"About six months. We met at Columbia, and we took the same subway home after class. We got to talking, found out we were both dreaming the same kind of dream, and became friends. You know. Misery loves company."

"Take the same classes at Columbia?"

"Only one. Creative Writing, from Professor Stonegell."

"Where'd you buy the poison?"

"I didn't. Al did. He bought it a while back and just kept it around. He kept saying if he didn't make a good sale soon he'd kill himself. But he didn't mean it. It was just a kind of gag."

Crawley pulled at his right earlobe. Levine knew, from his long experience with his partner, that that gesture meant that Crawley was confused. "You went there today to kill him?"

"That's right."

Levine shook his head. That wasn't right. Softly, he said, "Why did you bring the library books along?"

"I was on my way up to the library," said Perkins, twisting around in his seat to look at Levine.

"Look this way," snapped Crawley.

Perkins looked around at Crawley again, but not before Levine had seen that same burning deep in Perkins's eyes. Stronger, this time, and more like pleading. Pleading? What was Perkins pleading for?

"I was on my way to the library," Perkins said again. "Al had a couple of records out on my card, so I went over to get them. On the way, I decided to kill him."

"Why?" asked Crawley.

"Because he was a pompous ass," said Perkins, the same answer he'd given before.

"Because he got a story accepted by one of the literary magazines and you didn't?" suggested Crawley.

"Maybe. Partially. His whole attitude. He was smug. He knew more than anybody else in the world."

"Why did you kill him today? Why not last week or next week?"

"I felt like it today."

"Why did you give yourself up?"

"You would have gotten me anyway."

Levine asked, "Did you know that before you killed him?"

"I don't know," said Perkins, without looking around at Levine. "I didn't think about it till afterward. Then I knew the police would get me anyway—they'd talk to Professor Stonegell and the other people who knew us both and I didn't want to have to wait it out. So I went and confessed."

"You told the policeman," said Levine, "that you'd killed your best friend."

"That's right."

"Why did you use that phrase, best friend, if you hated him so much you wanted to kill him?"

"He was my best friend. At least, in New York. I didn't really know anyone else, except Professor Stonegell. Al was my best friend because he was just about my only friend."

"Are you sorry you killed him?" asked Levine.

This time, Perkins twisted around in the chair again,

ignoring Crawley. "No, sir," he said, and his eyes now were blank.

There was silence in the room, and Crawley and Levine looked at one another. Crawley questioned with his eyes, and Levine shrugged, shaking his head. Something was wrong, but he didn't know what. And Perkins was being so helpful that he wound up being no help at all.

Crawley turned to the stenographer. "Type it up formal," he said. "And have somebody come take the pigeon to his nest."

After the stenographer had left, Levine said, "Anything you want to say off the record, Perkins?"

Perkins grinned. His face was half-turned away from Crawley, and he was looking at the floor, as though he was amused by something he saw there. "Off the record?" he murmured. "As long as there are two of you in here, it's *on* the record."

"Do you want one of us to leave?"

Perkins looked up at Levine again, and stopped smiling. He seemed to think it over for a minute, and then he shook his head. "No," he said. "Thanks, anyway. But I don't think I have anything more to say. Not right now anyway."

Levine frowned and sat back in his chair, studying Perkins. The boy didn't ring true; he was constructed of too many contradictions. Levine reached out for a mental image of Perkins, but all he touched was air.

After Perkins was led out of the room by two uniformed cops, Crawley got to his feet, stretched, sighed, scratched, pulled his earlobe, and said, "What do you make of it, Abe?"

"I don't like it."

"I know that. I saw it in your face. But he confessed, so what else is there?"

"The phony confession is not exactly unheard of, you know."

"Not this time," said Crawley. "A guy confesses to a crime he didn't commit for one of two reasons. Either he's a crackpot who wants the publicity or to be punished or something like that, or he's protecting somebody else. Perkins doesn't read like a crackpot to me, and there's nobody else involved for him to be protecting."

"In a capital punishment state," suggested Levine, "a guy might confess to a murder he didn't commit so the state would do his suicide for him."

Crawley shook his head. "That still doesn't look like Perkins," he said.

"Nothing looks like Perkins. He's given us a blank wall to stare at. A couple of times it started to slip, and there was something else inside."

"Don't build a big thing, Abe. The kid confessed. He's the killer; let it go at that."

"The job's finished, I know that. But it still bothers me."

"Okay," said Crawley. He sat down behind the desk again and put his feet up on the scarred desk top. "Let's straighten it out. Where does it bother you?"

"All over. Number one, motivation. You don't kill a man for being a pompous ass. Not when you turn around a minute later and say he was your best friend."

"People do funny things when they're pushed far enough. Even to friends."

"Sure. Okay, number two. The murder method. It doesn't sound right. When a man kills impulsively, he grabs something and starts swinging. When he calms down, he goes and turns himself in. But when you *poison* somebody, you're using a pretty sneaky method. It doesn't make sense for you to run out and call a cop right after using poison. It isn't the same kind of mentality."

"He used the poison," said Crawley, "because it was handy. Gruber bought it, probably had it sitting on his dresser or something, and Perkins just picked it up on impulse and poured it into the beer."

"That's another thing," said Levine. "Do you drink much beer out of cans?"

Crawley grinned. "You know I do."

"I saw some empty beer cans sitting around the apartment, so that's where Gruber got his last beer from."

"Yeah. So what?"

"When you drink a can of beer, do you pour the beer out of the can into a glass, or do you just drink it straight from the can?"

"I drink it out of the can. But not everybody does."

"I know, I know. Okay, what about the library books? If you're going to kill somebody, are you going to bring library books along?"

"It was an impulse killing. He didn't know he was going to do it until he got there."

Levine got his feet. "That's the hell of it," he said. "You can explain away every single question in this business. But it's such a simple case. Why should there be so many questions that need explaining away?"

Crawley shrugged. "Beats me," he said. "All I know is, we've got a confession, and that's enough to satisfy me."

"Not me," said Levine. "I think I'll go poke around and see what happens. Want to come along?"

"Somebody's going to have to hand the pen to Perkins when he signs his confession," said Crawley.

"Mind if I take off for a while?"

"Go ahead. Have a big time," said Crawley, grinning at him. "Play detective."

Levine's first stop was back at Gruber's address. Gruber's apartment was empty now, having been sifted completely through normal routine procedure. Levine went down to the basement door under the stoop, but he didn't go back to Gruber's door. He stopped at the front apartment instead, where a ragged-edged strip of paper attached with peeling scotch tape to the door read, in awkward and childish lettering, SUPERINTENDENT. Levine rapped and waited. After a minute, the door opened a couple of inches, held by a chain. A round face peered out at him from a height of a little over five feet. The face said, "Who you looking for?"

"Police," Levine told him. He opened his wallet and held it up for the face to look at.

"Oh," said the face. "Sure thing." The door shut, and Levine waited while the chain was clinked free, and then the door opened wide.

The super was a short and round man, dressed in corduroy trousers and a grease-spotted undershirt. He wheezed, "Come in, come in," and stood back for Levine to come into his crowded and musty-smelling living room.

Levine said, "I want to talk to you about Al Gruber."

The super shut the door and waddled into the middle of the room, shaking his head. "Wasn't that a shame?" he asked. "Al was a nice boy. No money, but a nice boy. Sit down somewhere, anywhere."

Levine looked around. The room was full of low-slung, heavy, sagging, over-stuffed furniture, armchairs and sofas. He picked the least battered armchair of the lot, and sat on the very edge. Although he was a short man, his knees seemed to be almost up to his chin, and he had the feeling that if he relaxed he'd fall over backwards.

The super trundled across the room and dropped into one of the other armchairs, sinking into it as though he never intended to get to his feet again in his life. "A real shame," he said again. "And to think I maybe could have stopped it."

"You could have stopped it? How?"

"It was around noon," said the super. "I was watching the TV over there, and I heard a voice from the back apartment, shouting, 'Al! Al!' So I went out to the hall, but by the time I got there the shouting was all done. So I didn't know what to do. I waited a minute, and then I came back in and watched the TV again. That was probably when it was happening."

"There wasn't any noise while you were in the hall? Just the two shouts before you got out there?"

"That's all. At first, I thought it was another one of them arguments, and I was gonna bawl out the two of them, but it stopped before I even got the door open."

"Arguments?"

"Mr. Gruber and Mr. Perkins. They used to argue all the time, shout at each other, carry on like monkeys. The other tenants was always complaining about it. They'd do it late at night sometimes, two or three o'clock in the morning, and the tenants would all start phoning me to complain."

"What did they argue about?"

The super shrugged his massive shoulders. "Who knows? Names. People. Writers. They both think they're great writers or something."

"Did they ever get into a fist fight or anything like that? Ever threaten to kill each other?"

"Naw, they'd just shout at each other and call each other

stupid and ignorant and stuff like that. They liked each other, really, I guess. At least they always hung around together. They just loved to argue, that's all. You know how it is with college kids. I've had college kids renting here before, and they're all like that. They all love to argue. Course, I never had nothing like this happen before."

"What kind of person was Gruber, exactly?"

The super mulled it over for a while. "Kind of a quiet guy," he said at last. "Except when he was with Mr. Perkins, I mean. Then he'd shout just as loud and often as anybody. But most of the time he was quiet. And good-mannered. A real surprise, after most of the kids around today. He was always polite, and he'd lend a hand if you needed some help or something, like the time I was carrying a bed up to the third floor front. Mr. Gruber come along and pitched right in with me. He did more of the work than I did."

"And he was a writer, wasn't he? At least, he was trying to be a writer."

"Oh, sure. I'd hear that typewriter of his tappin' away in there at all hours. And he always carried a notebook around with him, writin' things down in it. I asked him once what he wrote in there, and he said descriptions, of places like Prospect Park up at the corner, and of the people he knew. He always said he wanted to be a writer like some guy named Wolfe, used to live in Brooklyn too."

"I see." Levine struggled out of the armchair. "Thanks for your time," he said.

"Not at all." The super waddled after Levine to the door. "Anything I can do," he said. "Any time at all."

"Thanks again," said Levine. He went outside and stood in the hallway, thinking things over, listening to the latch click in place behind him. Then he turned and walked down the hallway to Gruber's apartment, and knocked on the door.

As he'd expected, a uniformed cop had been left behind to keep an eye on the place for a while, and when he opened the door, Levine showed his identification and said, "I'm on the case. I'd like to take a look around."

The cop let him in, and Levine looked carefully through Gruber's personal property. He found the notebooks, finally, in the bottom drawer of the dresser. There were five of them, steno pad size loose-leaf fillers. Four of them were filled with writing, in pen, in a slow and careful hand, and the fifth was still half blank.

Levine carried the notebooks over to the card table, pushed the typewriter out of the way, sat down and began to skim through the books.

He found what he was looking for in the middle of the third one he tried. A description of Larry Perkins, written by the man Perkins had killed. The description, or character study, which it more closely resembled, was four pages long, beginning with a physical description and moving into a discussion of Perkins's personality. Levine noticed particular sentences in this latter part: "Larry doesn't want to write, he wants to be a writer, and that isn't the same thing. He wants the glamour and the fame and the money, and he thinks he'll get it from being a writer. That's why he's dabbled in acting and painting and all the other so-called glamorous professions. Larry and I are both being thwarted by the same thing: neither of us has anything to say worth saying. The difference is, I'm trying to find something to say, and Larry wants to make it on glibness alone. One of these days, he's going to find out he won't get anywhere that way. That's going to be a terrible day for him."

Levine closed the book, then picked up the last one, the

one that hadn't yet been filled, and leafed through that. One word kept showing up throughout the last notebook. "Nihilism." Gruber obviously hated the word, and he was also obviously afraid of it. "Nihilism is death," he wrote on one page. "It is the belief that there are no beliefs, that no effort is worthwhile. How could any writer believe such a thing? Writing is the most positive of acts. So how can it be used for negative purposes? The only expression of nihilism is death, not the written word. If I can say nothing hopeful, I shouldn't say anything at all."

Levine put the notebooks back in the dresser drawer finally, thanked the cop, and went out to the Chevy. He'd hoped to be able to fill in the blank spaces in Perkins's character through Gruber's notebooks, but Gruber had apparently had just as much trouble defining Perkins as Levine was now having. Levine had learned a lot about the dead man, that he was sincere and intense and self-demanding as only the young can be, but Perkins was still little more than a smooth and blank wall. "Glibness," Gruber had called it. What was beneath the glibness? A murderer, by Perkins's own admission. But what else?

Levine crawled wearily into the Chevy and headed for Manhattan.

Professor Harvey Stonegell was in class when Levine got to Columbia University, but the girl at the desk in the dean's outer office told him that Stonegell would be out of that class in just a few minutes, and would then be free for the rest of the afternoon. She gave him directions to Stonegell's office, and Levine thanked her.

Stonegell's office door was locked, so Levine waited in the hall, watching students hurrying by in both directions, and reading the notices of scholarships, grants, and fellowships thumbtacked to the bulletin board near the office door.

The professor showed up about fifteen minutes later, with two students in tow. He was a tall and slender man, with a gaunt face and a full head of gray-white hair. He could have been any age between fifty and seventy. He wore a tweed suit jacket, leather patches at the elbows, and non-matching gray slacks.

Levine said, "Professor Stonegell?"

"Yes?"

Levine introduced himself and showed his identification. "I'd like to talk to you for a minute or two."

"Of course. I'll just be a minute." Stonegell handed a book to one of the two students, telling him to read certain sections of it, and explained to the other student why he hadn't received a passing grade in his latest assignment. When both of them were taken care of, Levine stepped into Stonegell's crowded and tiny office, and sat down in the chair beside the desk.

Stonegell said, "Is this about one of my students?"

"Two of them. From your evening writing course. Gruber and Perkins."

"Those two? They aren't in trouble, are they?"

"I'm afraid so. Perkins has confessed to murdering Gruber."

Stonegell's thin face paled. "Gruber's dead? Murdered?"

"By Perkins. He turned himself in right after it happened. But, to be honest with you, the whole thing bothers me. It doesn't make sense. You knew them both. I thought you might be able to tell me something about them, so it *would* make sense."

Stonegell lit himself a cigarette and offered one to

Levine. Then he fussed rather vaguely with his messy desk-top, while Levine waited for him to gather his thoughts.

"This takes some getting used to," said Stonegell after a minute. "Gruber and Perkins. They were both good students in my class, Gruber perhaps a bit better. And they were friends."

"I'd heard they were friends."

"There was a friendly rivalry between them," said Stonegell. "Whenever one of them started a project, the other one started a similar project, intent on beating the first one at his own game. Actually, that was more Perkins than Gruber. And they always took opposite sides of every question, screamed at each other like sworn enemies. But actually they were very close friends. I can't understand either one of them murdering the other."

"Was Gruber similar to Perkins?"

"Did I give that impression? No, they were definitely unalike. The old business about opposites attracting. Gruber was by far the more sensitive and sincere of the two. I don't mean to imply that Perkins was insensitive or insincere at all. Perkins had his own sensitivity and his own sincerity, but they were almost exclusively directed within himself. He equated everything with himself, his own feelings and his own ambitions. But Gruber had more of the—oh, I don't know—more of a *world-view*, to badly translate the German. His sensitivity was directed outward, toward the feelings of other people. It showed up in their writing. Gruber's forte was characterization, subtle interplay between personalities. Perkins was deft, almost glib, with movement and action and plot, but his characters lacked substance. He wasn't really interested in anyone but himself."

"He doesn't sound like the kind of guy who'd confess to a murder right after he committed it."

"I know what you mean. That isn't like him. I don't imagine Perkins would ever feel remorse or guilt. I should think he would be one of the people who believes the only crime is in being caught."

"Yet we didn't catch him. He came to us." Levine studied the book titles on the shelf behind Stonegell. "What about their mental attitudes recently?" he asked. "Generally speaking, I mean. Were they happy or unhappy, impatient or content or what?"

"I think they were both rather depressed, actually," said Stonegell. "Though for somewhat different reasons. They had both come out of the Army less than a year ago, and had come to New York to try to make their mark as writers. Gruber was having difficulty with subject matter. We talked about it a few times. He couldn't find anything he really wanted to write about, nothing he felt strongly enough to give him direction in his writing."

"And Perkins?"

"He wasn't particularly worried about writing in that way. He was, as I say, deft and clever in his writing, but it was all too shallow. I think they might have been bad for one another, actually. Perkins could see that Gruber had the depth and sincerity that he lacked, and Gruber thought that Perkins was free from the soul-searching and self-doubt that was hampering him so much. In the last month or so, both of them have talked about dropping out of school, going back home and forgetting about the whole thing. But neither of them could have done that, at least not yet. Gruber couldn't have, because the desire to write was too strong in him. Perkins couldn't, because the desire to be a famous writer was too strong."

"A year seems like a pretty short time to get all that depressed," said Levine.

Stonegell smiled. "When you're young," he said, "a year can be eternity. Patience is an attribute of the old."

"I suppose you're right. What about girl friends, other people who knew them both?"

"Well, there was one girl whom both were dating rather steadily. The rivalry again. I don't think either of them was particularly serious about her, but both of them wanted to take her away from the other one."

"Do you know this girl's name?"

"Yes, of course. She was in the same class with Perkins and Gruber. I think I might have her home address here."

Stonegell opened a small file drawer atop his desk, and looked through it. "Yes, here it is," he said. "Her name is Anne Marie Stone, and she lives on Grove Street, down in the Village. Here you are."

Levine accepted the card from Stonegell, copied the name and address onto his pad, and gave the card back. He got to his feet. "Thank you for your trouble," he said.

"Not at all," said Stonegell, standing. He extended his hand, and Levine, shaking it, found it bony and almost parchment-thin, but surprisingly strong. "I don't know if I've been much help, though," he said.

"Neither do I, yet," said Levine. "I may be just wasting both our time. Perkins confessed, after all."

"Still—" said Stonegell.

Levine nodded. "I know. That's what's got me doing extra work."

"I'm still thinking of this thing as though—as though it were a story problem, if you know what I mean. It isn't real yet. Two young students, I've taken an interest in both of them, fifty years after the worms get me they'll still be around—and then you tell me one of them is already wormfood, and the other one is effectively just as dead. It isn't real to me yet. They won't be in class tomorrow night, but I still won't believe it."

"I know what you mean."

"Let me know if anything happens, will you?"

"Of course."

Anne Marie Stone lived in an apartment on the fifth floor of a walk-up on Grove Street in Greenwich Village, a block and a half from Sheridan Square. Levine found himself out of breath by the time he reached the third floor, and he stopped for a minute to get his wind back and to slow the pounding of his heart. There was no sound in the world quite as loud as the beating of his own heart these days, and when that beating grew too rapid or too irregular, Detective Levine felt a kind of panic that twenty-four years as a cop had never been able to produce.

He had to stop again at the fourth floor, and he remembered with envy what a Bostonian friend had told him about a City of Boston regulation that buildings used as residence had to have elevators if they were more than four stories high. Oh, to live in Boston. Or, even better, in Levittown, where there isn't a building higher than two stories anywhere.

He reached the fifth floor, finally, and knocked on the door of apartment 5B. Rustlings from within culminated in the peephole in the door being opened, and a blue eye peered suspiciously out at him. "Who is it?" asked a muffled voice.

"Police," said Levine. He dragged out his wallet, and held it high, so the eye in the peephole could read the identification.

"Second," said the muffled voice, and the peephole closed. A seemingly endless series of rattles and clicks indicated locks being released, and then the door opened, and a short, slender girl, dressed in pink toreador pants, gray bulky sweater and blonde pony tail, motioned to Levine to come in. "Have a seat," she said, closing the door after him.

"Thank you." Levine sat in a new-fangled basket chair, as uncomfortable as it looked, and the girl sat in another chair of the same type, facing him. But she managed to look comfortable in the thing.

"Is this something I did?" she asked him. "Jaywalking or something?"

Levine smiled. No matter how innocent, a citizen always presumes himself guilty when the police come calling. "No," he said. "It concerns two friends of yours, Al Gruber and Larry Perkins."

"Those two?" The girl seemed calm, though curious, but not at all worried or apprehensive. She was still thinking in terms of something no more serious than jaywalking or a neighbor calling the police to complain about loud noises. "What are they up to?"

"How close are you to them?"

The girl shrugged. "I've gone out with both of them, that's all. We all take courses at Columbia. They're both nice guys, but there's nothing serious, you know. Not with either of them."

"I don't know how to say this," said Levine, "except the blunt way. Early this afternoon, Perkins turned himself in and admitted he'd just killed Gruber."

The girl stared at him. Twice, she opened her mouth to speak, but both times she closed it again. The silence lengthened, and Levine wondered belatedly if the girl had been telling the truth, if perhaps there had been something serious in her relationship with one of the boys after all. Then she blinked and looked away from him, clearing her throat. She stared out the window for a second, then looked back and said, "He's pulling your leg."

Levine shook his head. "I'm afraid not."

"Larry's got a weird sense of humor sometimes," she said. "It's a sick joke, that's all. Al's still around. You haven't found the body, have you?"

"I'm afraid we have. He was poisoned, and Perkins admitted he was the one who gave him the poison."

"That little bottle Al had around the place? That was only a gag."

"Not anymore."

She thought about it a minute longer, then shrugged, as though giving up the struggle to either believe or disbelieve. "Why come to me?" she asked him.

"I'm not sure, to tell you the truth. Something smells wrong about the case, and I don't know what. There isn't any logic to it. I can't get through to Perkins, and it's too late to get through to Gruber. But I've got to get to know them both, if I'm going to understand what happened."

"And you want me to tell you about them."

"Yes."

"Where did you hear about me? From Larry?"

"No, he didn't mention you at all. The gentlemanly instinct, I suppose. I talked to your teacher, Professor Stonegell."

"I see." She stood up suddenly, in a single rapid and graceless movement, as though she had to make some motion, no matter how meaningless. "Do you want some coffee?"

"Thank you, yes."

"Come on along. We can talk while I get it ready."

He followed her through the apartment. A hallway led

from the long, narrow living room past bedroom and bathroom to a tiny kitchen. Levine sat down at the kitchen table, and Anne Marie Stone went through the motions of making coffee. As she worked, she talked.

"They're good friends," she said. "I mean, they *were* good friends. You know what I mean. Anyway, they're a lot different from each other. Oh, golly! I'm getting all loused up in tenses."

"Talk as though both were still alive," said Levine. "It should be easier that way."

"I don't really believe it anyway," she said. "Al—he's a lot quieter than Larry. Kind of intense, you know? He's got a kind of reversed Messiah complex. You know, he figures he's supposed to be something great, a great writer, but he's afraid he doesn't have the stuff for it. So he worries about himself, and keeps trying to analyze himself, and he hates everything he writes because he doesn't think it's good enough for what he's supposed to be doing. That bottle of poison, that was a gag, you know, just a gag, but it was the kind of joke that has some sort of truth behind it. With this thing driving him like this, I suppose even death begins to look like a good escape after a while."

She stopped her preparations with the coffee, and stood listening to what she had just said. "Now he did escape, didn't he? I wonder if he'd thank Larry for taking the decision out of his hands."

"Do you suppose he asked Larry to take the decision out of his hands?"

She shook her head. "No. In the first place, Al could never ask anyone else to help him fight the thing out in any way. I know, I tried to talk to him a couple of times, but he just couldn't listen. It wasn't that he didn't want to listen, he just couldn't. He had to figure it out for himself. And Larry isn't the helpful sort, so Larry would be the last person anybody would go to for help. Not that Larry's a bad guy, really. He's just awfully self-centered. They both are, but in different ways. Al's always worried about himself, but Larry's always proud of himself. You know. Larry would say, 'I'm for me first,' and Al would say, 'Am I worthy?' Something like that."

"Had the two of them had a quarrel or anything recently, anything that you know of that might have prompted Larry to murder?"

"Not that I know of. They've both been getting more and more depressed, but neither of them blamed the other. Al blamed himself for not getting anywhere, and Larry blamed the stupidity of the world. You know, Larry wanted the same thing Al did, but Larry didn't worry about whether he was worthy or capable or anything like that. He once told me he wanted to be a famous writer, and he'd be one if he had to rob banks and use the money to bribe every publisher and editor and critic in the business. That was a gag, too, like Al's bottle of poison, but I think that one had some truth behind it, too."

The coffee was ready, and she poured two cups, then sat down across from him. Levine added a bit of evaporated milk, but no sugar, and stirred the coffee distractedly. "I want to know why," he said. "Does that seem strange? Cops are supposed to want to know who, not why. I know who, but I want to know why."

"Larry's the only one who could tell you, and I don't think he will."

Levine drank some of the coffee, then got to his feet. "Mind if I use your phone?" he asked.

"Go right ahead. It's in the living room, next to the bookcase."

Levine walked back into the living room and called the station. He asked for Crawley. When his partner came on the line, Levine said, "Has Perkins signed the confession yet?"

"He's on the way down now. It's just been typed up."

"Hold him there after he signs it, okay? I want to talk to him. I'm in Manhattan, starting back now."

"What have you got?"

"I'm not sure I have anything. I just want to talk to Perkins again, that's all."

"Why sweat it? We got the body; we got the confession; we got the killer in a cell. Why make work for yourself?"

"I don't know. Maybe I'm just bored."

"Okay, I'll hold him. Same room as before."

Levine went back to the kitchen. "Thank you for the coffee," he said. "If there's nothing else you can think of, I'll be leaving now."

"Nothing," she said. "Larry's the only one can tell you why."

She walked him to the front door, and he thanked her again as he was leaving. The stairs were a lot easier going down.

When Levine got back to the station, he picked up another plainclothesman, a detective named Ricco, a tall, athletic man in his middle thirties who affected the Ivy League look. He resembled more closely someone from the District Attorney's office than a precinct cop. Levine gave him a part to play, and the two of them went down the hall to the room where Perkins was waiting with Crawley.

"Perkins," said Levine, the minute he walked in the room, before Crawley had a chance to give the game away by saying something to Ricco, "this is Dan Ricco, a reporter from the *Daily News*."

Perkins looked at Ricco with obvious interest, the first real display of interest and animation Levine had yet seen from him. "A reporter?"

"That's right," said Ricco. He looked at Levine. "What is this?" he asked. He was playing it straight and blank.

"College student," said Levine. "Name's Larry Perkins." He spelled the last name. "He poisoned a fellow student."

"Oh, yeah?" Ricco glanced at Perkins without much eagerness. "What for?" he asked, looking back at Levine. "Girl? Any sex in it?"

"Afraid not. It was some kind of intellectual motivation. They both wanted to be writers."

Ricco shrugged. "Two guys with the same job? What's so hot about that?"

"Well, the main thing," said Levine, "is that Perkins here wants to be famous. He tried to get famous by being a writer, but that wasn't working out. So he decided to be a famous murderer."

Ricco looked at Perkins. "Is that right?" he asked.

Perkins was glowering at them all, but especially at Levine. "What difference does it make?" he said.

"The kid's going to get the chair, of course," said Levine blandly. "We have his signed confession and everything. But I've kind of taken a liking to him. I'd hate to see him throw his life away without getting something for it. I thought maybe you could get him a nice headline on page two, something he could hang up on the wall of his cell."

Ricco chuckled and shook his head. "Not a chance of it," he said. "Even if I wrote the story big, the city desk would knock it down to nothing. This kind of story is a dime a dozen. People kill other people around New York twenty-four hours a day. Unless there's a good strong sex interest, or it's maybe one of those mass killings things like the guy who put the bomb in the airplane, a murder in New York is filler stuff. And who needs filler stuff in the spring, when the ball teams are just getting started?"

"You've got influence on the paper, Dan," said Levine. "Couldn't you at least get him picked up by the wire services?"

"Not a chance in a million. What's he done that a few hundred other clucks in New York don't do every year? Sorry, Abe, I'd like to do you the favor, but it's no go."

Levine sighed. "Okay, Dan," he said. "If you say so."

"Sorry," said Ricco. He grinned at Perkins. "Sorry, kid," he said. "You should of knifed a chorus girl or something."

Ricco left and Levine glanced at Crawley, who was industriously yanking on his earlobe and looking bewildered. Levine sat down facing Perkins and said, "Well?"

"Let me alone a minute," snarled Perkins. "I'm trying to think."

"I was right, wasn't I?" asked Levine. "You wanted to go out in a blaze of glory."

"All right, all right. Al took his way, I took mine. What's the difference?"

"No difference," said Levine. He got wearily to his feet, and headed for the door. "I'll have you sent back to your cell now."

"Listen," said Perkins suddenly. "You know I didn't kill him, don't you? You know he committed suicide, don't you?"

Levine opened the door and motioned to the two uniformed cops waiting in the hall.

"Wait," said Perkins desperately.

"I know, I know," said Levine. "Gruber really killed himself, and I suppose you burned the note he left."

"You know damn well I did."

"That's too bad, boy."

Perkins didn't want to leave. Levine watched deadpan as the boy was led away, and then he allowed himself to relax, let the tension drain out of him. He sagged into a chair and studied the veins on the backs of his hands.

Crawley said, into the silence, "What was all that about, Abe?"

"Just what you heard."

"Gruber committed suicide?"

"They both did."

"Well—what are we going to do now?"

"Nothing. We investigated; we got a confession; we made an arrest. Now we're done."

"But—"

"But hell!" Levine glared at his partner. "That little fool is gonna go to trial, Jack, and he's gonna be convicted and go to the chair. He chose it himself. It was *his* choice. I'm not railroading him; he chose his own end. And he's going to get what he wanted."

"But listen, Abe—"

"I won't listen!"

"Let me—let me get a word in."

Levine was on his feet suddenly, and now it all came boiling out, the indignation and the rage and the frustration. "Damn it, you don't know yet! You've got another six, seven years yet. You don't know what it feels like to lie awake in bed at night and listen to your heart skip a beat every once in a while, and wonder when it's going to skip two beats in a row and you're dead. You don't know what it feels like to know your body's starting to die, it's starting to get old and die and it's all downhill from now on."

"What's that got to do with—"

"I'll tell you what! They had the *choice*! Both of them young, both of them with sound bodies and sound hearts and years ahead of them, decades ahead of them. And they chose to throw it away! They chose to throw away what I don't have any more. Don't you think I wish *I* had that choice? All right! They chose to die, let 'em die!"

Levine was panting from exertion, leaning over the desk and shouting in Jack Crawley's face. And now, in the sudden silence while he wasn't speaking, he heard the ragged rustle of his breath, felt the tremblings of nerve and muscle throughout his body. He let himself carefully down into a chair and sat there, staring at the wall, trying to get his breath.

Jack Crawley was saying something, far away, but Levine couldn't hear him. He was listening to something else, the loudest sound in all the world. The fitful throbbing of his own heart.

THE MEN IN BLACK RAINCOATS

BY PETE HAMILL

South Slope

(Originally published in 1977)

I t was close to midnight on a Friday evening at Rattigan's Bar and Grill. There were no ball games on the television, old movies only made the clientele feel more ancient, and the jukebox was still broken from the afternoon of Red Cioffi's daughter's wedding. So it was time for Brendan Malachy McCone to take center stage. He motioned for a fresh beer, put his right foot on the brass rail, breathed in deeply, and started to sing.

> *Oh, the Garden of Eden has vanished, they say,*
> *But I know the lie of it still,*
> *Just turn to the left at the bridge of Finaghy,*
> *And meet me halfway to Coote Hill . . .*

The song was very Irish, sly and funny, the choruses full of the names of long-forgotten places, and the regulars loved Brendan for the quick jaunty singing of it. They loved the roguish glitter in his eyes, his energy, his good-natured boasting. He was, after all, a man in his fifties now, and yet here he was, still singing the bold songs of his youth. And on this night, as on so many nights, they joined him in the verses.

The boy is a man now,
He's toil-worn, he's tough,
He whispers, "Come over the sea"
Come back, Patty Reilly, to Bally James Duff,
Ah, come back, Patty Reilly, to me . . .

Outside, rain had begun to fall, a cold Brooklyn rain, driven by the wind off the harbor, and it made the noises and the singing and the laughter seem even better. Sardines and crackers joined the glasses on the bar. George the bartender filled the empties. And Brendan shifted from jauntiness to sorrow.

If you ever go across the sea to Ireland,
Then maybe at the closing of your day . . .

The mood of the regulars hushed now, as Brendan gave them the song as if it were a hymn. The bar was charged with the feeling they all had for Brendan, knowing that he had been an IRA man long ago, that he had left Ireland a step ahead of the British police who wanted him for the killing of a British soldier in the Border Campaign. This was their Brendan: the Transit Authority clerk who had once stood in the doorways of Belfast, with the cloth cap pulled tight on his brow, the pistol deep in the pockets of the trenchcoat, ready to kill or to die for Ireland.

Oh, the strangers came and tried to teach us their ways,
And scorned us just for being what we are . . .

The voice was a healthy baritone, a wealth of passion overwhelming a poverty of skill, and it touched all of them, making the younger ones imagine the streets of Belfast today, where their cousins were still fighting, reminding the older ones of peat fires, black creamy stout, buttermilk in the morning. The song was about a vanished time, before rock and roll and women's liberation, before they took Latin out of the Mass, before the blacks and the Puerto Ricans had begun to move in and the children of the Irish had begun to move out. The neighborhood was changing, all right. But Brendan Malachy McCone was still with them, still in the neighborhood.

A little after midnight two strangers came in, dressed in black raincoats. They were wet with rain. They ordered whiskey. Brendan kept singing. Nobody noticed that his voice faltered on the last lines of "Galway Bay," as he took the applause, glanced at the strangers, and again shifted the mood.

> Oh, Mister Patrick McGinty,
> An Irishman of note,
> He fell into a fortune—and
> He bought himself a goat . . .

The strangers drank in silence.

At closing time the rain was still pelting down. Brendan stood in the open doorway of the bar with Charlie the Pole and Scotch Eddie, while George the bartender counted the receipts. Everyone else had gone home.

"We'll have to make a run for it," Charlie said.

"Dammit," Scotch Eddie said.

"Yiz might as well run, cause yiz'll drown anyway," George said. He was finished counting and looked small and tired.

"I'll see you gents," Charlie said, and rushed into the rain, running lumpily down the darkened slope of 11th Street to his home. Eddie followed, cutting sharply to his left. But Brendan did not move. He had seen the strangers in the black raincoats, watched them in the mirror for a while as he moved through the songs, saw them leave an hour later.

And now he was afraid.

He looked up and down the avenue. The streetlamp scalloped a halo of light on the corner. Beyond the light there was nothing but the luminous darkness and the rain.

"Well, I've got to lock it up, Brendan."

"Right, George. Good night."

"God bless."

Brendan hurried up the street, head down, lashed by the rain, eyes searching the interiors of parked cars. He saw nothing. The cars were locked. He looked up at the apartments and there were no lights anywhere and he knew the lights would be out at home too, where Sarah and the kids would all be sleeping. Even the firehouse was dimly lit, its great red door closed, the firemen stretched out on their bunks in the upstairs loft.

Despite the drink and the rain, Brendan's mouth was dry. Once he thought he saw something move in the darkness of an areaway and his stomach lifted and fell. But again it was nothing. Shadows. Imagination. Get hold of yourself, Brendan.

He crossed the avenue. A half block to go. Away off he saw the twin red taillights of a city bus, groaning slowly toward Flatbush Avenue. Hurry. Another half block and he could enter the yard, hurry up the stairs, unlock the door, close it behind him, undress quickly in the darkened kitchen, dry off the rain with a warm rough towel, brush the beer off his teeth, and fall into the great deep warmth of bed with Sarah. And he would be safe again for another night. Hurry. Get the key out. Don't get caught naked on the stairs.

He turned into his yard, stepped over a spreading puddle at the base of the stoop, and hurried up the eight worn sandstone steps. He had the key out in the vestibule and quickly opened the inside door.

They were waiting for him in the hall.

The one in the front seat on the right was clearly the boss. The driver was only a chauffeur and did his work in proper silence. The strangers in the raincoats sat on either side of Brendan in the back seat and said nothing as the car moved through the wet darkness, down off the slope, into the Puerto Rican neighborhood near Williamsburg. They all clearly deferred to the one in the front seat right. All wore gloves. Except the boss.

"I'm telling you, this has to be some kind of mistake," Brendan said.

"Shut up," said the boss, without turning. His skin was pink in the light of the streetlamps, and dark hair curled over the edge of his collar. The accent was not New York. Maybe Boston. Maybe somewhere else. Not New York.

"I don't owe anybody money," Brendan said, choking back the dry panic. "I'm not into the bloody loan sharks. I'm telling you, this is—"

The boss said, "Is your name Brendan Malachy McCone?"

"Well, uh, yes, but—"

"Then we've made no mistake."

Williamsburg was behind them now and they were following the route of the Brooklyn-Queens Expressway while avoiding its brightly lit ramp. Brendan sat back. From that angle he could see more of the man in the front seat right— the velvet collar of his coat, the high protruding cheekbones, the longish nose, the pinkie ring glittering on his left hand when he lit a cigarette with a thin gold lighter. He could not see the man's eyes but he was certain he had never seen the man before tonight.

"Where are you taking me?"

The boss said calmly, "I told you to shut up. Shut up."

Brendan took a deep breath, and then let it out slowly. He looked to the men on either side of him, smiling his most innocent smile, as if hoping they would think well of him, believe in his innocence, intervene with the boss, plead his case. He wanted to tell them about his kids, explain that he had done nothing bad. Not for thirty years.

The men looked away from him, their nostrils seeming to quiver, as if he had already begun to stink of death. Brendan tried to remember the words of the Act of Contrition.

The men beside him stared out past the little rivers of rain on the windows, as if he were not even in the car. They watched the city turn into country, Queens into Nassau County, all the sleeping suburbs transform into the darker emptier reaches of Suffolk County, as the driver pushed on, driving farther away, out to Long Island, to the country of forests and frozen summer beaches. Far from Brooklyn. Far from the Friday nights at Rattigan's. Far from his children. Far from Sarah.

Until they pulled off the expressway at Southampton, moved down back roads for another fifteen minutes, and came to a marshy cove. A few summer houses were sealed for the winter. Rain spattered the still water of the cove. Patches of dirty snow clung to the shoreline, resisting the steady cold rain.

"This is fine," the boss said.

The driver pulled over, turned out the car lights, and turned off the engine. They all sat in the dark.

The boss said, "Did you ever hear of a man named Peter Devlin?"

Oh, my God, Brendan thought.

"Well?"

"Vaguely. The name sounds familiar."

"Just familiar?"

"Well, there was a Devlin where I came from. There were a lot of Devlins in the North. It's hard to remember. It was a long time ago."

"Yeah, it was. It was a long time ago."

"Aye."

"And you don't remember him more than just vaguely? Well, isn't that nice? I mean, you *were* best man at his wedding."

Brendan's lips moved, but no words came out.

"What else do you vaguely remember, McCone?"

There was a long pause. Then: "He died."

"No, not *died*. He was killed, wasn't he?"

"Aye."

"Who killed him, McCone?"

"He died for Ireland."

"Who *killed* him, McCone?"

"The Special Branch. The British Special Branch."

The boss took out his cigarettes and lit one with the gold lighter. He took a long drag. Brendan saw the muscles working tensely in his jaw. The rain drummed on the roof of the car.

"Tell me some more about him."

"They buried him with full military honors. They draped his coffin with the Tricolor and sang "The Soldier's

Song" over his grave. The whole town wore the Easter Lily. The B-Specials made a lot of arrests."

"You saw all this?"

"I was told."

"But you weren't there?"

"No, but—"

"What happened to his wife?"

"Katey?"

"Some people called her Katey," the boss said.

"She died too, soon after—the flu, was it?"

"Well, there was another version. That she died of a broken heart."

The boss stared straight ahead, watching the rain trickle down the windshield. He tapped an ash into the ashtray, took another deep drag, and said, "What did they pay you to set him up, Brendan?"

He called me Brendan. He's softening. Even a gunman can understand it was all long ago.

"What do you mean?"

"Don't play games, Brendan. Everyone in the North knew you set him up. The British told them."

"It was a long time ago, Mister. There were a lot of lies told. You can't believe every . . ."

The boss wasn't really listening. He took out his pack of cigarettes, flipped one higher than the others, gripped its filter in his teeth, and lit it with the butt of the other. Then he tamped out the first cigarette in the ashtray. He looked out past the rain to the darkness of the cove.

"Shoot him," he said.

The man on Brendan's left opened the door a foot.

"Oh, sweet sufferin' Jesus, Mister," Brendan said. "I've got five kids. They're all at home. One of them is making her first

Communion. Please. For the love of God. If Dublin Command has told you to get me, just tell them you couldn't find me. Tell them I'm dead. I can get you a piece of paper. From one of the politicians. Sayin' I'm dead. Yes. That's a way. And I'll just vanish. Just disappear. Please. I'm an old man now, I won't live much bloody longer. But the weans. The weans, Mister. And it was all thirty years ago. Christ knows I've paid for it. Please. Please."

The tears were blurring his vision now. He could hear the hard spatter of the rain through the open car door. He felt the man on his right move slightly and remove something from inside his coat.

The boss said, "You left out a few things, Brendan."

"I can send all my earnings to the lads. God knows they can use it in the North now. I've sent money already, I have, to the Provisionals. I never stopped being for them. For a United Ireland. Never stopped. I can have the weans work for the cause. I'll get a second job. My Sarah can go out and work too. Please, Mister. Jesus, Mister . . ."

"Katey Devlin didn't die of the flu," the boss said. "And she didn't die of a broken heart. Did she, Brendan?"

"I don't—"

"Katey Devlin killed herself. Didn't she?"

Brendan felt his stomach turn over.

The boss said, very quietly, "She loved Peter Devlin more than life itself. She didn't want him to die."

"But neither does Sarah want *me* to die. She's got the weans, the feedin' of them, and the clothin' of them, and the schoolin' of them to think of. Good God, man, have ye no mercy? I was a boy then. My own people were starvin'. We had no land, we were renters, we were city people, not farmers, and the war was on, and . . . They told me they would only arrest him. Intern him for the duration and let him out when the fightin' stopped, and they told me the IRA would take care of Kate while he was inside. Please, Mister, I've got five kids. Peter Devlin only had *two*."

"I know," said the man in the front seat right. "I was one of them."

For the first time he turned completely around. His eyes were a cold blue under the shock of curly dark hair. Kate's eyes in Peter's face. He stared at Brendan for a moment. He took another drag on the cigarette and let the smoke drift through his nose, creating lazy trails of gray in the crowded car.

"Shoot him," he said.

The man on his left touched Brendan's hand and opened the door wide.

THE DAY OF THE BULLET

BY STANLEY ELLIN

Bath Beach

(Originally published in 1959)

I believe that in each lifetime there is one day of destiny. It may be a day chosen by the Fates who sit clucking and crooning over a spinning wheel, or, perhaps, by the gods whose mill grinds slow, but grinds exceedingly fine. It may be a day of sunshine or rain, of heat or cold. It is probably a day which none of us is aware of at the time, or can even recall through hindsight.

But for every one of us there is that day. And when it leads to a bad end it's better not to look back and search it out. What you discover may hurt, and it's a futile hurt because nothing can be done about it any longer. Nothing at all.

I realize that there is a certain illogic in believing this, something almost mystical. Certainly it would win the ready disfavor of those modern exorcists and dabblers with crystal balls, those psychologists and sociologists and caseworkers who—using their own peculiar language to express it—believe that there may be a way of controlling the fantastic conjunction of time, place, and event that we must all meet at some invisible crossroads on the Day. But they are wrong. Like the rest of us they can only be wise after the event.

In this case—and the word "case" is particularly fitting here—the event was the murder of a man I had not seen for thirty-five years. Not since a summer day in 1923, or, to be even more exact, the evening of a summer day in 1923 when as boys we faced each other on a street in Brooklyn, and then went our ways, never to meet again.

We were only twelve years old then, he and I, but I remember the date because the next day my family moved to Manhattan, an earth-shaking event in itself. And with dreadful clarity I remember the scene when we parted, and the last thing said there. I understand it now, and know it was that boy's Day. The Day of the Bullet, it might be called—although the bullet itself was not to be fired until thirty-five years later.

I learned about the murder from the front page of the newspaper my wife was reading at the breakfast table. She held the paper upright and partly folded, but the fold could not conceal from me the unappetizing picture on the front page, the photograph of a man slumped behind the wheel of his car, head clotted with blood, eyes staring and mouth gaping in the throes of violent and horrifying death.

The picture meant nothing to me, any more than did its shouting headline—RACKETS BOSS SHOT TO DEATH. All I thought, in fact, was that there were pleasanter objects to stare at over one's coffee and toast.

Then my eye fell on the caption below the picture, and I almost dropped my cup of coffee. *The body of Ignace Kovac*, said the caption, *Brooklyn rackets boss who last night—*

I took the paper from my wife's hand while she looked at me in astonishment, and studied the picture closely. There was no question about it. I had not seen Ignace Kovac since we were kids together, but I could not mistake him, even in the guise of this dead and bloody hulk. And the most terrible part of it, perhaps, was that next to him, resting against the seat of the car, was a bag of golf clubs. Those golf clubs were all my memory needed to work on.

I was called back to the present by my wife's voice. "Well," she said with good-natured annoyance, "considering that I'm right in the middle of Walter Winchell—"

I returned the paper to her. "I'm sorry. I got a jolt when I saw that picture. I used to know him."

Her eyes lit up with the interest of one who—even at sec-ondhand—finds herself in the presence of the notorious. "You did? When?"

"Oh, when the folks still lived in Brooklyn. We were kids together. He was my best friend."

My wife was an inveterate tease. "Isn't that something? I never knew you hung around with juvenile delinquents when you were a kid."

"He wasn't a juvenile delinquent. Matter of fact—"

"If you aren't the serious one." She smiled at me in a kindly dismissal and went back to Winchell, who clearly offered fresher and more exciting tidings than mine. "Anyhow," she said, "I wouldn't let it bother me too much, dear. That was a long time ago."

It was a long time ago. You could play ball in the middle of the street then; few automobiles were to be seen in the far reaches of Brooklyn in 1923. And Bath Beach, where I lived, was one of the farthest reaches. It fronted on Gravesend Bay with Coney Island to the east a few minutes away by trolley car, and Dyker Heights and its golf course to the west a few minutes away by foot. Each was an entity separated from Bath Beach by a wasteland of weedgrown lots which building contractors had not yet discovered.

So, as I said, you could play ball in the streets without

fear of traffic. Or you could watch the gaslighter turning up the street lamps at dusk. Or you could wait around the fire-house on Eighteenth Avenue until, if you were lucky enough, an alarm would send three big horses there slewing the pump-engine out into the street in a spray of sparks from iron-shod wheels. Or, miracle of miracles, you could stand gaping up at the sky to follow the flight of a biplane proudly racketing along overhead.

Those were the things I did that summer, along with Iggy Kovac, who was my best friend, and who lived in the house next door. It was a two-story frame house painted in some sedate color, just as mine was. Most of the houses in Bath Beach were like that, each with a small garden in front and yard in back. The only example of ostentatious architecture on our block was the house on the corner owned by Mr Rose, a newcomer to the neighborhood. It was huge and stuccoed, almost a mansion, surrounded by an enormous lawn, and with a stuccoed two-car garage at the end of its driveway.

That driveway held a fascination for Iggy and me. On it, now and then, would be parked Mr Rose's automobile, a gray Packard, and it was the car that drew us like a magnet. It was not only beautiful to look at from the distance, but close up it loomed over us like a locomotive, giving off an aura of thunderous power even as it stood there quietly. And it had *two* running boards, one mounted over the other to make the climb into the tonneau easier. In fact, no one we knew had a car anywhere near as wonderful as that Packard.

So we would sneak down the driveway when it was parked there, hoping for a chance to mount those running boards without being caught. We never managed to do it. It seemed that an endless vigil was being kept over that car, either by Mr Rose himself or by someone who lived in the rooms over the garage. As soon as we were no more than a few yards down the driveway a window would open in the house or the garage, and a hoarse voice would bellow threats at us. Then we would turn tail and race down the driveway and out of sight.

We had not always done that. The first time we had seen the car we had sauntered up to it quite casually, all in the spirit of good neighbors, and had not even understood the nature of the threats. We only stood there and looked up in astonishment at Mr Rose, until he suddenly left the window and reappeared before us to grab Iggy's arm.

Iggy tried to pull away and couldn't. "Leggo of me!" he said in a high-pitched, frightened voice. "We weren't doing anything to your ole car! Leggo of me, or I'll tell my father on you. Then you'll see what'll happen!"

This did not seem to impress Mr Rose. He shook Iggy back and forth—not hard to do because Iggy was small and skinny even for his age—while I stood there, rooted to the spot in horror.

There were some cranky people in the neighborhood who would chase us away when we made any noise in front of their houses, but nobody had ever handled either of us the way Mr Rose was doing. I remember having some vague idea that it was because he was new around here, he didn't know yet how people around here were supposed to act, and when I look back now I think I may have been surprisingly close to the truth. But whatever the exact reasons for the storm he raised, it was enough of a storm to have Iggy blubbering out loud, and to make us approach the Packard warily after that. It was too much of a magnet to resist, but once we were on Mr Rose's territory we were like a pair of rabbits crossing open ground during the hunting season. And with just about as much luck.

I don't want to give the impression by all this that we were bad kids. For myself, I was acutely aware of the letter of the law, and had early discovered that the best course for anyone who was good-natured, pacific, and slow afoot—all of which I was in extra measure—was to try and stay within bounds. And Iggy's vices were plain high spirits and reckless-ness. He was like quicksilver and was always on the go and full of mischief.

And smart. Those were the days when at the end of each school week your marks were appraised and you would be reseated according to your class standing—best students in the first row, next best in the second row, and so on. And I think the thing that best explains Iggy was the way his posi-tion in class would fluctuate between the first and sixth rows. Most of us never moved more than one row either way at the end of the week; Iggy would suddenly be shoved from the first row to the ignominy of the sixth, and then the Friday after would just as suddenly ascend the heights back to the first row. That was the sure sign that Mr Kovac had got wind of the bad tidings and had taken measures.

Not physical measures, either. I once asked Iggy about that, and he said, "Nah, he don't wallop me, but he kind of says don't be so dumb, and, well—you know—"

I did know, because I suspect that I shared a good deal of Iggy's feeling for Mr Kovac, a fervent hero worship. For one thing, most of the fathers in the neighborhood "worked in the city"—to use the Bath Beach phrase—meaning that six days a week they ascended the Eighteenth Avenue station of the BMT and were borne off to desks in Manhattan. Mr Kovac, on the other hand, was a conductor on the Bath Avenue trolleycar line, a powerful and imposing figure in his official cap and blue uniform with the brass buttons on it.

The cars on the Bath Avenue line were without side walls, closely lined with benches from front to back, and were manned by conductors who had to swing along narrow platforms on the outside to collect fares. It was something to see Mr Kovac in action. The only thing comparable was the man who swung himself around a Coney Island merry-go-round to take your tickets.

And for another thing, most of the fathers—at least when they had reached the age mine had—were not much on athletics, while Mr Kovac was a terrific baseball player. Every fair Sunday afternoon down at the little park by the bay there was a pick-up ball game where the young fellows of the neighborhood played a regulation nine innings on a marked-off diamond, and Mr Kovac was always the star. As far as Iggy and I were concerned, he could pitch like Vance and hit like Zack Wheat, and no more than that could be desired. It was something to watch Iggy when his father was at bat. He'd sit chewing his nails right through every windup of the pitcher, and if Mr Kovac came through with a hit, Iggy would be up and screaming so loud you'd think your head was coming off.

Then after the game was over we'd hustle a case of pop over to the team, and they would sit around on the park benches and talk things over. Iggy was his father's shadow then; he'd be hanging around that close to him, taking it all in and eating it up. I wasn't so very far away myself, but since I couldn't claim possession as Iggy could, I amiably kept at a proper distance. And when I went home those afternoons it seemed to me that my father looked terribly stodgy, sitting there on the porch the way he did, with loose pages of the Sunday paper around him.

When I first learned that I was going to have to leave all

this, that my family was going to move from Brooklyn to Manhattan, I was completely dazed. Manhattan was a place where on occasional Saturday afternoons you went, all dressed up in your best suit, to shop with your mother at Wanamakers or Macy's, or, with luck, went to the Hippodrome with your father, or maybe to the Museum of Natural History. It had never struck me as a place where people *lived*.

But as the days went by my feelings changed, became a sort of apprehensive excitement. After all, I was doing something pretty heroic, pushing off into the Unknown this way, and the glamor of it was brought home to me by the way the kids on the block talked to me about it.

However, none of that meant anything the day before we moved. The house looked strange with everything in it packed and crated and bundled together; my mother and father were in a harried state of mind; and the knowledge of impending change—it was the first time in my life I had ever moved from one house to another—now had me scared stiff.

That was the mood I was in when after an early supper I pushed through the opening in the hedge between our backyard and the Kovacs's, and sat down on the steps before their kitchen door. Iggy came out and sat down beside me. He could see how I felt, and it must have made him uncomfortable.

"Jeez, don't be such a baby," he said. "It'll be great, living in the city. Look at all the things you'll have to see there."

I told him I didn't want to see anything there.

"All right, then don't," he said. "You want to read something good? I got a new Tarzan, and I got *The Boy Allies at Jutland*. You can have your pick, and I'll take the other one."

This was a more than generous offer, but I said I didn't feel like reading, either.

"Well, we can't just sit here being mopey," Iggy said reasonably. "Let's do something. What do you want to do?"

This was the opening of the ritual where by rejecting various possibilities—it was too late to go swimming, too hot to play ball, to early to go into the house—we would arrive at a choice. We dutifully went through this process of elimination, and it was Iggy as usual who came up with the choice.

"I know," he said. "Let's go over to Dyker Heights and fish for golf balls. It's pretty near the best time now, anyhow."

He was right about that, because the best time to fish for balls that had been driven into the lone water hazard of the course and never recovered by their owners was at sunset when, chances were, the place would be deserted but there would still be enough light to see by. The way we did this kind of fishing was to pull off our sneakers and stockings, buckle our knickerbockers over our knees, then slowly and speculatively wade through the ooze of the pond, trying to feel out sunken golf balls with our bare feet. It was pleasant work, and occasionally profitable, because the next day any ball you found could be sold to a passing golfer for five cents. I don't remember how we came to fix on the price of five cents as a fair one, but there it was. The golfers seemed to be satisfied with it, and we certainly were.

In all our fishing that summer I don't believe we found more than a total of half a dozen balls, but thirty cents was largesse in those days. My share went fast enough for anything that struck my fancy: Iggy, however, had a great dream. What he wanted more than anything else in the world was a golf club, and every cent he could scrape together was deposited in a tin can with a hole punched in its top and its seam bound with bicycle tape.

He would never open the can, but would shake it now and then to estimate its contents. It was his theory that when the can was full to the top it would hold just about enough to pay for the putter he had picked out in the window of Leo's Sporting Goods Store on 86th Street. Two or three times a week he would have me walk with him down to Leo's, so that we could see the putter, and in between he would talk about it at length, and demonstrate the proper grip for holding it, and the way you have to line up a long putt on a rolling green. Iggy Kovac was the first person I knew—I have known many since—who was really golf crazy. But I think that his case was the most unique, considering that at the time he had never in his life even had his hands on a real club.

So that evening, knowing how he felt about it, I said all right, if he wanted to go fish for golf balls I would go with him. It wasn't much of a walk down Bath Avenue; the only hard part was when we entered the course at its far side where we had to climb over mountains of what was politely called "fill." It made hot and smoky going, then there was a swampy patch, and finally the course itself and the water hazard.

I've never been back there since that day, but not long ago I happened to read an article about the Dyker Heights golf course in some magazine or other. According to the article, it was now the busiest public golf course in the world. Its eighteen well-kept greens were packed with players from dawn to dusk, and on weekends you had to get in line at the clubhouse at three or four o'clock in the morning if you wanted a chance to play a round.

Well, each to his own taste, but it wasn't like that when Iggy and I used to fish for golf balls there. For one thing, I don't think it had eighteen holes; I seem to remember it as a nine-hole layout. For another thing, it was usually pretty empty, either because not many people in Brooklyn played golf in those days, or because it was not a very enticing spot at best.

The fact is, it smelled bad. They were reclaiming the swampy land all around it by filling it with refuse, and the smoldering fires in the refuse laid a black pall over the place. No matter when you went there, there was that dirty haze in the air around you, and in a few minutes you'd find your eyes smarting and your nose full of a curious acrid smell.

Not that we minded it, Iggy and I. We accepted it casually as part of the scenery, as much a part as the occasional Mack truck loaded with trash that would rumble along the dirt road to the swamp, its chain-drive chattering and whining as it went. The only thing we did mind sometimes was the heat of the refuse underfoot when we climbed over it. We never dared enter the course from the clubhouse side; the attendant there had once caught us in the pond trying to plunder his preserve, and we knew he had us marked. The back entrance may have been hotter, but it was the more practical way in.

When we reached the pond there was no one else in sight. It was a hot, still evening with a flaming red sun now dipping toward the horizon, and once we had our sneakers and stockings off—long, black cotton stockings they were—we wasted no time wading into the water. It felt good, too, as did the slick texture of the mud oozing up between my toes when I pressed down. I suspect that I had the spirit of the true fisherman in me then. The pleasure lay in the activity, not in the catch.

Still, the catch made a worthy objective, and the idea was

to walk along with slow, probing steps, and to stop whenever you felt anything small and solid underfoot. I had just stopped short with the excited feeling that I had pinned down a golf ball in the muck when I heard the sound of a motor moving along the dirt track nearby. My first thought was that it was one of the dump trucks carrying another load to add to the mountain of fill, but then I knew that it didn't sound like a Mack truck.

I looked around to see what kind of car it was, still keeping my foot planted on my prize, but the row of bunkers between the pond and the road blocked my view. Then the sound of the motor suddenly stopped, and that was all I needed to send me splashing out of the water in a panic. All Iggy needed, too, for that matter. In one second we had grabbed up our shoes and stockings and headed around the corner of the nearest bunker where we would be out of sight. In about five more seconds we had our stockings and shoes on without even bothering to dry our legs, ready to take flight if anyone approached.

The reason we moved so fast was simply that we weren't too clear about our legal right to fish for golf balls. Iggy and I had talked it over a couple of times, and while he vehemently maintained that we had every right to—there were the balls, with nobody but the dopey caretaker doing anything about it—he admitted that the smart thing was not to put the theory to the test, but to work at our trade unobserved. And I am sure that when the car stopped nearby he had the same idea I did: somebody had reported us, and now the long hand of authority was reaching out for us.

So we waited, crouching in breathless silence against the grassy wall of the bunker, until Iggy could not contain himself any longer. He crawled on hands and knees to the corner of the bunker and peered around it toward the road. "Holy smoke, look at that!" he whispered in an awed voice, and waggled his hand at me to come over.

I looked over his shoulder, and with shocked disbelief I saw a gray Packard, a car with double running boards, one mounted over the other, the only car of its kind I had ever seen. There was no mistaking it, and there was no mistaking Mr Rose who stood with two men near it, talking to the smaller one of them, and making angry chopping motions of his hands as he talked.

Looking back now, I think that what made the scene such a strange one was its setting. There was the deserted golf course all around us, and the piles of smoldering fill in the distance, everything seeming so raw and uncitylike and made crimson by the setting sun; and there in the middle of it was this sleek car and the three men with straw hats and jackets and neckties, all looking completely out of place.

Even more fascinating was the smell of danger around them, because while I couldn't hear what was being said I could see that Mr Rose was in the same mood he had been in when he caught Iggy and me in his driveway. The big man next to him said almost nothing, but the little man Mr Rose was talking to shook his head, tried to answer, and kept backing away slowly, so that Mr Rose had to follow him. Then suddenly the little man wheeled around and ran right toward the bunker where Iggy and I lay hidden. We ducked back, but he ran past the far side of it, and he was almost past the pond when the big man caught up with him and grabbed him, Mr Rose running up after them with his hat in his hand. That is when we could have got away without being seen, but we didn't. We crouched there spellbound, watching something we would never have dreamed of seeing—grownups having it out right in front of us the way it happens in the movies.

I was, as I have said, twelve years old that summer. I can now mark it as the time I learned that there was a difference between seeing things in the movies and seeing them in real life. Because never in watching the most bruising movie, with Tom Mix or Hoot Gibson or any of my heroes, did I feel what I felt there watching what happened to that little man. And I think that Iggy must have felt it even more acutely than I did, because he was so small and skinny himself, and while he was tough in a fight he was always being outweighed and overpowered. He must have felt that he was right there inside that little man, his arms pinned tight behind his back by the bully who had grabbed him, while Mr Rose hit him back and forth with an open hand across the face, snarling at him all the while.

"You dirty dog," Mr Rose said. "Do you know who I am? Do you think I'm one of those lousy small-time bootleggers you double-cross for the fun of it? *This* is who I am!" And with the little man screaming and kicking out at him he started punching away as hard as he could at the belly and face until the screaming and kicking suddenly stopped. Then he jerked his head toward the pond, and his pal heaved the little man right into it headfirst, the straw hat flying off and bobbing up and down in the water a few feet away.

They stood watching until the man in the water managed to get on his hands and knees, blowing out dirty water, shaking his head in a daze, and then without another word they walked off toward the car. I heard its doors slam, and the roar of the motor as it moved off, and then the sound faded away.

All I wanted to do then was get away from there. What I had just seen was too much to comprehend or even believe in; it was like waking up from a nightmare to find it real. Home was where I wanted to be.

I stood up cautiously, but before I could scramble off to home and safety, Iggy clutched the back of my shirt so hard that he almost pulled me down on top of him.

"What're you doing?" he whispered hotly. "Where do you think you're going?"

I pulled myself free. "Are you crazy?" I whispered back. "You expect to hang around here all night? I'm going home, that's where I'm going."

Iggy's face was ashy white, his nostrils flaring. "But that guy's hurt. You just gonna let him stay there?"

"Sure I'm gonna let him stay there. What's it my business?"

"You saw what happened. You think it's right to beat up a guy like that?"

What he said and the way he said it in a tight, choked voice made me wonder if he really had gone crazy just then. I said weakly, "It's none of my business, that's all. Anyhow, I have to go home. My folks'll be sore if I don't get home on time."

Iggy pointed an accusing finger at me. "All right, if that's the way you feel!" he said, and then before I could stop him he turned and dashed out of concealment toward the pond. Whether it was the sense of being left alone in a hostile world, or whether it was some wild streak of loyalty that acted on me, I don't know. But I hesitated only an instant and then ran after him.

He stood at the edge of the pond looking at the man in it who was still on his hands and knees and shaking his head vaguely from side to side. "Hey, mister," Iggy said, and there was none of the assurance in his voice that there had been before, "are you hurt?"

The man looked slowly around at us, and his face was

fearful to behold. It was bruised and swollen and glassy-eyed, and his dripping hair hung in long strings down his forehead. It was enough to make Iggy and me back up a step, the way he looked.

With a great effort he pushed himself to his feet and stood there swaying. Then he lurched forward, staring at us blindly, and we hastily backed up a few more steps. He stopped short and suddenly reached down and scooped up a handful of mud from under the water.

"Get out of here!" he cried like a woman screaming. "Get out of here, you little sneaks!"—and without warning flung the mud at us.

It didn't hit me, but it didn't have to. I let out one yell of panic and ran wildly, my heart thudding, my legs pumping as fast as they could. Iggy was almost at my shoulder—I could hear him gasping as we climbed the smoldering hill of refuse that barred the way to the avenue, slid down the other side in a cloud of dirt and ashes, and raced toward the avenue without looking back. It was only when we reached the first street-light that we stopped and stood there trembling, our mouths wide open, trying to suck in air, our clothes fouled from top to bottom.

But the shock I had undergone was nothing compared to what I felt when Iggy finally got his wind back enough to speak up.

"Did you see that guy?" he said, still struggling for breath. "Did you see what they did to him? Come on, I'm gonna tell the cops."

I couldn't believe my ears. "The cops? What do you want to get mixed up with the cops for? What do you care what they did to him, for Pete's sake?"

"Because they beat him up, didn't they? And the cops

can stick them in jail for fifty years if somebody tells them, and I'm a witness. I saw what happened and so did you. So you're a witness too."

I didn't like it. I certainly had no sympathy for the evillooking apparition from which I had just fled, and, more than that, I balked at the idea of having anything to do with the police. It was just that, like most other kids I knew, I was nervous in the presence of a police uniform. It left me even more mystified by Iggy than ever. The idea of any kid voluntarily walking up to report something to a policeman was beyond comprehension.

I said bitterly, "All right, so I'm a witness. But why can't the guy that got beat up go and tell the cops about it? Why do we have to go and do it?"

"Because he wouldn't tell anybody about it. Didn't you see the way he was scared of Mr Rose? You think it's all right for Mr Rose to go around like that, beating up anybody he wants to, and nobody does anything about it?"

Then I understood. Beneath all this weird talk, this sudden display of nobility, was solid logic, something I could get hold of. It was not the man in the water Iggy was concerned with, it was himself. Mr Rose had pushed *him* around, and now he had a perfect way of getting even.

I didn't reveal this thought to Iggy, though, because when your best friend has been shoved around and humiliated in front of you, you don't want to remind him of it. But at least it put everything into proper perspective. Somebody hurts you, so you hurt him back, and that's all there is to it.

It also made it much easier to go along with Iggy in his plan. I wasn't really being called on to ally myself with some stupid grownup who had got into trouble with Mr Rose; I was being a good pal to Iggy.

All of a sudden, the prospect of walking into the police

station and telling my story to somebody seemed highly intriguing. And, the reassuring thought went, far in back of my head, none of this could mean trouble for me later on, because tomorrow I was moving to Manhattan anyhow; wasn't I?

So I was right there, a step behind Iggy, when we walked up between the two green globes which still seemed vaguely menacing to me, and into the police station. There was a tall desk there, like a judge's bench, at which a gray-haired man sat writing, and at its foot was another desk at which sat a very fat uniformed man reading a magazine. He put the magazine down when we approached and looked at us with raised eyebrows.

"Yeah?" he said. "What's the trouble?"

I had been mentally rehearsing a description of what I had seen back there on the golf course, but I never had a chance to speak my piece. Iggy started off with a rush, and there was no way of getting a word in. The fat man listened with a puzzled expression, every now and then pinching his lower lip between his thumb and forefinger. Then he looked up at the one behind the tall desk and said, "Hey, sergeant, here's a couple of kids say they saw an assault over at Dyker Heights. You want to listen to this?"

The sergeant didn't even look at us, but kept on writing. "Why?" he said. "What's wrong with your ears?"

The fat policeman leaned back in his chair and smiled. "I don't know," he said, "only it seems to me some guy named Rose is mixed up in this."

The sergeant suddenly stopped writing. "What's that?" he said.

"Some guy named Rose," the fat policeman said, and he appeared to be enjoying himself a good deal. "You know anybody with that name who drives a big gray Packard?"

The sergeant motioned with his head for us to come right up to the platform his desk was on. "All right, kid," he said to Iggy, "what's bothering you?"

So Iggy went through it again, and when he was finished the sergeant just sat there looking at him, tapping his pen on the desk. He looked at him so long and kept tapping that pen so steadily—tap, tap, tap—that my skin started to crawl. It didn't surprise me when he finally said to Iggy in a hard voice, "You're a pretty wise kid."

"What do you mean?" Iggy said. "I saw it!" He pointed at me. "He saw it, too. He'll tell you!"

I braced myself for the worst and then noted with relief that the sergeant was paying no attention to me. He shook his head at Iggy and said, "I do the telling around here, kid. And I'm telling you you've got an awful big mouth for someone your size. Don't you have more sense than to go around trying to get people into trouble?"

This, I thought, was the time to get away from there, because if I ever needed proof that you don't mix into grownup business I had it now. But Iggy didn't budge. He was always pretty good at arguing himself out of spots where he was wrong; now that he knew he was right he was getting hot with outraged virtue.

"Don't you believe me?" he demanded. "For Pete's sake, I was right there when it happened! I was this close!"

The sergeant looked like a thundercloud. "All right, you were that close," he said. "Now beat it, kid, and keep that big mouth shut. I got no time to fool around any more. Go on, get out of here!"

Iggy was so enraged that not even the big gold badge a foot from his nose could intimidate him now. "I don't care if you don't believe me. Wait'll I tell my father. You'll see!"

I could hear my ears ringing in the silence that followed. The sergeant sat staring at Iggy, and Iggy, a little scared by his own outburst, stared back. He must have had the same idea I did then. Yelling at a cop was probably as bad as hitting one, and we'd both end up in jail for the rest of our lives. Not for a second did I feel any of the righteous indignation Iggy did. As far as I was concerned, he had led me into this trap, and I was going to pay for his lunacy. I guess I hated him then even more than the sergeant did.

It didn't help any when the sergeant finally turned to the fat policeman with the air of a man who had made up his mind.

"Take the car and drive over to Rose's place," he said. "You can explain all this to him, and ask him to come along back with you. Oh yes, and get this kid's name and address, and bring his father along, too. Then we'll see."

So I had my first and only experience of sitting on a bench in a police station watching the pendulum of the big clock on the wall swinging back and forth, and recounting all my past sins to myself. It couldn't have been more than a half hour before the fat policeman walked in with Mr Rose and Iggy's father, but it seemed like a year. And a long, miserable year at that.

The surprising thing was the way Mr Rose looked. I had half expected them to bring him in fighting and struggling, because while the sergeant may not have believed Iggy's story, Mr Rose would know it was so.

But far from struggling, Mr Rose looked as if he had dropped in for a friendly visit. He was dressed in a fine summer suit and sporty-looking black-and-white shoes and he was smoking a cigar. He was perfectly calm and pleasant, and, in some strange way, he almost gave the impression that he was in charge there.

It was different with Iggy's father. Mr Kovac must have been reading the paper out on the porch in his undershirt, because his regular shirt had been stuffed into his pants carelessly and part of it hung out. And from his manner you'd think that he was the one who had done something wrong. He kept swallowing hard, and twisting his neck in his collar, and now and then glancing nervously at Mr Rose. He didn't look at all impressive as he did at other times.

The sergeant pointed at Iggy. "All right, kid," he said. "Now tell everybody here what you told me. Stand up so we can all hear it."

Since Iggy had already told it twice he really had it down pat now, and he told it without a break from start to finish, no one interrupting him. And all the while Mr Rose stood there listening politely, and Mr Kovac kept twisting his neck in his collar.

When Iggy was finished the sergeant said, "I'll put it to you straight out, Mr Rose. Were you near that golf course today?"

Mr Rose smiled. "I was not."

"Of course not," said the sergeant. "But you can see what we're up against."

"Sure I can," said Mr Rose. He went over to Iggy and put a hand on his shoulder. "And you know what?" he said. "I don't even blame the kid for trying this trick. He and I had a little trouble some time back about the way he was always climbing over my car, and I guess he's just trying to get square with me. I'd say he's got a lot of spirit in him. Don't you, sonny?" he asked, squeezing Iggy's shoulder in a friendly way.

I was stunned by the accuracy of this shot, but Iggy reacted like a firecracker going off. He pulled away from Mr Rose's hand and ran over to his father. "I'm *not* lying!" he said desperately and grabbed Mr Kovac's shirt, tugging at it. "Honest to God, pop, we both saw it. Honest to God, pop!"

Mr Kovac looked down at him and then looked around at all of us. When his eyes were on Mr Rose it seemed as if his collar were tighter than ever. Meanwhile, Iggy was pulling at his shirt, yelling that we saw it, we saw it, and he wasn't lying, until Mr Kovac shook him once, very hard, and that shut him up.

"Iggy," said Mr Kovac, "I don't want you to go around telling stories about people. Do you hear me?"

Iggy heard him, all right. He stepped back as if he had been walloped across the face, and then stood there looking at Mr Kovac in a funny way. He didn't say anything, didn't even move when Mr Rose came up and put a hand on his shoulder again.

"You heard your father, didn't you, kid?" Mr Rose said.

Iggy still didn't say anything.

"Sure you did," Mr Rose said. "And you and I understand each other a lot better now, kiddo, so there's no hard feelings. Matter of fact, any time you want to come over to the house you come on over, and I'll bet there's plenty of odd jobs you can do there. I pay good, too, so don't you worry about that." He reached into his pocket and took out a bill. "Here," he said, stuffing it into Iggy's hand, "this'll give you an idea. Now go on out and have yourself some fun."

Iggy looked at the money like a sleepwalker. I was baffled by that. As far as I could see, this was a triumph, and here was Iggy in a daze, instead of openly rejoicing. It was only when the sergeant spoke to us that he seemed to wake up.

"All right, you kids," the sergeant said, "beat it home now. The rest of us got some things to talk over."

I didn't need a second invitation. I got out of there in a

hurry and went down the street fast, with Iggy tagging along behind me not saying a word. It was three blocks down and one block over, and I didn't slow down until I was in front of my house again. I had never appreciated those familiar outlines and lights in the windows any more than I did at that moment. But I didn't go right in. It suddenly struck me that this was the last time I'd be seeing Iggy, so I waited there awkwardly. I was never very good at goodbyes.

"That was all right," I said finally. "I mean Mr Rose giving you that dollar. That's as good as twenty golf balls."

"Yeah?" said Iggy, and he was looking at me in the same funny way he had looked at his father. "I'll bet it's as good as a whole new golf club. Come on down to Leo's with me, and I'll show you."

I wanted to, but I wanted to get inside the house even more. "Ahh, my folks'll be sore if I stay out too late tonight," I said. "Anyhow, you can't buy a club for a dollar. You'll need way more than that."

"You think so?" Iggy said, and then held out his hand and slowly opened it so that I could see what he was holding. It was not a one-dollar bill. It was, to my awe, a five-dollar bill.

That, as my wife said, was a long time ago. Thirty-five years before a photograph was taken of little Ignace Kovac, a man wise in the way of the rackets, slumped in a death agony over the wheel of his big car, a bullet hole in the middle of his forehead, a bag of golf clubs leaning against the seat next to him. Thirty-five years before I understood the meaning of the last things said and done when we faced each other on a street in Brooklyn, and then went off, each in his own direction.

I gaped at the money in Iggy's hand. It was the hoard of Croesus, and its very magnitude alarmed me.

"Hey," I said. "That's five bucks. That's a lot of money! You better give it to your old man, or he'll really jump on you."

Then I saw to my surprise that the hand holding the money was shaking. Iggy was suddenly shuddering all over as if he had just plunged into icy water.

"My old man?" he yelled wildly at me, and his lips back showing his teeth clenched together hard, as if that could stop the shuddering. "You know what I'll do if my old man tries anything? I'll tell Mr Rose on him, that's what! Then you'll see!"

And wheeled and ran blindly away from me down the street to his destiny.

PART IV

Wartime Brooklyn

TRALALA

BY HUBERT SELBY, JR.

South Brooklyn

(Originally published in 1957)

I will rise now, and go about the city in the streets, and in the broad ways I will seek him whom my soul loveth: I sought him, but I found him not.

The watchmen that go about the city found me: to whom I said, Saw ye him whom my soul loveth?

Song of Solomon 3: 2, 3

Tralala was 15 the first time she was laid. There was no real passion. Just diversion. She hungout in the Greeks with the other neighborhood kids. Nothin to do. Sit and talk. Listen to the jukebox. Drink coffee. Bum cigarettes. Everything a drag. She said yes. In the park. 3 or 4 couples finding their own tree and grass. Actually she didnt say yes. She said nothing. Tony or Vinnie or whoever it was just continued. They all met later at the exit. They grinned at each other. The guys felt real sharp. The girls walked in front and talked about it. They giggled and alluded. Tralala shrugged her shoulders. Getting laid was getting laid. Why all the bullshit? She went to the park often. She always had her pick. The other girls were as willing, but played games. They liked to tease. And giggle. Tralala didnt fuckaround. Nobody likes a cockteaser. Either you put out or you dont. Thats all.

And she had big tits. She was built like a woman. Not like some kid. They preferred her. And even before the first summer was over she played games. Different ones though. She didnt tease the guys. No sense in that. No money either. Some of the girls bugged her and she broke their balls. If a girl liked one of the guys or tried to get him for any reason Tralala cut in. For kicks. The girls hated her. So what. Who needs them. The guys had what she wanted. Especially when they lushed a drunk. Or pulled a job. She always got something out of it. Theyd take her to the movies. Buy cigarettes. Go to a PIZZERIA for a pie. There was no end of drunks. Everybody had money during the war. The waterfront was filled with drunken seamen. And of course the base was filled with doggies. And they were always good for a few bucks at least. Sometimes more. And Tralala always got her share. No tricks. All very simple. The guys had a ball and she got a few bucks. If there was no room to go to there was always the Wolffe Building cellar. Miles and miles of cellar. One screwed and the others played chick. Sometimes for hours. But she got what she wanted. All she had to do was putout. It was kicks too. Sometimes. If not, so what? It made no difference. Lay on your back. Or bend over a garbage can. Better than working. And its kicks. For a while anyway. But time always passes. They grew older. Werent satisfied with the few bucks they got from drunks. Why wait for a drunk to passout. After theyve spent most of their loot. Drop them on their way back to the Armybase. Every night dozens left Willies, a bar across the street from the Greeks. Theyd get them on their way back to the base or the docks. They usually let the doggies go. They didn't have too much. But the seamen were usually loaded. If they were too big or too sober theyd hit them over the head with a brick. If they looked easy one would hold him and the other(s) would lump him. A few times they got one in the lot on 57th street. That was a ball. It was real dark back by the fence. Theyd hit him until their arms were tired. Good kicks. Then a pie and beer. And Tralala. She was always there. As more time passed they acquired valuable experience. They were more selective. And stronger. They didn't need bricks anymore. Theyd make the rounds of the bars and spot some guy with a roll. When he left theyd lush him. Sometimes Tralala would set him up. Walk him to a doorway. Sometimes through the lot. It worked beautifully. They all had new clothes. Tralala dressed well. She wore a clean sweater every few days. They had no trouble. Just stick to the seamen. They come and go and who knows the difference. Who gives a shit. They have more than they need anyway. And whats a few lumps. They might get killed so whats the difference. They stayed away from doggies. Usually. They played it smart and nobody bothered them. But Tralala wanted more than the small share she was getting. It was about time she got something on her own. If she was going to get laid by a couple of guys for a few bucks she figured it would be smarter to get laid by one guy and get it all. All the drunks gave her the eye. And stared at her tits. It would be a slopeout. Just be sure to pick a liveone. Not some bum with a few lousy bucks. None of that shit. She waited, alone, in the Greeks. A doggie came in and ordered coffee and a hamburger. He asked her if she wanted something. Why not. He smiled. He pulled a bill from a thick roll and dropped it on the counter. She pushed her chest out. He told her about his ribbons. And medals. Bronze Star. And a Purpleheart with 2 Oakleaf Clusters. Been overseas 2 years. Going home. He talked and slobbered and she smiled. She hoped he didnt have all ones. She wanted to get him out before anybody else came. They got in a cab and drove to a downtown hotel. He bought a bottle of whiskey and they sat and drank and he talked. She kept filling his glass. He kept talking. About the war. How he was shot up. About home. What he was going to do. About the months in the hospital and all the operations. She kept pouring but he wouldnt pass out. The bastard. He said he just wanted to be near her for a while. Talk to her and have a few drinks. She waited. Cursed him and his goddamn mother. And who gives a shit about your leg gettin all shotup. She had been there over an hour. If hed fucker maybe she could get the money out of his pocket. But he just talked. The hell with it. She hit him over the head with the bottle. She emptied his pockets and left. She took the money out of his wallet and threw the wallet away. She counted it on the subway. 50 bucks. Not bad. Never had this much at once before. Shouldve gotten more though. Listenin to all that bullshit. Yeah. That sonofabitch. I shoulda hitim again. A lousy 50 bucks and hes talkin like a wheel or somethin. She kept 10 and stashed the rest and hurried back to the Greeks. Tony and Al were there and asked her where she was. Alex says ya cutout with a drunken doggie a couple a hours ago. Yeah. Some creep. I thought he was loaded. Didju score? Yeah. How much? 10 bucks. He kept bullshitin how much he had and alls he had was a lousy 10. Yeah? Lets see. She showed them the money. Yasure thats all yagot? Ya wanna search me? Yathink I got somethin stashed up my ass or somethin? We/ll take a look later. Yeah. How about you? Score? We got a few. But you dont have ta worry aboutit. You got enough. She said nothing and shrugged her shoulders. She smiled and offered to buy them coffee. And? Krist. What a bunch of bloodsuckers. OK Hey Alex . . . They were still sitting at the counter when the doggie came in. He was holding a bloodied handkerchief to his head and blood had caked on his wrist and cheek. He grabbed Tralala by the arm and pulled her from the stool. Give me my wallet you goddamn whore. She spit in his face and told him ta go fuckhimself. Al and Tony pushed him against the wall and asked him who he thought he was. Look, I dont know you and you dont know me. I got no call to fight with you boys. All I want is my wallet. I need my ID Card or I cant get back in the Base. You can keep the goddamn money. I dont care. Tralala screamed in his face that he was a no good mothafuckin sonofabitch and then started kicking him, afraid he might say how much she had taken. Ya lousy fuckin hero. Go peddle a couple of medals if yaneed money so fuckin bad. She spit in his face again, no longer afraid he might say something, but mad. Goddamn mad. A lousy 50 bucks and he was cryin. And anyway, he shouldve had more. Ya lousy fuckin creep. She kicked him in the balls. He grabbed her again. He was crying and bent over struggling to breathe from the pain of the kick. If I dont have the pass I cant get in the Base. I have to get back. Theyre going to fly me home tomorrow. I havent been home for almost 3 years. Ive been all shot up. Please, PLEASE. Just the wallet. Thats all I want. Just the ID Card. PLEASE PLEASE!!! The tears streaked the caked blood and he hung on Tonys and Als grip and Tralala swung at his face, spitting, cursing and kicking. Alex yelled to stop and get out. I dont want trouble in here. Tony grabbed the doggie around the neck and Al shoved the bloodied handkerchief in his mouth and they dragged him outside and into a darkened doorway. He was still crying and begging for his ID Card and trying to tell them he wanted to go home when Tony pulled his head up by his hair and Al punched him a few times in the stomach and then in the face, then held him up while Tony hit

him a few times; but they soon stopped, not afraid that the
cops might come, but they knew he didnt have any money
and they were tired from hitting the seaman they had lushed
earlier, so they dropped him and he fell to the ground on his
back. Before they left Tralala stomped on his face until both
eyes were bleeding and his nose was split and broken then
kicked him a few times in the balls. Ya rotten scumbag, then
they left and walked slowly to 4th avenue and took a subway
to manhattan. Just in case somebody might put up a stink. In
a day or two he/ll be shipped out and nobodyll know the difference. Just another fuckin doggie. And anyway he deserved
it. They ate in a cafeteria and went to an allnight movie. The
next day they got a couple of rooms in a hotel on the east side
and stayed in manhattan until the following night. When
they went back to the Greeks Alex told them some MPs and
a detective were in asking about the guys who beat up a soldier the other night. They said he was in bad shape. Had to
operate on him and he may go blind in one eye. Ain't that
just too bad. The MPs said if they get ahold of the guys who
did it theyd killem. Those fuckin punks. Whad the law say.
Nottin. You know. Yeah. Killus! The creeps. We oughtta
dumpem on general principles. Tralala laughed. I shoulda
pressed charges fa rape. I wont be 18 for a week. He raped me
the dirty freaky sonofabitch. They laughed and ordered cof-
feeand. When they finished Al and Tony figured theyd better
make the rounds of a few of the bars and see what was doin.
In one of the bars they noticed the bartender slip an envelope
in a tin box behind the bar. It looked like a pile of bills on the
bottom of the box. They checked the window in the MENS
ROOM and the alley behind it then left the bar and went
back to the Greeks. They told Tralala what they were going
to do and went to a furnished room they had rented over one

of the bars on 1st avenue. When the bars closed they took a heavy duty screwdriver and walked to the bar. Tralala stood outside and watched the street while they broke in. It only took a few minutes to force open the window, drop inside, crawl to the bar, pickup the box and climb out the window and drop to the alley. They pried open the box in the alley and started to count. They almost panicked when they finished counting. They had almost 2 thousand dollars. They stared at it for a moment then jammed it into their pockets. Then Tony took a few hundred and put it into another pocket and told Al theyd tell Tralala that that was all they got. They smiled and almost laughed then calmed themselves before leaving the alley and meeting Tralala. They took the box with them and dropped it into a sewer then walked back to the room. When they stepped from the alley Tralala ran over to them asking them how they made out and how much they got and Tony told her to keep quiet that they got a couple a hundred and to play it cool until they got back to the room. When they got back to the room Al started telling her what a snap it was and how they just climbed in and took the box but Tralala ignored him and kept asking how much they got. Tony took the lump of money from his pocket and they counted it. Not bad eh Tral? 250 clams. Yeah. How about giving me 50 now. What for? You aint going no where now. She shrugged and they went to bed. The next afternoon they went to the Greeks for coffee and two detectives came in and told them to come outside. They searched them, took the money from their pockets and pushed them into their car. The detectives waved the money in front of their faces and shook their heads. Dont you know better than to knock over a bookie drop? Huh? Huh, Huh! Real clever arent you. The detectives laughed and actually felt a professional amazement as they looked at their dumb expressions and realized that they really didnt know who they had robbed. Tony slowly started to come out of the coma and started to protest that they didnt do nothin. One of the detectives slapped his face and told him to shutup. For Christs sake dont give us any of that horseshit. I suppose you just found a couple of grand lying in an empty lot? Tralala screeched, a what? The detectives looked at her briefly then turned back to Tony and Al. You can lush a few drunken seamen now and then and get away with it, but when you start taking money from my pocket youre going too far sonny. What a pair of stupid punks . . . OK sister, beat it. Unless you want to come along for the ride? She automatically backed away from the car, still staring at Tony and Al. The doors slammed shut and they drove away. Tralala went back to the Greeks and sat at the counter cursing Tony and Al and then the bulls for pickinem up before she could get hers. Didnt even spend a penny of it. The goddamn bastards. The rotten stinkin sonsofbitches. Those thievin flatfooted bastards. She sat drinking coffee all afternoon then left and went across the street to Willies. She walked to the end of the bar and started talking with Ruthy, the barmaid, telling her what happened, stopping every few minutes to curse Tony, Al, the bulls and lousy luck. The bar was slowly filling and Ruthy left her every few minutes to pour a drink and when she came back Tralala would repeat the story from the beginning, yelling about the 2 grand and they never even got a chance to spend a penny. With the repeating of the story she forgot about Tony and Al and just cursed the bulls and her luck and an occasional seaman or doggie who passed by and asked her if she wanted a drink or just looked at her. Ruthy kept filling Tralalas glass as soon as she emptied it and told her to forget about it. Thats the breaks. No sense in beatin yahead against the wall about it. Theres plenty more. Maybe not that much, but enough. Tralala snarled, finished her drink and told Ruthy to fill it up. Eventually she absorbed her anger and quieted down and when a young seaman staggered over to her she glanced at him and said yes. Ruthy brought them two drinks and smiled. Tralala watched him take the money out of his pocket and figured it might be worthwhile. She told him there were better places to drink than this crummy dump. Well, lez go baby. He gulped his drink and Tralala left hers on the bar and they left. They got into a cab and the seaman asked her whereto and she said she didnt care, anywhere. OK. Takeus to Times Square. He offered her a cigarette and started telling her about everything. His name was Harry. He came from Idaho. He just got back from Italy. He was going to—she didnt bother smiling but watched him, trying to figure out how soon he would pass out. Sometimes they last allnight. Cant really tell. She relaxed and gave it thought. Cant konkim here. Just have ta wait until he passes out or maybe just ask for some money. The way they throw it around. Just gotta getim in a room alone. If he dont pass out I/ll just rapim with somethin—and you should see what we did to that little ol . . . He talked on and Tralala smoked and the lampposts flicked by and the meter ticked. He stopped talking when the cab stopped in front of the Crossroads. They got out and tried to get in the Crossroads but the bartender looked at the drunken seaman and shook his head no. So they crossed the street and went to another bar. The bar was jammed, but they found a small table in the rear and sat down. They ordered drinks and Tralala sipped hers then pushed her unfinished drink across the table to him when he finished his. He started talking again but the lights and the music slowly affected him and the subject matter was changed and he started telling Tralala what a good lookin girl she was and what a good time he was going to show her; and she told him that she would show him the time of his life and didnt bother to hide a yawn. He beamed and drank faster and Tralala asked him if he would give her some money. She was broke and had to have some money or she/d be locked out of her room. He told her not to worry that hed find a place for her to stay tonight and he winked and Tralala wanted to shove her cigarette in his face, the cheap sonofabitch, but figured she/d better wait and get his money before she did anything. He toyed with her hand and she looked around the bar and noticed an Army Officer staring at her. He had a lot of ribbons just like the one she had rolled and she figured hed have more money than Harry. Officers are usually loaded. She got up from the table telling Harry she was going to the ladies room. The Officer swayed slightly as she walked up to him and smiled. He took her arm and asked her where she was going. Nowhere. O, we cant have a pretty girl like you going nowhere. I have a place thats all empty and a sack of whiskey. Well . . . She told him to wait and went back to the table. Harry was almost asleep and she tried to get the money from his pocket and he started to stir. When his eyes opened she started shaking him, taking her hand out of his pocket, and telling him to wakeup. I thought yawere goin to show me a good time. You bet. He nodded his head and it slowly descended toward the table. Hey Harry, wakeup. The waiter wants to know if yahave any money. Showem ya money so I wont have to pay. You bet. He slowly took the crumpled mess of bills from his pocket and Tralala grabbed it from his hand and said I toldya he had money. She picked up the cigarettes from the table, put the money in her pocketbook and walked back to the bar. My friend is sleeping so I dont think he/ll mind, but I think we/d better leave. They left the bar and walked to his hotel. Tralala hoped she didnt make a mistake. Harry mightta had more money stashed somewhere. The Officer should have more though and anyway she probably got everything Harry had and she could get more from this jerk if he has any. She looked at him trying to determine how much he could have, but all Officers look the same. Thats the trouble with a goddamn uniform. And then she wondered how much she had gotten from Harry and how long she would have to wait to count it. When they got to his room she went right into the bathroom, smoothed out the bills a little and counted them. 45. Shit. Fuckit. She folded the money, left the bathroom and stuffed the money in a coat pocket. He poured two small drinks and they sat and talked for a few minutes then put the light out. Tralala figured there was no sense in trying anything now so she relaxed and enjoyed herself. They were having a smoke and another drink when he turned and kissed her and told her she had the most beautiful pair of tits he had ever seen. He continued talking for a few minutes, but she didnt pay any attention. She thought about her tits and what he had said and how she could get anybody with her tits and the hell with Willies and those slobs, she'd hang around here for a while and do alright. They put out their cigarettes and for the rest of the night she didnt wonder how much money he had. At breakfast the next morning he tried to remember everything that had happened in the bar, but Harry was only vaguely remembered and he didnt want to ask her. A few times he tried speaking, but when he looked at her he started feeling vaguely guilty. When they had finished eating he lit her cigarette, smiled, and asked her if he could buy her something. A dress or something like that. I mean, well you know

. . . Id like to buy you a little present. He tried not to sound maudlin or look sheepish, but he found it hard to say what he felt, now, in the morning, with a slight hangover, and she looked to him pretty and even a little innocent. Primarily he didnt want her to think he was offering to pay her or think he was insulting her by insinuating that she was just another prostitute; but much of his loneliness was gone and he wanted to thank her. You see, I only have a few days leave left before I go back and I thought perhaps we could—that is I thought we could spend some more time together . . . he stammered on apologetically hoping she understood what he was trying to say but the words bounced off her and when she noticed that he had finished talking she said sure. What thefuck. This is much better than wresslin with a drunk and she felt good this morning, much better than yesterday (briefly remembering the bulls and the money they took from her) and he might even give her his money before he went back overseas (what could he do with it) and with her tits she could always makeout and whatthehell, it was the best screwin she ever had . . . They went shopping and and she bought a dress, a couple of sweaters (2 sizes too small), shoes, stockings, a pocketbook and an overnight bag to put her clothes in. She protested slightly when he told her to buy a cosmetic case (not knowing what it was when he handed it to her and she saw no sense in spending money on that when he could as well give her cash), and he enjoyed her modesty in not wanting to spend too much of his money; and he chuckled at her childlike excitement at being in the stores, looking and buying. They took all the packages back to the hotel and Tralala put on her new dress and shoes and they went out to eat and then to a movie. For the next few days they went to movies, restaurants (Tralala trying to make a mental note of the ones where the Officers hungout), a few more stores and back to the hotel. When they woke on the 4th day he told her he had to leave and asked her if she would come with him to the station. She went thinking he might give her his money and she stood awkwardly on the station with him, their bags around them, waiting for him to go on the train and leave. Finally the time came for him to leave and he handed her an envelope and kissed her before boarding the train. She felt the envelope as she lifted her face slightly so he could kiss her. It was thin and she figured it might be a check. She put it in her pocketbook, picked up her bag and went to the waiting room and sat on a bench and opened the envelope. She opened the paper and started reading: Dear Tral: There are many things I would like to say and should have said, but—A letter. A goddamn LETTER. She ripped the envelope apart and turned the letter over a few times. Not a cent. I hope you understand what I mean and am unable to say—she looked at the words—if you do feel as I hope you do Im writing my address at the bottom. I dont know if I/ll live through this war, but—Shit. Not vehemently but factually. She dropped the letter and rode the subway to Brooklyn. She went to Willies to display her finery. Ruthy was behind the bar and Waterman Annie was sitting in a booth with a seaman. She stood at the bar talking with Ruthy for a few minutes answering her questions about the clothes and telling her about the rich john she was living with and how much money he gave her and where they went. Ruthy left occasionally to pour a drink and when she came back Tralala continued her story, but soon Ruthy tired of listening to her bullshit as Tralalas short imagination bogged down. Tralala turned and looked at Annie and asked her when they leter out. Annie told her ta go screw herself. Youre the only one who would. Annie laughed and Tralala told her ta keep her shiteatin mouth shut. The seaman got up from the booth and staggered toward Tralala. You shouldnt talk to my girl friend like that. That douchebag? You should be able ta do betteran that. She smiled and pushed her chest out. The seaman laughed and leaned on the bar and asked her if she would like a drink. Sure. But not in this crummy place. Lets go ta some place thats not crawlin with stinkin whores. The seaman roared, walked back to the table, finished his drink and left with Tralala. Annie screamed at them and tried to throw a glass at Tralala but someone grabbed her arm. Tralala and Jack (he was an oiler and he . . .) got into a cab and drove downtown. Tralala thought of ditching him rightaway (she only wanted to break Annies balls), but figured she ought to wait and see. She stayed with him and they went to a hotel and when he passedout she took what he had and went back uptown. She went to a bar in Times Square and sat at the bar. It was filled with servicemen and a few drunken sailors smiled at her as she looked around, but she ignored them and the others in the bar ignored her. She wanted to be sure she picked up a live one. No drunken twobit sailor or doggie for her. O no. Ya bet ya sweetass no. With her clothes and tits? Who inthehell do those punks think they are. I oughtta go spit in their stinkin faces. Shit! They couldnt kiss my ass. She jammed her cigarette out and took a short sip of her drink. She waited. She smiled at a few Officers she thought might have loot, but they were with women. She cursed the dames under her breath, pulled the top of her dress down, looked around and sipped her drink. Even with sipping the drink was soon gone and she had to order another. The bartender refilled her glass and marked her for an amateur. He smiled and was almost tempted to tell her that she was trying the wrong place, but didnt. He just refilled her glass thinking she would be better off in one of the 8th avenue bars. She sipped the new drink and lit another cigarette. Why was she still alone? What was with this joint? Everybody with a few bucks had a dame. Goddamn pigs. Not one ofem had a pair half as big as hers. She could have any sonofabitch in Willies or any bum stumbling into the Greeks. Whats with the creeps in here. They should be all around her. She shouldnt be sitting alone. She/d been there 2 hours already. She felt like standing up and yelling fuck you to everybody in the joint. Youre all a bunch of goddamn creeps. She snarled at the women who passed. She pulled her dress tight and forced her shoulders back. Time still passed. She still ignored the drunks figuring somebody with gelt would popup. She didnt touch her third drink, but sat looking around, cursing every sonofabitch in the joint and growing more defiant and desperate. Soon she was screaming in her mind and wishing takrist she had a blade, she/d cut their goddamn balls off. A CPO came up to her and asked her if she wanted a drink and she damn near spit in his face, but just mumbled as she looked at the clock and said shit. Yeah, yeah, lets go. She gulped down her drink and they left. Her mind was still such a fury of screechings (and that sonofabitch gives me nothin but a fuckin letter) that she just lay in bed staring at the ceiling and ignored the sailor as he screwed her and when he finally rolled off for the last time and fell asleep she continued staring and cursing for hours before falling asleep. The next afternoon she demanded that he giver some money and he laughed. She tried to hit him but he grabbed her arm, slapped her across the face and told her she was out of her mind. He laughed and told her to take it easy. He had a few days leave and he had enough money for both of them.

They could have a good time. She cursed him and spit and he told her to grab her gear and shove off. She stopped in a cafeteria and went to the ladies room and threw some water on her face and bought a cup of coffee and a bun. She left and went back to the same bar. It was not very crowded being filled mostly with servicemen trying to drink away hangovers, and she sat and sipped a few drinks until the bar started filling. She tried looking for a liveone, but after an hour or so, and a few drinks, she ignored everyone and waited. A couple of sailors asked her if she wanted a drink and she said whatthefuck and left with them. They roamed around for hours drinking and then she went to a room with two of them and they gave her a few bucks in the morning so she stayed with them for a few days, 2 or 3, staying drunk most of the time and going back to the room now and then with them and their friends. And then they left or went somewhere and she went back to the bar to look for another one or a whole damn ship. Whats the difference. She pulled her dress tight but didnt think of washing. She hadnt reached the bar when someone grabbed her arm, walked her to the side door and told her to leave. She stood on the corner of 42nd & Broadway cursing them and wanting to know why they let those scabby whores in but kick a nice young girl out, ya lousy bunch apricks. She turned and crossed the street, still mumbling to herself, and went in another bar. It was jammed and she worked her way to the back near the jukebox and looked. When someone came back to play a number she smiled, threw her shoulders back and pushed the hair from her face. She stood there drinking and smiling and eventually left with a drunken soldier. They screwed most of the night, slept for a short time then awoke and started drinking and screwing again. She stayed with him for a day or two, perhaps

longer, she wasnt sure and it didnt make any difference anyway, then he was gone and she was back in a bar looking. She
bounced from one bar to another still pulling her dress tight
and occasionally throwing some water on her face before
leaving a hotel room, slobbering drinks and soon not looking
but just saying yeah, yeah, whatthefuck and pushing an
empty glass toward the bartender and sometimes never seeing the face of the drunk buying her drinks and rolling on and
off her belly and slobbering over her tits; just drinking then
pulling off her clothes and spreading her legs and drifting off
to sleep or a drunken stupor with the first lunge. Time
passed—months, maybe years, who knows, and the dress was
gone and just a beatup skirt and sweater and the Broadway
bars were 8th avenue bars, but soon even these joints with
their hustlers, pushers, pimps, queens and wouldbe thugs
kicked her out and the inlaid linoleum turned to wood and
then was covered with sawdust and she hung over a beer in
a dump on the waterfront, snarling and cursing every sonofabitch who fucked herup and left with anyone who looked at
her or had a place to flop. The honeymoon was over and still
she pulled the sweater tight but there was no one there to
look. When she crawled out of a flophouse she fell in the
nearest bar and stayed until another offer of a flop was made.
But each night she would shove her tits out and look around
for a liveone, not wanting any goddamn wino but the bums
only looked at their beers and she waited for the liveone who
had an extra 50¢ he didnt mind spending on beer for a piece
of ass and she flopped from one joint to another growing dirt-
ier and scabbier. She was in a South street bar and a seaman
bought her a beer and his friends who depended on him for
their drinks got panicky fearing he would leave them and
spend their beer money on her so when he went to the head

they took the beer from her and threw her out into the street. She sat on the curb yelling until a cop came along and kicked her and told her to move. She sprawled to her feet cursing every sonofabitch and his brother and told them they could stick their fuckin beer up their ass. She didnt need any goddamn skell to buy her a drink. She could get anything she wanted in Willies. She had her kicks. She/d go back to Willies where what she said goes. That was the joint. There was always somebody in there with money. No bums like these cruds. Did they think she/d let any goddamn bum in her pants and play with her tits just for a few bucks. Shit! She could get a seamans whole payoff just sittin in Willies. People knew who she was in Willies. You bet yasweet ass they did. She stumbled down the subway and rode to Brooklyn, muttering and cursing, sweat streaking the dirt on her face. She walked up the 3 steps to the door and was briefly disappointed that the door wasnt closed so she could throw it open. She stood for just a second in the doorway looking around then walked to the rear where Waterman Annie, Ruthy and a seaman were sitting. She stood beside the seaman, leaned in front of him and smiled at Annie and Ruthy then ordered a drink. The bartender looked at her and asked her if she had any money. She told him it was none of his goddamn business. My friend here is going to pay for it. Wontya honey. The seaman laughed and pushed a bill forward and she got her drink and sneered at the ignorant sonofabitchin bartender. The rotten scumbag. Annie pulled her aside and told her if she tried cuttin her throat she/d dump her guts on the floor. Mean Ruthys gonna leave as soon as Jacks friend comes and if ya screw it up youll be a sorry sonofabitch. Tralala yanked her arm away and went back to the bar and leaned against the seaman and rubbed her tits against his arm. He laughed and told her to drinkup. Ruthy told Annie not ta botha witha, Fredll be here soon and we/ll go, and they talked with Jack and Tralala leaned over and interrupted their conversation and snarled at Annie hoping she burns like hell when Jack left with *her* and Jack laughed at everything and pounded the bar and bought drinks and Tralala smiled and drank and the jukebox blared hillbilly songs and an occasional blues song, and the red and blue neon lights around the mirror behind the bar sputtered and winked and the soldiers seamen and whores in the booths and hanging on the bar yelled and laughed and Tralala lifted her drink and said chugalug and banged her glass on the bar and she rubbed her tits against Jacks arm and he looked at her wondering how many blackheads she had on her face and if that large pimple on her cheek would burst and ooze and he said something to Annie then roared and slapped her leg and Annie smiled and wrote Tralala off and the cash register kachanged and the smoke just hung and Fred came and joined the party and Tralala yelled for another drink and asked Fred how he liked her tits and he poked them with a finger and said I guess theyre real and Jack pounded the bar and laughed and Annie cursed Tralala and tried to get them to leave and they said lets stay for a while, we/re having fun and Fred winked and someone rapped a table and roared and a glass fell to the floor and the smoke fell when it reached the door and Tralala opened Jacks fly and smiled and he closed it 5 6 7 times laughing and stared at the pimple and the lights blinked and the cashregister crooned kachang kachang and Tralala told Jack she had big tits and he pounded the bar and laughed and Fred winked and laughed and Ruthy and Annie wanted to leave before something screwed up their deal and wondered how much money they had and hating to see them spend it on

Tralala and Tralala gulped her drinks and yelled for more and Fred and Jack laughed and winked and pounded the bar and another glass fell to the floor and someone bemoaned the loss of a beer and two hands fought their way up a skirt under a table and she blew smoke in their faces and someone passed-out and his head fell on the table and a beer was grabbed before it fell and Tralala glowed she had it made and she/d shove it up Annies ass or anybody elses and she gulped another drink and it spilled down her chin and she hung on Jacks neck and rubbed her chest against his cheek and he reached up and turned them like knobs and roared and Tralala smiled and O she had it made now and piss on all those mothafuckas and someone walked a mile for a smile and someone pulled the drunk out of the booth and dropped him out the back door and Tralala pulled her sweater up and bounced her tits on the palms of her hands and grinned and grinned and grinned and Jack and Fred whooped and roared and the bartender told her to put those goddamn things away and get thehelloutahere and Ruthy and Annie winked and Tralala slowly turned around bouncing them hard on her hands exhibiting her pride to the bar and she smiled and bounced the biggest most beautiful pair of tits in the world on her hands and someone yelled is that for real and Tralala shoved them in his face and everyone laughed and another glass fell from a table and guys stood and looked and the hands came out from under the skirt and beer was poured on Tralalas tits and someone yelled that she had been christened and the beer ran down her stomach and dripped from her nipples and she slapped his face with her tits and someone yelled youll smotherim ta death—what a way to die—hey, whats for desert—I said taput those goddamn things away ya fuckin hippopotamus and Tralala told him she had the pret-

tiest tits in the world and she fell against the jukebox and the
needle scraped along the record sounding like a long belch
and someone yelled all tits and no cunt and Tralala told him
to comeon and find out and a drunken soldier banged out of
a booth and said comeon and glasses fell and Jack knocked
over his stool and fell on Fred and they hung over the bar
nearing hysteria and Ruthy hoped she wouldnt get fired
because this was a good deal and Annie closed her eyes and
laughed relieved that they wouldnt have to worry about
Tralala and they didnt spend too much money and Tralala
still bounced her tits on the palms of her hands turning to
everyone as she was dragged out the door by the arm by 2 or
3 and she yelled to Jack to comeon and she/d fuckim blind
not like that fuckin douchebag he was with and someone
yelled we/re coming and she was dragged down the steps tripping over someones feet and scraping her ankles on the stone
steps and yelling but the mob not slowing their pace dragged
her by an arm and Jack and Fred still hung on the bar roaring and Ruthy took off her apron getting ready to leave
before something happened to louse up their deal and the 10
or 15 drunks dragged Tralala to a wrecked car in the lot on
the corner of 57th street and yanked her clothes off and
pushed her inside and a few guys fought to see who would be
first and finally a sort of line was formed everyone yelling and
laughing and someone yelled to the guys on the end to go get
some beer and they left and came back with cans of beer
which were passed around the daisychain and the guys from
the Greeks cameover and some of the other kids from the
neighborhood stood around watching and waiting and
Tralala yelled and shoved her tits into the faces as they
occurred before her and beers were passed around and the
empties dropped or thrown and guys left the car and went

back on line and had a few beers and waited their turn again and more guys came from Willies and a phone call to the Armybase brought more seamen and doggies and more beer was brought from Willies and Tralala drank beer while being laid and someone asked if anyone was keeping score and someone yelled who can count that far and Tralalas back was streaked with dirt and sweat and her ankles stung from the sweat and dirt in the scrapes from the steps and sweat and beer dripped from the faces onto hers but she kept yelling she had the biggest goddamn pair of tits in the world and someone answered ya bet ya sweet ass yado and more came 40 maybe 50 and they screwed her and went back on line and had a beer and yelled and laughed and someone yelled that the car stunk of cunt so Tralala and the seat were taken out of the car and laid in the lot and she lay there naked on the seat and their shadows hid her pimples and scabs and she drank flipping her tits with the other hand and somebody shoved the beer can against her mouth and they all laughed and Tralala cursed and spit out a piece of tooth and someone shoved it again and they laughed and yelled and the next one mounted her and her lips were split this time and the blood trickled to her chin and someone mopped her brow with a beer soaked handkerchief and another can of beer was handed to her and she drank and yelled about her tits and another tooth was chipped and the split in her lips was widened and everyone laughed and she laughed and she drank more and more and soon she passedout and they slapped her a few times and she mumbled and turned her head but they couldnt revive her so they continued to fuck her as she lay unconscious on the seat in the lot and soon they tired of the dead piece and the daisychain brokeup and they went back to Willies the Greeks and the base and the kids who were watching and waiting to take a turn took out their disappointment on Tralala and tore her clothes to small scraps put out a few cigarettes on her nipples pissed on her jerkedoff on her jammed a broomstick up her snatch then bored they left her lying amongst the broken bottles rusty cans and rubble of the lot and Jack and Fred and Ruthy and Annie stumbled into a cab still laughing and they leaned toward the window as they passed the lot and got a good look at Tralala lying naked covered with blood urine and semen and a small blot forming on the seat between her legs as blood seeped from her crotch and Ruthy and Annie happy and completely relaxed now that they were on their way downtown and their deal wasnt lousedup and they would have plenty of money and Fred looking through the rear window and Jack pounding his leg and roaring with laughter . . . .

THE BOYS OF BENSONHURST

SALVATORE LA PUMA

Bensonhurst

(Originally published in 1987)

1942

The angel whispering in Frankie's ear warned him to be careful going to New Jersey, but he said, "Scram," to the pest, which the other guys thought might be a fly, and they all went up from the BMT subway to Times Square, where lights on billboards, movie houses, restaurants, and shops blinked nervously, and where even the scrounging pigeons were hemmed in. Mobs of people drifted out of step but mostly in two-way lanes, and nearly everyone, including the legless beggar man squatting and rolling along the sidewalk, seemed to know exactly where he belonged, and cars looked packed in the streets as in lots at Yankee games.

They went west on 42nd Street: Frankie, the oldest at seventeen; Nick, the altar boy; Rocco, the killer in the ring and with dames; and Gene, wild on the drums and the youngest at fifteen.

"I love this place," said Rocco, shadowboxing in the street.

"Lots of dames around," said Frankie.

Cardboard dames in underpants and bras were posted by the lurid movie houses, and live dames in split skirts and open blouses were in doorways, all looking for customers. Bells were ringing in arcades for pinball, miniature bowling, and peep shows. Greasy smoke blew from narrow shops grilling hot dogs, hamburgers, and knishes, shops which would be closed for a few hours before dawn with see-through steel gates. White-hat hawkers urged the guys to buy beers, orange drinks, cotton candy, caramel popcorn, and homemade fudge. Almost anything a guy could want was for sale.

The pedestrians were all sizes, ages, colors, sexes, rich and poor. They gawked at the hustlers and pimps who gawked back. Horns and tail pipes played flat, while loud-speakers from record shops played the hits so far in 1942. In a bookstore window the nudist magazine *Sunbathers* had on its cover naked dames with pubic hair. So the guys went inside. Frankie Primo often read magazines and books, rode on an old Harley, was secretly in love with an older dame, and didn't want to go in the Army. Of Sicilian blood, he was a little ashamed that he wasn't eager to kill Japs and Nazis. Every other Sicilian guy he knew of couldn't wait.

"You ever read this?" said Frankie.

"It must be about screwing," said Nick Consoli, who wanted to be one of the boys, and often went along, but at the crucial moment he could hold back, remembering what sin was, as he was doing now, shaking his head. "Screwing's bad for the soul."

"Everything's about screwing," said Frankie, acting the man of the world.

The man in charge crooked his finger at them, so Frankie and his friends moved to the shadowy back of the store. There the man dealt out cards face-down on the glass show-case like hands of poker. When he flipped them over, they weren't aces and kings; they were snapshots of naked dames turning themselves inside out to show how they were made. The guys got frog eyes.

"How much?" said Frankie.

"A fin," said the man.

"Five bucks for pictures?" said Frankie. "You're kidding?"

"Get *out*," said the man. "*Out*. Before I kick asses. Scummy kids."

Farther down 42nd was the bus terminal with snaking lines at ticket windows, with sitters on suitcases and hard benches, and blind-looking people hurrying somewhere, and others dragging, unhappy to go where they were going. Not knowing which line to get in, the boys went to Information.

"You don't want the Greyhound," said the colored guy. "It don't stop in Union City. You want the Madison line. It's red and white. It goes to Jersey by the Skyway."

At the first and only stop in Union City everybody got off, as if the only reason to go there was to see the show. It was almost June and the light was still out, and they all went up the hilly street, passing old brick buildings with boarded-up windows, dark warehouses where nothing useful could be kept, scurrying rats, and drunks nursing like babies from bottles in paper bags.

"Poor bastards. We ought to help them out. But we ain't got time," said Frankie, and his angel whispered her agreement.

The boys kept their eyes peeled in case a derelict should pounce from a doorway with a filthy proposition. They were a little scared, except for Rocco Marino. He threw a left jab at an invisible opponent to dare trouble to come out. But then, without being asked, Rocco gave a dollar to the old man with a balding beard and one-tooth grin.

"I got dough from my fights," Rocco said to his friends, who didn't have as much. He didn't want them to think he was a show-off.

When the crowd turned the corner, the street was in the

glaring spotlight of thousands of burning white bulbs on the Hudson Theater's marquee, reading in capital letters:

BURLESQUE

"We have half an hour still," said Frankie.

"How about a beer?" said Gene Dragoni, hoping the bar next to the theater wouldn't find him too young.

"First, let's get tickets," said Nick. "If they sold out while we're sipping suds, it would be a waste. After that trip."

They got in line. But the seats weren't reserved. So instead of drinking their beers in Little Lil's Bar, bought from Lil herself, who was built like a wrestler and who winked at Gene although she knew they were all underage, they took their bottles to seats in the third row of the balcony.

The orchestra's lower half was already mostly filled, though not entirely by servicemen and other men. Dames too were in the audience, with dates, or in groups of dames together. That girls were there at all seemed to the guys a little odd. But at the back of their minds they knew things existed that they couldn't explain yet. They hoped that later on, when they weren't boys any longer, they would understand such minor mysteries.

Two rows down and over to the side in the balcony were two dames by themselves not much older than Frankie and his friends, and one had rusting blonde hair. The guys couldn't take their eyes off the dames, and the dames, not taking their eyes off the guys either, even waved first. The guys elbowed each other and thought they were easily recognizable as Romeos. They talked about moving their seats next to the dames, or asking them up to seats in their row. But they were filled up on each other's friendship and were anticipating the pleasure of other dames showing off their legs, breasts, and behinds, so for now they just didn't need these dames.

People in the aisles were still looking for seats when a guy in a white jacket and black tie came onstage. His grin was so broad it was almost a mirror reflecting flashes in code. "Ladies and gentlemen, tonight we have a *sensational* offer. The most sensational in the *history* of the Hudson Theater. Tonight we have this *lovely* box of delicious Whitman's chocolates made with *imported* chocolate. Crunchy *nuts*. Chewy *carmels*. Buttery *creams*. All for *one* dollar. Let me repeat this sensational *bargain* price. All for one *little* dollar. This special sale is from the maker *exclusively* to you, to introduce their *fine* quality. And not only *one pound* of chocolates, but in each ten boxes is a *special* bonus. A *Bulova watch*. Can you believe *your* good luck? One out of ten leaves here tonight with a Bulova worth $25 *on his wrist*. What a terrific deal. I'm buying ten boxes myself. And even if you don't win, these delicious chocolates make you *feel* like a winner. So, *please*, have your dollars ready. We have only seventy-five boxes for this *limited* offer. When we're sold out, there just won't be anymore."

"Let's split one," said Rocco, taking out a dollar. The other three each passed him a quarter.

"But who gets the watch?" said Nick, believing it possible to win one.

"We can toss for it," said Gene, since the laws of chance, unlike arm wrestling, would favor them equally.

"No watches in those boxes," said Frankie. "It's the worm on the hook."

The box had space for twice as much candy as was there, not a pound, but eight pieces, quickly chewed, as the boys shrugged off their disappointment.

Another guy came onstage in his white jacket which was a little too long. He was short and square and talked up to the microphone. "All you people who didn't win the watch. In case you won one, you *can't* be in on this. This is only if you didn't buy the candy, or if you did, you didn't get a Bulova, which *now you can get*. Really, *really* cheap. But only one to a person. I know people here want to buy two, three to take home to their wife, and to their mother. But we have to limit *one each*, since we don't have too many. It's the most *fantastic* deal Bulova ever made. For just *two dollars*. That's right, two American dollars, you get a *100 percent guaranteed* Bulova. You *never* heard such a bargain. How can we do it? Very simple. They have more watches than orders. But they couldn't get rid of the extras through the stores which sell them for the *high* price. In fact, you'll notice the name Bulova doesn't appear on the face of this watch. It doesn't want regular stores knowing how *cheap* they're selling them here tonight. In stores you pay $25. But tonight, for *one* night only, you pay just *two dollars*. The man's. Or the lady's. *Solid* gold-plated. *Genuine* leather strap. But we have to move fast, ladies and gentlemen. Only ten minutes to curtain time. So have your money ready, *please*. Don't miss this *amazing* offer. It won't happen *ever again*."

"We should get a watch," said Nick, the altar boy.

"I have one," said Gene.

"Me too," said Rocco. "But for two bucks, it sounds good."

"It's probably a Dick Tracy," said Frankie. "I wouldn't buy anything from *these* guys."

"My mother could use a watch," said Nick. "I'll get the lady's." He fished out his money. Then they all looked at the watch imprisoned in cellophane and staples. Frankie cut the paper with his Barlow knife. The watch was definitely a watch.

So Nick started winding it. He was winding it and winding it. When it didn't come to an end, he handed the watch to Frankie. Frankie looked at it for a minute and then tapped it in his palm. Then he passed it to Rocco, who shook it with his featherweight grace. Then Gene weighed it in his hand and passed it back to Nick. Gene didn't want to be unkind to his friend Nick and didn't say that the watch felt empty.

Nick was still trying to get it to run when the curtain went up and the lights went out. To the beat from the orchestra in the pit, the line of dames kicked onstage with pink feathers in their hair and sparkling sequins on their underwear. They weren't dolls exactly. The guys were expecting to see the beauties who existed in their imaginations, but instead they saw average dames, with all the mistakes Mother Nature makes in faces and figures. Since they looked so human, the boys felt slightly embarrassed, as if they were leering at their own mothers or sisters, and they drooped a little.

"One on the end's cute," said Nick.

"Too skinny," said Rocco. "But mama mia, the one in the middle."

"No," said Frankie. "The blonde."

The blonde's smile looked sincere, while the other smiles looked like something was too tight, or a snapshot in the hot sun was about to be taken. The girls in the chorus were showing their teeth as if the audience was a convention of dentists. They pranced and kicked and then they bowed their behinds to applause. Frankie thought none was as sexy as Sylvia tightening her garter in her office when once he just happened to walk in.

Then the stage went dark and the spotlight was on two

hands holding a sign that read MISS SUGAR BUNS. The spotlight danced to the other side of the stage where a bride in
her wedding gown danced out to a jazzy wedding march. One
glove, one button, and one thread at a time was a slow boil
for the crowd, and she was still in her underwear ten minutes
later. The drumbeat seemed to be in her hips and breasts
where she was big, and every guy was raving. Gene, who
played the drums in his school orchestra, was thinking that
he might come here to the Hudson Theater when he gradu-
ated in a few years and get a job at the skins in the pit from
where he could look up at dames every night until, if it were
ever possible, he would get his fill.

Miss Sugar Buns was down to her hairnet bra and spangled G-string, and the guys were quiet as if words had more
value now by their absence. The theater was heating up and
everyone was sweating and holding his breath. The drum
rolled. Poised in the spotlight, to clashes of the symbols, the
stripper tore off her hairnet bra. Then her G-string. The boys
thought they saw everything, but from the balcony, it was
hard to be sure. She didn't seem to have any pubic hair. And
it all happened so fast. But they acted to each other as if they
had seen the most precious thing a man would want to see.

Altogether, they saw four comedy acts, the chorus six or
seven times, and three other strippers. The last was Miss
Floppy Candy. Then the show was over and the guys were
almost dead from loving all the dames. They had loved even
the ugly ones, which a few were, but noses, love handles,
bowlegs, and buck-teeth had been disguised by the music and
by their dreams of dames.

The crowd moved up the aisles, and when the guys were
out on the sidewalk in front of the theater their eyes lit up
again. The two dolls from the balcony were licking ice cream

cones, bought from the Good Humor Man at the curb. One was almost a Miss Sugar Buns herself, and the other was blonde, but not as pretty close up.

"It's kind of late," said Frankie, worried about the time as usual, and reminded by that wispy voice that strange dames could be carrying strange germs.

"Let's go over," said Rocco.

"They won't give us the time," said Nick, who thought of the pain of confessing his sins that weren't even too bad.

"What can we lose?" said Gene, who aspired to brazen acts.

Frankie for his reasons, and Nick for his, hung back, and Frankie said, "We'll go take the bus. You guys can stay."

But Nick, not ready to admit he wouldn't screw one of the dolls, said, unconvincingly, "They're something."

"They are," said Frankie. "But not for me."

Rocco said, "Go have a beer, you guys. Let me and Gene try."

"Okay," they said.

Before Rocco and Gene could approach the girls, the girls came to them. The blonde said, "It's five dollars apiece. That's the discount price if we take you four."

The guys had thought the dolls admired them as handsome young lions who stood out for their Sicilian dark looks, thick manes, and straight backs. The boys had money in their pockets to pay the dolls for their services, and they weren't cheap about spending it. But they felt insulted now that the dolls weren't wanting to be kissed and petted in their tight arms. The dolls just wanted their five bucks. "Shit," said Rocco, in a mutter. So they all got on the bus and went back to Bensonhurst.

* * *

"It's nice you let me come over. I was thinking who I could talk to," said Frankie in the hall.

Sylvia Cohen wasn't asking him inside. She was looking him over, trying to guess what he would say and what she would do with him. He didn't work for Tony Tempesta or other gangsters, but delivered small packages between them on his Harley. Frankie had swaggered into Sylvia's olive oil office unafraid of anything, but his grin said he wouldn't swat a fly, and both those things tickled her.

"Saturday night's a lousy time to call a girl. The only reason I'm here's the guy got a flat. But I was going out anyway," said Sylvia, her lipstick chewed off and her hair in a mess, and Frankie guessed she wasn't going anywhere like that.

"This thing's been on my mind," he said.

"So what is it?" she said.

"You think we could sit down?"

"Look, Frankie, just because we had an ice cream a couple of times and you held my hand once, don't mean we can hang out. You're seventeen, for Pete's sake. Everybody'll say Sylvia's hard up. And I ain't. So I hope you ain't planning on asking me on no date."

She eyed him as if he was a crook, but one who wanted to steal only a fresh baked pie, and she thought she might spare a slice if he was nice and polite.

"I was just wanting to talk. You always give me a big smile," said Frankie, now worried that he wouldn't get her interested, since she thought he was a kid even though he had a heavyweight's build. Besides, she was too beautiful, with her buttery hair and stripper's figure, to give it all away easily.

"I'm thirsty. You thirsty? C'mon in the parlor. I'll get something." She didn't leave, but instead, they stood on the parlor rug, wondering what they were doing there together.

"You have iced tea?" said Frankie.

"Last night this guy was feeding me brandy alexanders. Which I loved. And he thought he was going to get somewhere. He's an accountant. So he thinks each day's a sheet in his ledger. He's so boring. His voice comes out a word at a time. You could die waiting. Almost I could've screamed. Then I had another brandy. So, actually, I'm glad to talk to you. You're not boring, but I sure wish you was older."

"I'm sorry I'm not," said Frankie. "But then I'd be drafted."

"Sit down," said Sylvia. "I'll be right back."

"I'll be quiet so I won't wake anybody."

"Yeah. Be real, real quiet. But even if you was loud, they wouldn't hear you. My folks went to Miami Beach," said Sylvia, walking away swinging her hips.

"No kidding?" said Frankie, dropping to the sofa and crossing his feet on the coffee table. Chinese-pagoda lamps and cupid lamps were on the tables, and porcelain poodles, cats, teacups, dishes, vases, World's Fair trylons and perispheres were on shelves in the corner.

The artificial flowers and artificial fruits on two tables saddened Frankie, although he didn't know why, since they were beautiful in their own right. Before Sylvia came back, he hid the flowers behind one stuffed chair, and then hid the fruit too. He helped himself to a cigarette from the brass box on the coffee table, but when Sylvia was coming back he took his feet off the table.

"I do it myself. Except I take my shoes off," she said, slipping out of hers.

They both put their feet up on the coffee table and slouched back in the plush sofa and sipped tea. Frankie was crazy about Sylvia because she always acted herself. There was no bullshit to work through. And to find out if she would be anxious to be rid of him in a few minutes, or whether she was lonely and would talk for hours, Frankie tested her by saying, "I won't stay long. Since you're going out someplace?"

"You know what they do in Miami?" she said, ignoring his question and asking one of her own, which she was prepared to answer herself. "My mother and father? They go sit on the sand. The men talk business. Jewish men always do. The women play Mah-Jongg. They go for Christmas. And now they go in the water. I went once. Almost died for something, *anything*, to happen."

"Didn't guys on the beach come over?"

"They were old enough to be my father. I just turned twenty-two. Last Saturday. May 21."

"I didn't even know you had a birthday," said Frankie. "You suppose a birthday kiss a week late is okay to give?"

"Here on the cheek," she said.

He kissed both gardenia-smelling checks, and then she steered him back to his place on the sofa and took his hand to keep him in check.

"You smell good," he said.

"Holding hands is one of the nicest things," said Sylvia. "It has to be somebody you like. Then it feels right. So what's on your mind, Frankie?"

He had wanted her opinion of his dilemma, since she lived on 18th Avenue and wasn't connected to any Sicilian family on 79th Street, and wouldn't have their same ideas, and wouldn't gossip. But they were having a good time now and no one else was home, and no telling what miracle might happen. Still, he had to prove that he wasn't just making it up that he wanted to talk to her, so he told her.

"I'll be eighteen in three months," he said. "Then I get

drafted. But I don't want to kill nobody. So I don't know what to do." He was surprised that Sylvia looked interested.

"Somebody has to kill the Nazis," she said.

"They should be killed," he said. "But I can't be the guy pulls the trigger."

"Are you afraid?"

"No more than anybody else."

"It ain't against your religion?" she said.

"No. What's worse, guys from the neighborhood can't wait to get in. Their mothers cry, but they want their sons to go. It's patriotic. We have to show we don't side with Italy."

"What does your father say?"

"I asked him. He said it's up to me. That it's bad either way. It's which trouble I can handle. My father ran away from Sicily so he wouldn't go in. He took care of my mother three years. In bed, in the parlor, where there's more light and people passing by. I watched her dying but couldn't do anything."

"Maybe you're a weak guy," said Sylvia.

"Maybe that's true," said Frankie, but he knew he really wasn't a scared rabbit, and seeing his mother dying, he wasn't even scared of dying himself.

"Can't you go work in a hospital? Instead of the infantry?"

"I asked that," said Frankie. "The draft board said my beliefs need proof. Which I don't have. They can't accept my word. And, besides, even if they did, a Sicilian guy who won't put up his hands, or won't kill Nazis, everybody figures is a fairy."

"Are you, Frankie? I heard some fairies ride Harleys. Tony says cops on them are. Personally, I wouldn't know. I met one once in Miami. He did my hair. And he wasn't so bad. My motto is, Live and let live. So I wouldn't care if you was."

"I don't know if I am," said Frankie, sensing the door of opportunity swinging open. "I hang around with guys. And we like each other. And I'm a little shy with dames."

"You called me," said Sylvia. "And when I said to come over, you did. You ain't shy."

Frankie thought his guardian angel might have followed him into the house to stand behind the sofa to protect him from sin, but when he looked around he didn't see her. He thought she looked like the nun he had for catechism when he was seven. The angel had been trailing him since his mother died. He tried burning candles and saying rosaries for years, to send her away, but she kept whispering in his ear, but at least she wasn't behind the sofa.

"I don't think of you as just a dame," he said.

"Then what as?" said Sylvia, her femininity never before challenged by any male. And while a catty friend couldn't hurt her, it was much harder to shrug off Frankie's sting. "I ain't a dame?"

"You're a person a guy can talk to," said Frankie.

"I appreciate that," said Sylvia. "But if you don't see me as a dame, you have a problem."

"It could be."

"There's nothing I can do. And it's getting late. So why don't you go to a burlesque? See how it makes you feel?"

"That's a good idea," he said.

"If you went in the Army, you might like the boys. That would be a pity."

"I like holding your hand, Sylvia. And kissing your cheek."

"That doesn't count. Let me know how it comes out."

"Any chance you could give me a test? I might be turning queer and not know it. Jesus, if you saved me, I'd respect you all my life."

"I can't," said Sylvia. "This guy, works for Tony, he's married. He's Sicilian too. And, you know, he'd get sore. He ain't no pussycat, which's, I guess, why I like him. But I wouldn't want him on my bad side."

"I see," said Frankie, crushed that another guy was in the picture. He could still secretly love her, but he couldn't compete with a gangster.

Sylvia observed his sinking face, but couldn't guess how deep was his disappointment. She might encourage Frankie now, if not with a test, possibly with a sample. He could be a fine man someday. He could love women who all needed to be loved. He could fight just battles. Many such men were already in the service, and it worried her slightly that if she helped him he would go too. But someone should help him. It was the right thing to do. Otherwise, he could be a miserable coward, and miss the pleasure of having a woman in his bed, and sharing his daily life.

"I've an idea," she said. "We'll go in my bedroom. And talk privately. Which wouldn't feel right here in the parlor."

"You're wonderful," said Frankie.

"Don't think I'm double-crossing my boyfriend."

Sylvia put the light on. On her ruffled bed were dolls from newborns to first-graders. Frankie thought his first visit to a dame's bedroom might be an intrusion on her privacy. Her bra and underpants were on her bedroom chair, and her slip, stockings, and nightgown made a pink puddle on the floor. She sat on the edge of her bed and patted the space next to her. His heart upped its beat. Then he worried that nothing ever was as easy as he thought. Never having done it before, would he be nervous? And would his angel kick him in the ass?

"Sicilian girls ain't so beautiful as you," he said.

"A girl in a bathing suit excite you?" she said.

"Is she supposed to?" he said, faking.

"Suppose she's in underclothes?"

"I've never seen any girl like that."

"Would you like to?" She turned on other lamps, filling the room almost with sunlight near midnight. Standing a few feet from Frankie, she dropped her skirt, and then her blouse. Miss Sylvia Cohen could be Miss Double Cones.

Frankie's biological system reacted as it hadn't at the burlesque, but he stayed icy to wait for the scoops themselves to be presented. Then he grinned. When she pulled down her underpants, he went to take her in his arms. She examined him from the outside and she was pleased.

"I think I'm in love with you," he blurted out.

"Well, that's healthy," she said, not believing it, but taking it as a compliment to her figure. "I think you're just a little too sensitive, Frankie. Which a girl wouldn't expect, the way you're built. Sensitive's nice, but we all have to grow up, and go to war, in one way or another. Now, you have to go home, Frankie."

"Don't make me," he said.

"I gave you a show and you sneaked a feel, but that's that. Kids brag."

Since she kept her lips out of reach, Frankie kissed her neck like a starved madman. Then her shoulders turned down. She was surrendering, but then, mustering her resolve, she pushed free. They stood there, he in all his clothes and she naked.

"I wouldn't ever tell anyone."

"You had enough."

"Okay, I'll go," said Frankie. "But you think . . . I'm embarrassed asking, but could I, you know, take a look? I could be sure then. That I ain't queer. I might even volunteer for the Army."

Sylvia sat on the bed and Frankie kneeled, but she was shy and kept her feet together. So he put his cheek on her thigh and kissed the white pillow that was her belly. Then she fingered his hair and closed her eyes. And he looked. Her thighs were warm petals on his cheeks. Her hair was darker blonde, curlier, and in a halo. She hummed while Frankie seemed to be praying. Then she pulled his hair, not to hurt him but to draw him up to the bed.

"I love you, Sylvia."

"I love you too, Frankie," she said, about a mild illness that would cure itself. "The nice Jewish boys I went to school with, that my mother said I should marry one, they're in the service. Two are gold stars hanging in their windows. Sometimes I cry thinking about guys I had bagels with. Not that I loved them, or even kissed them."

Frankie thought he could grow old there, holding her breasts until he died, and he thought Sylvia was the most perfect thing in the world, and that maybe women everywhere were the most perfect things God ever made. "Can we always be friends, Sylvia? Can we do this again?" And, not seeing his guardian angel in the room, he made his move with Sylvia and she didn't try to stop him.

"Only one other guy touched me," said Sylvia. "Which wasn't right I let him. But I liked him so much. And now you. There must be something wrong with me that I chose that other guy. And that I chose you."

"I appreciate you chose me," said Frankie.

"You loved me good," said Sylvia. "So I doubt you wouldn't do the right thing."

"Let's again," he said.

"You mustn't ever tell anyone," she said. "Bruno would kill me."

"I promise, Sylvia. I'll never say anything. But I'm asking you to be my steady, even though I know it's impossible. Would you?" She didn't answer, but they made love again, and were still in each other's arms, not wanting to untie the knot. It was a comforting illusion to think that one was part of the other. Then Sylvia was crying and sniffling. "Did I hurt you?" he said.

"You did it nice," she said, laughing now, tears running down her cheeks. "Someday I'll marry an accountant. I'll have a boy and a girl. I'll get a little fat. And I'll go to Miami Beach."

"Maybe *I'll* marry you," said Frankie.

"You're a goyim. No good Jewish girl marries a goyim. You're not even circumcised." She laughed. "Maybe one of these days the war'll be over."

For a long while they lay in bed, not sleeping. Sylvia wasn't crying or laughing now, and they weren't talking, but their naked sides still touched.

Sylvia thought about the Jewish boys in the Army, about Frankie who was too young to be her lover, and about Bruno in bed with his wife. Nothing good would ever come from Bruno. She liked Bruno's looks and that he was smooth on the dance floor and sure of himself. But now she had a boy who wasn't sure of himself, and it wasn't as awful as she thought it might be, and, in fact, was kind of nice. Sylvia wasn't sure now that she could give up Frankie as easily as she thought she could give up Bruno.

With just one lamp on, and both Sylvia and Frankie under the bed sheet, Frankie thought he was no nearer to deciding whether or not to put on the uniform. But he was deliciously drowsy from love's wine, which also made him feel manly, strong, and knowing. Then he turned on his belly to sleep while Sylvia was still on her back, and he put his arm lightly around her. "You asleep, Sylvia?" Her slow regular breathing convinced him that she was, so he didn't ask again. "Good night, sweetheart," he said, and heard someone's distant radio playing love songs.

The war was in the newspapers, on every radio, in classrooms, in newsreels and movies, in letters from guys in the service, in most conversations between housewives buying chickens, workers building ships at the Brooklyn Navy Yard, and between the old men at the Sicilian Social Society. Young men lied about their youth or health to dress their punches in olive drab in order to knock out the enemy sooner.

Gene Dragoni was planning to join up that summer before coming of age. He took the elevated downtown to the Marine Corps recruiting office on Fulton Street. The recruiting sergeant said, "Fill this out. Answer every question." The sergeant didn't believe that Gene was seventeen and a half, the minimum age, but he accepted the application anyway, and would tell his captain later.

Gene went home to wait for his notice. Then, he thought, he would leave a note for his parents saying he was running away, and would go into boot training as a recruit. A week later a letter came from the Marine Corps captain. He said he appreciated Gene's patriotism, but that he had called the teacher Gene put down as a character reference and the teacher had told him Gene's true age. So Gene would have to wait for a few years. Then the Marines would be proud to have him.

Next, Gene decided to be a fighter pilot. Hearing of a

Navy program that would train Utrecht graduates to fly, he went downtown again. The chief petty officer with a bunched-up old rug for a face put a nickel in the vending machine and handed a Hershey's to Gene and slapped him on the back. "Send in your older brother," he said. And after he thought for a moment, added, "You have any sisters at home?"

Gene wouldn't give up trying to get into uniform, to do the manly thing, as he saw it. He had grown up with his father's uniform, a cop's, around the house or in the closet, but he didn't see himself as a cop, since his father as a cop was often scolded by his mother for being away day and night. But the cop's uniform, and all uniforms, but especially the Marines' dress blues, seemed to bestow on the men who wore them modern-day knighthood. Rocco scoffed at that.

The uniform could put a guy on equal footing with his father, could make him as tall as a cop, and mitt-to-mitt with a heavyweight champ. Rocco didn't buy that either.

"I'll go in in two years. When my notice comes," said Rocco, but he wasn't crazy about fighting for a private's pay when he was making three, four times that with his gloves, and with much less chance of coming home in a pine box.

Some 79th Street kids, when they tried to hit a homer, or get an A, but failed, next time didn't even try, and thereby avoided the failure too. Others, such as Rocco, who was flattened to the canvas a few times, always got up to win the fight. And Gene wouldn't quit either. So when he heard on the radio that the 69th Regiment of the New York State Guard was asking for volunteers, he went to their armory.

The sergeant, a grocer in daytime, was forming his new company. Most of his soldiers so far were older guys like himself who wouldn't be drafted because they had kids, flatfeet, a punctured eardrum, or a weak heart. Still, they would do their bit in the Guard, which didn't give physicals, and would protect the home shores in case the enemy got some crazy idea it could invade. So when Gene Dragoni showed up, the grocer-sergeant had high hopes that some young blood would be coming in too.

"You're seventeen?"

"Yeah."

"Why're you joining?"

"To get training. For when I get drafted."

"You ever shoot a gun?"

"No. But I ain't afraid to."

"You sick or anything?"

"I'm an ox," said Gene, who was more like a bantam.

"Let's go meet the colonel."

The chicken colonel wasn't saying much. Through his thick glasses, he looked at the paper on which Gene had written his name, address, and religion, not required to give references this time. The colonel glanced up a few times and then went back to reading the paper. Gene thought that if the colonel didn't hurry up he would piss in his pants, partly because he was nervous. He thought the colonel knew he was too young, but was taking him anyway.

Finally, the colonel stood up and shook hands, and Gene thought it was a puny shake. "Welcome to the Guard, Private Dragoni," said the colonel.

With the signed requisition in his hand, Private Dragoni was sent to the quartermaster. That sergeant worked during the day in Macy's men's wear stockroom. The quartermaster asked Gene his sizes and loaded up his duffel bag with two sets of olive-drab fatigues for training, a khaki uniform for summer parades, and dress olive woolens for winter parades, and Gene stored his clothes in Rocco's garage.

He went to three meetings in fatigues, and marched around the armory, which was as big as St. Finbar's if all the pews were taken out. The recruits were instructed on how to strip down a rifle, clean it, oil it, and reassemble all the parts. Not only did they learn to do it, but they had to do it very fast. Gene was getting fed up with doing it over and over, and with marching back and forth.

Then the regiment was going upstate for the weekend. They would fire weapons. That ignited Gene's interest again. He convinced his father that he was going to pick vegetables for the war effort, as he had done once before as a class project one weekend.

The M-1 was almost as tall as he was when he brought it down from carrying it on his shoulder. He got into the standing shooting position as ordered, as the other recruits did too, hoisting the butt end against his shoulder, sighting down the barrel, getting ready to fire.

"It has a kick," said the sergeant. "You have to lean into it. Cup it inside your shoulder."

"Like this?" said Gene, who didn't have much weight to put behind the butt.

"And spread your feet, to keep your balance when it comes back on you."

"I can do it."

"You men, you each got a clip. When you hear the whistle, fire at will from the standing position. When you hear it again, you stop. Even if you ain't fired all your rounds. Ready. Aim. Fire."

The sergeant blew the brass whistle hanging from his neck. The live men shot at the cardboard men against the hill. The hill sponged up the bullets that went through the targets or missed them. Gene drove the bolt forward, and then, as he had learned, squeezed the trigger gently. The rifle fired with a small explosion, but it recoiled violently, knocking him on his ass, and the weapon was almost out of his hands. Taking his stance again, he pushed on the bolt to load the chamber, but forgot to squeeze. The pulled trigger exploded the round and the rifle shot back, again knocking him down.

"It takes getting used to," said the sergeant.

"My arm hurts too," said Gene.

"Your size, you should have a carbine. But only a noncom gets it. If you made corporal you'd have it. And it ain't so heavy."

"I don't think I can shoot in the prone position now. I hurt."

"Get down there, Private Dragoni."

"I don't think I can run anymore, sarge."

"Get the lead out of your ass, private."

By the time the weekend was over, Gene had had enough of being a soldier. But he had been sworn in, as in the regular Army, and he had been at the lecture that warned against going AWOL, which could land a guy in the stockade the same as a GI in the South Pacific leaving to screw a native girl. The sergeant had put it that way to give them a piece of candy on the side. The guys puffed their chests to show they were loyal GIs who wouldn't run out on the sergeant. They also wanted to show they were the kind of guys that, if they had a legitimate pass signed by the CO, would go out to the grass huts and knock off a piece of native tail.

At church on Sunday, Gene asked God to get him out of the Guard. He was too young. He was too small. He was too bored. When he grew up in a few years, he would be happy to be drafted at eighteen. Then he would serve his country as other guys on the street were already doing. It was his duty too. He had no doubt of that, but in the meantime, if God could arrange a miracle and get him honorably discharged, he would say a novena to St. Anthony and wouldn't ever go to another burlesque show.

With all the suffering in the world, God didn't have time to get back to Gene, who was more impatient after another Guard meeting. He was lectured on how to clean his brass buttons and his brass belt buckle, polish his boots, and arrange his underwear and personal items in his footlocker. He thought he was too quick-minded to worry about such crap. He wanted to do something daring and brave, but knew now that he had to wait.

When Frankie was grinding up 79th on his Harley one evening, Gene flagged him down, but Frankie was going too fast as usual and couldn't stop, so he made a U-turn up ahead, and even though 79th was one-way, rode his motorcycle back the wrong way to talk to Gene.

"You're oldest," said Gene, "so I have to ask for some advice. I wouldn't trust asking guys my own age. They can be dumb. And I can't ask my father, since he thinks I'm smart."

"Shoot," said Frankie.

Gene winced, but it meant he should get on with it, so he did. "I joined up, but I hate it. I got to get out."

Frankie turned his bike the legal way and got off and took off his black leather jacket that was warm in the cold wind generated by his speeding. But the jacket was too warm now that they were going to talk on New Utrecht's steps across the way. Gene told him his story from the beginning, and a few times Frankie laughed, especially since he was the opposite of Gene and wanted to stay out of the service. For a while

Frankie was stumped about how he could help, but then his own birthday coming up gave him an idea.

The night of the next meeting, they packed all Gene's Guard clothes from Rocco's garage and strapped the duffel bag on Frankie's Harley. Gene straddled the duffel bag and held on and they rode to the armory. An hour early, Gene shouldered his stuff and they went in. Ten minutes later the colonel came in, and Gene saluted and asked for permission to speak to the commanding officer.

"At ease," said the colonel. "Say your piece."

"I hate to admit this, sir."

"Yes?"

"I lied when I joined up, sir."

"So?"

"So I'm too young, sir."

"You took the oath, didn't you?"

"Yes, sir."

"Then you're in the Guard, private."

"But I can't be in, sir."

"Why not?"

"I haven't grown up yet, sir."

"You're the right age. I don't think you lied. You're dismissed now," said the colonel. He picked up a piece of paper and began reading through his heavy glasses. Then he looked up and Gene was still there. "I said you're dismissed, soldier."

Now Frankie stepped up and sat on the corner of the officer's desk. He snapped another piece of paper in the colonel's face. "What I have here, *sir*," said Frankie, "is my friend's birth certificate."

"So what?" said the colonel.

"So look at it," said Frankie.

"I don't know who the hell you are, but get off my desk and out of this government building or you'll be thrown out."

"This is your last chance," said Frankie.

So then the colonel grabbed the certificate, glanced at it, and said, "It's a forgery."

"We'll go to the *New York Times*. Show them Gene's birth certificate. And say you, Colonel Whitcomb, are holding him in the Guard against his wishes."

The colonel took the birth certificate again and studied it for such a long time that Gene was sure he would piss in his pants now.

"I have no use for crybabies in my command," said the colonel, finally. "We'll send you your goddamned discharge. And don't ever come back here again."

After Frankie slept with Sylvia that Saturday night, he called her every night of the next week. Two of those nights she said for him to come over when it was dark. He should walk, since his Harley made a racket and people watched where it went. If the porch light was off, it meant a neighbor had dropped by and he should come back in twenty, thirty minutes.

In the subsequent weeks and months they ate, talked, played games and cards together, and they went to movies, restaurants, a picnic on Long Island, with Sylvia driving her old Studebaker, and across the George Washington Bridge to Palisades Amusement Park in New Jersey, and they rode the 69th Street Ferry from Brooklyn to Staten Island. If her parents weren't going out of town, they made love in their rented room in Borough Park, and Frankie learned that Sylvia wasn't a moll even though her other boyfriend was a gangster. She was just a little too hungry for excitement and a little too sad over the war from which her fellow Jews were running for their lives. Otherwise, she was a little tough, medium sweet, and very smart, and he loved her a little more now that he knew her human weaknesses.

For her part, Sylvia learned that Frankie kept his word, that if he said he would arrive at six he did, if he said he would bring wine he did, and that he hadn't told his friends he was sleeping with her. They grew used to each other, and loved each other, and were careful that Bruno didn't find out. Since Bruno was married and, according to him, had a Sicilian wife who would roast his nuts in olive oil, he wasn't around much, and Sylvia, using her clever mind, cut back even on the few demands he did make. She slept with him twice in June (including Frankie's graduation night) and twice in July and twice again in August, and by then Bruno was making her sick.

The only thing that Bruno was doing differently was making the most of the few times they had together. But Sylvia was feeling more and more like the whore who screws for money but doesn't get paid. If she was paid by Bruno, perhaps she could go on with it, especially if she bought gold jewelry with the money. But Bruno didn't even bring her flowers, which Frankie did, from his father's garden, once a fragrant bunch of lilies of the valley, and another time zinnias with the colors of crayons.

"I'll tell him something," she said.

"It's better I talk to him man-to-man."

"Don't be dumb, Frankie. He carries a gun. He'll blow your brains out."

"Better me than you," he said, and the voice in his ear said indeed it would be him and not her.

"That's very brave," she said.

"He doesn't scare me."

"I know that."

"So I'll go have it out with him."

"You won't. That's an order."

"I don't take orders."

"You will from me."

"Sylvia, I can't let you risk your pretty neck."

"Kiss my toes."

"Jesus."

"Kiss them. You said you would if I asked. So do it."

"What's that going to prove?"

"That you love me enough to do what I say. I'm waiting."

Frankie got down on his knees and kissed her red painted toenails. Her toes didn't smell sour as his could, but of perfume, which seemed to be hidden everywhere on her body.

"I could almost make love to your toes," he said, getting up and rewarded with a deep kiss.

"The bum's a bully," she said. "So we have to play him careful. So neither of us gets hurt."

"Tell him it's over."

"He won't accept that. He'd keep after me, thinking he said something wrong, or did something. He'd apologize. Slobber over me. Hoping everything would be hunky-dory."

"Write a letter. Say you're pregnant. Going to Puerto Rico for an abortion. You don't want to get knocked up again."

"Are you kidding? With *him* Sicilian? You think he'd let me get an abortion of his kid? He'd pass out cigars. My God, I'd never get rid of the bum."

"So then what?" said Frankie.

"I could always shoot him. With his own gun. In the motel. He always signs in as Jones." She seemed very serious, looking Frankie in the eyes.

"*Jesus.*"

"After we do it, he passes out. Then I'd hit him between the eyes. He wouldn't know he got killed."

"*No.* No, Sylvia. *Jesus,* no."

"You *believed* me?"

"I did."

"I really wouldn't."

"Don't, Sylvia."

"Hey, Frankie, I'm not that kind of girl. I couldn't do that, take his gun and kill the SOB, even if he is a rat by trade."

"I'm glad. Killing is the worst thing. It makes us rotten as him. My father says that."

"Not that I'm saying it's right in this case, Frankie. But you have to kill rats *sometimes,* or they can nibble a person to death."

"Jesus. Don't do it. Not for my sake," he said.

"It ain't only for your sake. It's for mine too. And I just got a great idea. It's getting us out of this mess. Out of Bruno's clutches."

"Yeah? What's the idea?"

"I can't tell you yet. After I figure out all the answers to all his questions."

"You sure I can't tell him nice myself?" said Frankie.

"You want to kiss my toes again?"

"Something else this time."

"You listening to me? And not talking to Bruno?" she said.

"I'm listening to you," he said.

"Good. Later we'll go out for macaroni and clams."

For her performance Sylvia bought a nice sensible dress that came up to her neck and down to her knees and had plenty of room for her breasts. Ordinarily, her breasts were pushing against the fabric. She was just too big-busted, the shopgirls in the dress stores would say. And her new dress was also in white to look cherry. She had had a sexy look since puberty but had kept her cherry until giving it to Bruno, which was the biggest mistake of her life.

Actually, Sylvia had two plans. If the first didn't work, then she would ask Tony to get Bruno off her back. Bruno would kiss Tony's toes. Bruno worked for Tony, and was scared of Tony. And Tony had told Sylvia, who was his secretary in the olive oil office, that whatever her problem, it didn't matter if it was money or love or hate, he, Tony Tempesta, wanted first crack at solving it for her. Even though she was Jewish, she was in his family like his sister and he wouldn't let any harm come to her.

Before Bruno asked for their next date at the motel on Long Island, she asked him to have a drink when she got off. She was in her modest white dress and almost looked like a nun in the summer habit, and Bruno didn't give her the usual slap on her ass as soon as they were alone, and not getting it now, Sylvia knew her idea was working. He took her in his Caddie to The 19th Hole on the corner of 14th Avenue across from the Dyker Heights Golf Course. At the back of the bar they took the red leather booth where no one else was around.

Bruno's long black hair was combed straight back, his teeth were slightly irregular, his face was square and strong, and he still wasn't fat from all the food he ate, and he had the kind of smile that one minute could love a person to bits and the next minute could chop a person in pieces. The bad part of Bruno's smile came from his eyes, which were brown, but not warm as brown eyes often are. His eyes were like dried blood, scabby and mean, and if they weren't disguised by his smiling mouth, then the average person could feel a chill that no amount of clothing could warm up.

"I don't know how to tell you this, Bruno."

"So tell me. I won't bite."

"I got this marriage proposal," said Sylvia, very calmly. "He's a nice guy."

"He screw you?" he said.

"You know I wouldn't," she said.

"But he wants to get hitched anyway?" he said.

"Yeah. He's Jewish."

"I thought my Sicilian cock converted you."

"He's an accountant. He'll make a good father for my kids someday," she said.

"Accountant. That's pretty good. So you're quitting your job?" he said.

"Not till I get pregnant."

"I wouldn't screw up your wedding plans."

"I knew you'd understand, Bruno."

"Hey, I ain't no animal. I respect a woman who tells me what she has to do in her life. So, do I get an invite to the wedding? Like I'm just a friend from the office?"

"It's going to be a civil ceremony. At city hall. Just us."

"When you set the date and all, you let me know. So I can give you a wedding present. What can I give to show I appreciate all the good times we had?"

"I wouldn't ask for anything, Bruno. I had good times too. But thanks just the same."

"You finishing your drink?" he said.

"I had enough."

"Let's get out of here. I'll drop you off at your house. Don't worry, I ain't asking for a last piece of nookie. By the way, what's his name?"

"His name?" she said. "He's just a guy."

"I'm curious."

"Oh. Herbie."

"Herbie what?"

"Herbie Schwartz," she said, biting her tongue too late.

"So, pretty soon, you're going to be Sylvia Schwartz. Is that the truth, Sylvia?"

"Of course."

"Well, that's pretty good for Herbie. Not so good for Bruno. But what the hell, I'm married anyway. Maybe I'll go give Marie a good screwing for a change. You know, that butterball, she gained another five pounds last month."

Frankie and Sylvia waited for weeks to see if anything would go wrong from her dumping Bruno. Then they had a rip-roaring celebration, just the two of them, at Le Petit Cabaret in Greenwich Village. There Frankie spent his money on French champagne, escargots, and calf brains in brown butter. The show had Apache dancers, cancan girls, a comedian, and a canary, blonde, small, but with the voice of a choir.

They sat close, touching hands and thighs under the table, and saying clichés they meant. They danced cheek-to-cheek on the crowded floor. But their golden hour wouldn't last. Frankie, in order not to spoil the evening, didn't mention the greetings from the draft board in his pocket. He would tell her, if not that night, and not when they awoke in the morning in their rented room with other things on their minds, then another night.

A week went by and, not being able to tell her his notice had come, he just handed it to her. She read the place, Whitehall Street in downtown Manhattan by the financial district, and the date, Monday, November 30, 1942, at 8:00 A.M., and she wept.

Frankie now had another reason to resist going into uniform: his furious and singular passion for Sylvia, equally matched by her passion. That reason, of course, wouldn't excuse any man from the service. So he had no acceptable excuse, and they both knew it.

"I'm going in."

"We could run away. Change our names. Get a forged 4F card," she said.

"I couldn't," said Frankie, and was surprised to hear his angel say that Sylvia's plan was pretty good and that he should take her up on it.

"If you go, and won't kill them, you won't last. Not five minutes. The Nazis will aim at you first. You can't go in, Frankie."

"It would be a disgrace to Bensonhurst."

"Screw Bensonhurst," she said.

"We still have fifty days," he said.

"Think about it, honey. We could set up housekeeping. Get jobs in a war factory. What a wonderful time we could have."

"I'll think about it," he said, but he knew he wouldn't change his mind. The right thing to do, as everyone saw it, was to go in and be a soldier.

To store up on love and lovemaking, they were together every free minute. Frankie even met her for lunch a few times in the next weeks, and once Bruno got a glimpse of them. And they moved into the rented room and played house, cooking on a hot plate and going down to the basement to do the laundry. They put the calendar in the trash and lived as if it hadn't been invented.

When Frankie came home one evening with cartons of chow mein and sweet-and-sour pork, carried from the restaurant on his Harley, Sylvia wasn't there. Neither were her clothes and things. Her note said she couldn't see him for a while, but that she would explain everything in her letter when she had time to write it, and that she still loved him and always would.

For Frankie, losing the woman he loved was no easier at eighteen than it would be for another man losing his wife after decades. He brooded for a night and a day, not leaving the room. The mystery of her departure finally drove him into the street and he phoned her house, but her father said she wasn't there. Then Frankie had to make a run to Tony Tempesta's office where Sylvia was the secretary, but she wasn't on the job either. So then he really got worried and went and rang her father's doorbell. When no one answered, he went to the back door and jimmied the lock with his Barlow knife and went inside to Sylvia's bedroom. She was in bed in bandages.

"Jesus! What happened?"

"How'd you get in? You shouldn't've come here. Leave, Frankie, leave." Sylvia was a little hysterical, which was unlike her.

"I ain't leaving," he said, sitting on her bed, touching the gauze on her face and arms. "Does it hurt? How'd you get all that?"

"It doesn't matter. I'll heal. Then I'll do what I have to," said Sylvia.

"Were you in an accident?" said Frankie, who had the true explanation in his ear, but as always it was something he didn't want to hear.

"Yeah, an accident," she said. "And I don't want you getting in one too. So don't come around no more. But write me which camp you go to. Maybe I'll send you cookies, and if it ain't too far, come and see you."

"Make a list of anything you need. I'll come back tomorrow. And bring you roses. Red roses."

"You're my honey," she said.

"You ain't getting in no more accidents," he said.

"What's that mean?" she said, sitting up, extending her arm, and he came back and took her hand again.

He loosened up to put on his wouldn't-swat-a-fly grin. "You know that angel? She's been a pain. So I'm leaving her here. And she'll watch out for you."

Frankie looked around the room, looked under Sylvia's bed, but in her closet he thought he saw her. She was a frail and pretty young thing, with bright round eyes of sky, which she dimmed shyly.

"You stay here," said Frankie. "Don't leave Sylvia. If you follow me this time I'll get sore. And besides, you could get hurt out there too."

Sylvia said, "You have a screw loose, Frankie?"

"It could be."

"It doesn't matter," she said. "I made one mistake. Herbie's name."

"Is Herbie okay?" he said.

"Yeah. He just shit in his pants."

"I won't."

The next morning Frankie was a hot boiler with a head of steam that had to be let out, so he raced his Harley to the olive oil office, but Bruno wouldn't be in until two. Tony could feel Frankie's anger, so slowly Tony prodded him. Then Frankie realized that Tony didn't know the real reason Sylvia wasn't on the job, and remembering that Tony would watch out for her, he told him what had happened.

"Beating up Sylvia wasn't nice," said Tony. "You go home, kid. I have a talk with Bruno. He belongs to me."

Frankie was still steaming when he rode off. He tried to cool down by bringing the roses to Sylvia, but when he saw her bandages again his steam rose a few more degrees. Getting back on his bike, he charged around too fast and almost spilled, but he couldn't decide on a place to go, so he steered back to the olive oil office. He had to give that bully a broken nose.

He had been waiting outside the office for a half hour, straddling his bike, when he saw Bruno walking up the street. Without any planning, Frankie turned on the ignition, gunned it, shifted into first, and, speeding up, shifted into second. With his bike roaring like a cannon going off, he aimed it at Bruno. Bruno didn't jump out of the way soon enough to avoid the bike entirely. One leg was hit.

Frankie had tried to kill Bruno by running him down, but he had killed himself instead, by missing Bruno and hitting the brick wall beside the plate-glass windows of the office. His neck was broken.

Tony came out. When he saw that Bruno was still alive, he helped him inside and away from the crowd. In the back room where the counterfeit olive oil was mixed, Tony sat Bruno on the work bench and lit a smoke for him. When he returned from the front room with coffee, Bruno sipped it. Then, with a pistol that had a silencer, Tony shot Bruno in the head and put the body in an empty oil drum.

Frankie was laid out at the Califano Funeral Parlor and, in her bandages, Sylvia sat next to his father, Giovanni, for the three days that the body was on view. Gene, Rocco, and Nick were also there every day, in suits and ties, not knowing what to say to anyone. They had known Frankie better than they had the members of their own families. They had loved him as boys do each other, simply and without question, before they must turn to the richer love of a man for a woman, complicated and always questioning.

The last night of their vigil, an hour before the funeral parlor locked its doors for the night, Rocco hid himself in an unused room. Then, Gene at the handlebars of Frankie's Harley and Nick behind him in a swiped priest's cassock, they rode across the Brooklyn Bridge. Following the Madison bus on the Skyway, they arrived in Union City and at the Hudson Theater once again. As they had anticipated, the priest's cassock got Nick in the stage door when he said to the guard, "It's an errand of mercy."

Miss Sugar Buns believed that Nick was a priest, and since he was also willing to pay her $50 to perform for a dying man, she said, "Why the hell not?"

She straddled the Harley too, showing her thighs that Nick, behind her, thought were like moonlight in bottles, and with the cassock flaring out behind him like a ghost in the night trying to keep up with them, Nick was holding on around her waist as she held onto Gene in front, who was letting all the untamed juice out of the Harley and speeding in a race of one. Nick was deciding now that he was too old to be an altar boy anymore. He wanted girls, dozens, hundreds of girls.

"This isn't a hospital," said Miss Sugar Buns, as Gene knocked three times on the funeral parlor's back door, and then repeated it.

"You still get fifty bucks," said Gene.

"What took you guys so long?" said Rocco, letting them in. "I was getting scared in here by myself."

"God, he's dead," she said. "He won't enjoy it."

"Give him a chance," said Gene, doing a practice drum roll, his drums unpacked by Rocco while he was waiting.

"He can't see so good lying down," said Rocco. "Let's get him up."

"He's too big," said Nick, standing at the casket.

"Give me a hand," said Rocco, at Frankie's head.

"Where to? His legs're stiff," said Nick.

"Let's stand him some place," said Rocco, looking around, as he and Nick gripped Frankie at each end.

Miss Sugar Buns said, "First, let's see the scratch."

"You ain't only seeing it," said Gene, taking out the money, "but you're getting it. *In advance.*"

"That's sweet. I never been paid in advance." She stashed the bills in her purse.

Frankie was a heavy and stiff lead soldier that Rocco and Nick were standing in the corner now, where they pried open his aggie eyes. To keep Frankie from keeling over, they straddled chairs at each side of him. Then, by candlelight, less noticeable from the street than electric light, and by Gene's drumbeat, Miss Sugar Buns loosened and discarded, stretching it out, peeling one garment so slowly, bumping and grinding, for the pleasure of the dead Frankie.

She stripped off all her clothes, until she got down to her hairnet bra and spangled G-string. She wore them even under her street clothes when she went to buy groceries. And when those gossamer items flew from her body, the guys all nodded. They thought they had again seen everything she had, although the funeral parlor wasn't ablaze in a spotlight, and their eyes weren't dry, and their view was filtered, on purpose, through the fingers of Frankie's angel.

STEELWORK

GILBERT SORRENTINO

Bay Ridge

(Originally published in 1970)

1941
To Arms

McGinn

On Pearl Harbor Day, McGinn heard the news of the attack playing touch football in the playground. The Japanese had done it! There they were out there. Far away. He didn't quite know what they looked like but they had big swords and shit like that. Rising Sun? They tortured the Chinese a lot. He remembered the War cards he had collected for years.

Naked Chinese charging across a bridge against machine guns. The card's dominant color was red, for the blood. All the cards had a lot of red in them. Severed heads, children in Barcelona? with ragged holes where their eyes should be. A lot of crazy jigs in the desert throwing spears at Italian planes. Let the boogies an wops kill each other, Cockroach once told him.

Now America was in it. He'd get to go in, too. Get the fuck away from here an kill some fuckin Japs. Or somebody. He was sixteen and could easy make it. The war wouldn't end so quick.

They were out there. They sneaked in, the yella basteds,

right in an bombed the shit outa all the ships, on Sunday! Sunday! They got no rules, rape kids an nuns. There were nuns on the War cards. He thought of Sister Margaret Mary, dirty little basteds running after her. He stood in front of them an kicked their balls off! The rat fucks.

Maybe he could even get in now. School was a mystery to him and his grandma might be able to sign a paper or something. Get to be a pilot and bomb the ass off them, with a scarf. Plenty of snatch back on leave. You could fly off a carrier.

He started to run to Yodel's where he could talk about it. Jesus Christ! A fuckin war!

1946
Monte the Count
The Baptism

McGinn leaned, drunk, against the bar in Lento's. His right eye was swollen shut where a cop had laid a nightstick across his face two nights before. Under and around the metal plate in his head there was an unwavering current of sharp pain that wouldn't stop, that, in fact, the liquor seemed to intensify. I should be dead, he thought. I should be dead far away from here, far away, O far away . . . she loved him in the springtime and he's far far away, he sang, and downed his shot. Black Mac turned to look at him. Have another John, he said, I got some money, have another.

McGinn rubbed at his swollen eye tenderly and moved his hand up to the cold, shiny surface of the plate covering his brain. My head hurts me, Mac, he said. Jesus, I mean it hurts me terrible. Ah, ya fuck, ya got all that disability money

comin soon for the resta ya life. You got it by the balls. He sig-
naled the bartender for two more boilermakers, then turned
to continue talking with Ziggy.

It was red in front of McGinn's eyes after he had drunk
the whiskey. He retched, then calmed, then retched again,
but finally kept the shot down. Then he very carefully set the
shot glass down, picked up his beer and drank it all slowly. As
he was setting the beer glass down, it got very red. He looked
at Mac and saw him as if he were looking at him through a
piece of red cellophane. Like when they were all kids before
the war, looking at the green park through the cellophane,
the new world, intense, red and weird before them. It was
silent, he saw everybody's mouth moving but he could only
hear the jukebox, clear, day clear, the mouths, the movement
of the men at the bar, Frank the bartender drawing two beers.
The pain in his head was down in his ears now, in his neck,
clean and sharp into the swollen eye. I should be dead.

He was standing on the bar now, surprised to find himself
there and the noise of the saloon came back. The pain in his
head was gone and he saw them all clearly, they had sent him
to the war. You bastards! he shouted, you bastards! You ain't
got a plate in your head! Mac was touching, gently, his ankle,
motioning with his head for him to get down, and Frank was
drying his hands patiently, giving McGinn time to get down
by himself. A good kid he was, got hurt a little in the war but
a good kid.

You bastards, McGinn shouted. The bar was dead quiet
now, the jukebox stopped, the customers watching him
standing there, high above them. He lifted his hand up over
his head, gloriously, and saw himself, outside himself, above
them all, the men of the king's guard, McGinn in a cloak, soft
boots, a rapier elegant, pointed straight up. He raised his

hand high. I am the Count of Monte Cristo! he shouted, I am the Count of Monte Cristo! He kicked at Mac's drink and smashed it to the floor, then kicked at the glasses next to him on the bar, hearing them break, shouting through the absolute clarity now in his head, I am the Count of Monte Cristo! You bastards, you sent the Count to the war! He was screaming now, and someone at the far end of the bar started for the door. Hold it, you bastard! Hold it! You ain't callin no bulls on me! The man stopped, shrugged, walked back to the bar. Frank began moving quietly and casually down toward McGinn, smiling sickly. I am the Count! I am the Count, he was crying now, weeping freely, his arms at his side, the pain back in his head, his eye, his ears, the bar had gone silent to him, there were movements, feet scuffling, he saw them through the tears, out there they moved through their lives in dead silence, I am the Count of Monte Cristo, you mothers' cunts! he screamed, the tears running down his face, dropping down on his faded fatigue jacket, dark stains spreading on its front as Mac and Frank helped him to the floor.

1951
Fading Out
Monte the Count

His open Irish face had become coarsened and brutalized, and he frequently, now, forgot his name, his real name. He always answered to "Monte" or "Count." A broken nose, reddened face with the ruptured capillaries speckling its surface. At times, through the alcoholic murk, the pain screwing his face up.

Let the pricks jus hit me one good shot on the toppa the head. Jus one, jus one. He would cry at times, racked with sobbing, holding himself together, one hand on his belly and the other on top of his head, squeezing the life back into himself. (Beeoo Gesty! Beeoo Gesty! Cantering down toward Pep.)

Hermes Pavolites, one of three brothers who shot pool in Sal's, fair sticks, hit him a hard uppercut in the Melody Room one night, while Monte was looking at the bar in a daze, his head on his chest. Some bitter revenge taken at an opportune moment, for some old wrong done in the years just after the war. His two brothers stood near, in case Monte got up, but he simply sagged and oozed across the bar, spilling his beer and change into the rinse water. Everyone watched the Greeks walk out, laughing, then the place emptied.

Monte tried for months to find out who'd creamed him. Nobody had been there. Not me, Monte, I heard about the lousy fuckin thing, musta been some spicks come inna bar. To watch him walk the streets, asking questions, then finally stop, just look accusingly at everyone. One night he hit Frank Bull in Henry's, and Frank simply tore the arms off his shirt, laughing at him.

A little while later, the cops broke his arm outside Papa Joe's, one kneeling in the small of his back, holding his face down, pressed into the sidewalk, while the other casually whaled at his arms and legs with his nightstick. He broke Papa Joe's front window with the cast when he got out of Raymond Street jail.

1951
Monte the Count
The Last Stand

After he smashed Papa Joe's window with his cast, he stood for a moment, then, very wisely, walked rapidly down the block toward the bay. It would take a while for the cops to come, he'd sit in some driveway till morning, then just go down to the ferry and ride back and forth a while. It was almost five anyway. But he stopped in the middle of the block and started back, stood then on Papa Joe's corner and watched the prowl car coming down Third Avenue, slow to a halt. The first cop got out, swinging his nightstick, grinning at him. Monte walked over slowly, humbly, then when he got to within a few feet of the cop, kicked him in the balls. He fell backward, and Monte smashed him across the skull with the cast. Then he ran around to the driver's side as the cop was getting out there, the door just about a foot open, the cop's foot grazing the street. Monte kicked at the door with all his strength, slamming the cop's ankle between it and the car frame. He saw the cop's face go white and he started to laugh. The cop drew his gun and leveled it at Monte, pushed the door all the way open, his nightstick high over his shoulder in his other hand. Monte drew the cast back to paste him and the cop put the stick across the side of his head and laid him out. He sat in the open door of the car, the gun still trained on him, thinking about firing.

ABOUT THE CONTRIBUTORS:

LAWRENCE BLOCK is one of the acknowledged masters of the mystery genre, winning numerous accolades, including the Edgar, Maltese Falcon, Nero Wolfe, and Shamus awards. His column on fiction writing was a popular feature of *Writer's Digest* magazine for many years, and his books for writers include the classic *Telling Lies for Fun & Profit*. A longtime New Yorker, his books about Matthew Scudder and Bernie Rhodenbarr, like his big New York novel *Small Town*, span the five boroughs. Block lived on Manhattan Avenue in Greenpoint, Brooklyn for a year and a half in the early '80s; these days he's at home in Greenwich Village.

STANLEY ELLIN was born in Brooklyn in 1916 and lived off and on in the borough his entire life. A three-time Edgar Award winner, Ellin wrote psychological thrillers, frequently dealing with the theme of revenge. In 1981 he received the Mystery Writers of America's Grand Master Award. His first published story, "The Specialty of the House," appeared in 1948 in *Ellery Queen's Mystery Magazine* and won the Ellery Queen Award for Best First Story. Ellin died in Brooklyn in 1986.

MAGGIE ESTEP has published five books, most recently *Gargantuan*, the second in a series of crime novels involving horse racing. She is currently working on a third crime novel as well as a nonfiction book entitled *Bangtails: Ten Dazzling Horses and the American Rogues Who Raced Them*. Maggie lives in Brooklyn.

PETE HAMILL was born in Brooklyn in 1935. He is for many the living embodiment of New York City. In his writing for the *New York Times,* the *New York Daily News,* the *New York Post,* the *New Yorker,* and *Newsday,* he has brought the city to life for millions of readers. He is the author of many bestselling books, including the novels *Forever* and *Snow in August,* as well the memoir *A Drinking Life*. He currently divides his time between New York City and Cuernavaca, Mexico.

SALVATORE LA PUMA was born in Brooklyn in 1929. A novelist and short story writer, La Puma received the 1987 Flannery O'Connor Award for Short Fiction and a 1988 American Book

Award for his first story collection, *The Boys of Bensonhurst.* That book was followed in 1991 by *A Time for Wedding Cake,* a novel, and in 1992 by a second story collection, *Teaching Angels to Fly.* Most of La Puma's fiction takes place in Bensonhurst, Brooklyn, his own neighborhood until 1959. He now lives in Santa Barbara, California.

JONATHAN LETHEM, a Brooklyn native, has written about the borough in his novels *The Fortress of Solitude* and *Motherless Brooklyn,* and in several published essays. He is the author of six novels, two story collections, and a book of essays, *The Disappointment Artist.* His writings have appeared in the *New Yorker, Harper's, Rolling Stone, McSweeney's,* and many other periodicals.

H.P. LOVECRAFT was born in 1890 in Providence, Rhode Island, where he lived most of his life. Frequent illnesses in his youth disrupted his schooling, but Lovecraft gained a wide knowledge of many subjects through independent reading and study. He wrote many essays and poems early in his career, but gradually focused on the writing of horror stories, after the advent in 1923 of the pulp magazine *Weird Tales,* to which he contributed most of his fiction. His relatively small corpus of fiction—three short novels and about sixty short stories—has exercised a wide influence on subsequent work in the field, and he is regarded as the leading twentieth-century American author of supernatural fiction. Lovecraft lived in Brooklyn from 1924 to 1926, and he died in Providence in 1937.

TIM MCLOUGHLIN was born and raised in Brooklyn, where he still resides. He is the author of *Heart of the Old Country* (Akashic, 2001), a selection of the Barnes & Noble Discover Great New Writers Program and winner of Italy's Premio Penne Award. McLoughlin edited the first *Brooklyn Noir* anthology, to which he also contributed the story "When All This Was Bay Ridge."

HUBERT SELBY, JR. was born in Brooklyn in 1928. He dropped out of school at age fifteen and joined the Merchant Marine. Physically disabled by tuberculosis, he lost a lung at the age of eighteen and was sent home, not expected to live long. For the next decade, Selby remained bedridden and frequently hospitalized with a variety of lung-related ailments. Unable to make a living due to health concerns, Selby decided to become a writer. After the publication of *Last Exit to Brooklyn* in 1964, Selby became addicted to heroin, a problem that eventually landed him behind bars. After his release from prison, he moved to Los Angeles and kicked his habit. Selby was married three times and had four children. In recent years, *Last Exit to Brooklyn* and *Requiem for a Dream* have been adapted to film. He died in Los Angeles of chronic lung disease in April 2004.

IRWIN SHAW was born in 1913 in the Bronx and moved early in life to Brooklyn. He received a B.A. from Brooklyn College in 1934 and began his career as a scriptwriter for popular radio programs of the 1930s, before moving to Hollywood to write for the movies. Disillusioned with the film industry, Shaw returned to New York. His first piece of serious writing, an antiwar play entitled *Bury the Dead,* was produced on Broadway in 1936. His first collection of stories, *Sailor off the Bremen and Other Stories* (1939), earned him an immediate and lasting reputation as a writer of fiction. His first novel, *The Young Lions,* published in 1948, won high critical praise as one of the most important books to come out of World War II. The commercial success of the book and the movie adaptation brought Shaw financial independence and allowed him to devote the rest of his career to writing novels, among them *The Troubled Air* (1951), *Lucy Crown* (1956), *Rich Man, Poor Man* (1970), and *Acceptable Losses* (1982). His stories are collected in *Short Stories: Five Decades* (1978). He died in Davos, Switzerland in 1984.

GILBERT SORRENTINO was born in Brooklyn in 1929. He has published over thirty volumes of fiction, poetry, and essays. For much of the 1950s and '60s he published literary journals and magazines, and in 1965 he took a job at Grove Press where his first editing assignment was Alex Haley's *The Autobiography of Malcolm X.* Sorrentino's first novel, *The Sky Changes,* was published in 1966 and was soon followed by *Steelwork,* in which he draws upon memories of his Brooklyn childhood. He taught literature at Stanford University for many years, and rumor has it that he is currently living in Brooklyn.

DONALD E. WESTLAKE was born in Brooklyn, but didn't stay long, moving to Manhattan, Yonkers, Albany, Binghamton, and Manhattan again, before returning to deepest Brooklyn, a.k.a., Canarsie. That was a two-year stay, followed by Manhattan, Queens, Manhattan, New Jersey (the dark years), more Manhattan, a year in London, Manhattan again, and finally Columbia County in upstate New York. What he was doing among all those moves was attending college (no degrees) and the Air Force (no medals), getting married more than once, raising children, and writing. He has published about forty-five novels, others under different names, along with movie scripts, notably *The Grifters*, for which he received an Academy Award nomination. Westlake has won four Edgar Awards from the Mystery Writers of America—for best novel, best short story, best screenplay, and Grand Master. In 2002 he received a lifetime achievement award from the Writers Guild of America, East, but kept on writing anyway.

CAROLYN WHEAT lived in New York City for twenty-three years, where she practiced law and wrote mystery stories. She now lives and writes in California, where she is at work on her latest Cass Jameson novel and conducts writing workshops whenever she can.

COLSON WHITEHEAD was born and raised in New York City. He is the author of *The Intuitionist, John Henry Days,* and *The Colossus of New York,* and is a recipient of a Whiting Award and a MacArthur Fellowship. He lives in Brooklyn.

THOMAS WOLFE was born in 1900 in Asheville, North Carolina. An important twentieth-century American novelist, Wolfe authored four long novels, including *Look Homeward, Angel* and *The Web and the Rock.* Wolfe's early efforts to become a playwright met with frustration and failure. In 1924 he became an instructor at New York University, teaching there until 1930; thereafter he wrote mostly in New York City or abroad. He lived off and on in Brooklyn from 1931 to 1935, and he died in Baltimore in 1938.

Also available from Akashic Books

BROOKLYN NOIR edited by Tim McLoughlin
350 pages, a trade paperback original, $15.95, ISBN: 1-888451-58-0
*Finalist stories for EDGAR AWARD, PUSHCART PRIZE

Twenty brand new crime stories from New York's punchiest borough.
Contributors include: Pete Hamill, Arthur Nersesian, Maggie Estep,
Nelson George, Neal Pollack, Sidney Offit, Ken Bruen, and others.

"*Brooklyn Noir* is such a stunningly perfect combination that you
can't believe you haven't read an anthology like this before. But trust
me—you haven't. Story after story is a revelation, filled with the
requisite sense of place, but also the perfect twists that crime stories
demand. The writing is flat-out superb, filled with lines that will sing
in your head for a long time to come."
—Laura Lippman, winner of the Edgar, Agatha, and Shamus awards

HEART OF THE OLD COUNTRY
by Tim McLoughlin
217 pages, a trade paperback original, $14.95, ISBN: 1-888451-15-7
*A BARNES & NOBLE DISCOVER GREAT NEW WRITERS selection

"This novel reads like an inspired cross between Richard Price's
Bloodbrothers and Ross McDonald's *The Chill.*"
—*Entertainment Weekly*

"Tim McLoughlin is a master storyteller in the tradition of such great
New York City writers as Hubert Selby Jr. and Richard Price. I can't
wait for his second book!"
—Kaylie Jones, author of *Speak Now*

THE COCAINE CHRONICLES
edited by Gary Phillips & Jervey Tervalon
269 pages, a trade paperback original, $14.95, ISBN: 1-888451-75-0

The best fiction anthology of cocaine-themed tales to blow through
in years, featuring seventeen original stories by Susan Straight, Lee
Child, Laura Lippman, Ken Bruen, Jerry Stahl, Nina Revoyr, and
others.

"*The Cocaine Chronicles* is a pure, jangled hit of urban, gritty, and raw
noir. Caution: These stories are addicting."
—Harlan Coben, award-winning author of *Just One Look*

SOUTHLAND by Nina Revoyr

348 pages, a trade paperback original, $15.95, ISBN: 1-888451-41-6
*Winner of a LAMBDA LITERARY AWARD & FERRO-GRUMLEY AWARD
*EDGAR AWARD finalist

"If Oprah still had her book club, this novel likely would be at the top of her list . . . With prose that is beautiful, precise, but never pretentious . . ."

—*Booklist*

"*Southland* merges elements of literature and social history with the propulsive drive of a mystery, while evoking Southern California as a character, a key player in the tale. Such aesthetics have motivated other Southland writers, most notably Walter Mosley."

—*Los Angeles Times*

ADIOS MUCHACHOS by Daniel Chavarría

245 pages, a trade paperback original, $13.95, ISBN: 1-888451-16-5
*Winner of the EDGAR AWARD

"Out of the mystery wrapped in an enigma that, over the last forty years, has been Cuba for the U.S., comes a Uruguayan voice so cheerful, a face so laughing, and a mind so deviously optimistic that we can only hope this is but the beginning of a flood of Latin America's indomitable novelists, playwrights, storytellers. Welcome, Daniel Chavarría."

—Donald Westlake, author of *Trust Me on This*

HAIRSTYLES OF THE DAMNED
by Joe Meno

290 pages, a trade paperback original, $13.95, ISBN: 1-888451-70-X
*PUNK PLANET BOOKS, a BARNES & NOBLE DISCOVER PROGRAM selection

"Joe Meno writes with the energy, honesty, and emotional impact of the best punk rock. From the opening sentence to the very last word, *Hairstyles of the Damned* held me in his grip."

—Jim DeRogatis, pop music critic, *Chicago Sun-Times*

These books are available at local bookstores.
They can also be purchased with a credit card online through www.akashicbooks.com.
To order by mail send a check or money order to:

AKASHIC BOOKS
PO Box 1456, New York, NY 10009
www.akashicbooks.com, Akashic7@aol.com

(Prices include shipping. Outside the U.S., add $8 to each book ordered.)